Judy Astley was born in Lancashire but has lived for most of her life in Twickenham. She has been a dress designer and painter before writing her first novel, *Just for the Summer*, in 1994. She has now written twelve novels, all published by Black Swan. She has two grown-up daughters and lives with her husband in Twickenham and Cornwall.

*and published by Black Swan*

# ALL INCLUSIVE

## Judy Astley

**BLACK SWAN**

**ALL INCLUSIVE**
**A BLACK SWAN BOOK : 0 552 77186 4**

First publication in Great Britain

PRINTING HISTORY
Black Swan edition published 2005

1 3 5 7 9 10 8 6 4 2

Set in 11/13pt Melior by
Falcon Oast Graphic Art Ltd.

Black Swan Books are published by Transworld Publishers,
61–63 Uxbridge Road, London W5 5SA,
a division of The Random House Group Ltd,
in Australia by Random House Australia (Pty) Ltd,
20 Alfred Street, Milsons Point, Sydney, NSW 2061, Australia,
in New Zealand by Random House New Zealand Ltd,
18 Poland Road, Glenfield, Auckland 10, New Zealand
and in South Africa by Random House (Pty) Ltd,
Endulini, 5a Jubilee Road, Parktown 2193, South Africa.

Printed and bound in Great Britain by
Cox & Wyman Ltd, Reading, Berkshire.

Papers used by Transworld Publishers are natural, recyclable
products made from wood grown in sustainable forests.
The manufacturing processes conform to the environmental
regulations of the country of origin.

With love to the regular November/December La Source returners, especially Arnie, Vicki, Geoff, Diana, Rebecca, Gaffar, Susan, Dave, Jan, Morag, Karsten, David, Jennifer, Bob, Lynne, Vivian, Shirley, David, Diane, Nick (Jasper Carrot), Sue, Mel, Marion, Maryse, Tony, Jude, Boyd, Barbara, Robin (and in memory of Melanie), the hotel staff and management, especially Leon, Niron, CJ, Adrian, Gavin, Fabian, Jeremy, Petra, Cassie, Jennifer, Alicia, Ray, Miriam, Dean, Eric and the brilliant Denis Thomas.

You will be highly relieved to know that, incredibly inspiring as you all are, none of you are in this book.

# The Mango Experience (Sport 'n' Spa)

## Cocktail List

# 1

# Champagne Classic

21 ml brandy
1 sugar cube (white)
Angostura bitters
champagne

'Cyn! Cynthia! Hi! I didn't recognize you with your clothes on!'

Oh Lordy that came out all wrong, Ned realized as the words tumbled out loud and witless. What kind of a conversation-opener was that? People were staring, as well they might, both at him and at the woman on the far side of the Harrods meat counter, weighing up an oven-ready pheasant in each hand. All the same, what he'd said was true enough: here in the bustling Food Hall Cyn was elegantly wrapped up against the February frost in a honey-gold suede coat, shimmery olive velvet scarf and spike-heeled pointy brown boots. Last time he'd seen her, on that hot-sun holiday back in November, she'd been poolside on a lounger in a pink and scarlet bikini with matching sarong and shell-trimmed flip-flops.

'Ned! Good heavens, how *are* you? What are you doing in here?'

There was the dazzling flash of a fabulous smile that was just as sunburst-radiant even with the tan long faded. She had that high-maintenance high-gloss look, as if she began each day by having her skin gently buffed by handfuls of lightly oiled pearls.

Ned hesitated, stopping short of blurting out that he was in urgent pursuit of meat in case that too could be misinterpreted and result in a hasty summons to Security. He pushed his way through the lunchtime customers towards Cyn and kissed her on each cheek. He caught a hint of vanilla and coconut and was at once transported back to the beach bar on the island of St George, lining up the cocktails at sundown. Her choice was always a rum punch, he remembered, its surface thickly flecked with nutmeg and cinnamon. There would be a chunk of coconut on a cocktail stick and she'd dunk it in her drink and bite off little slivers of the flesh.

'I'm after a big slab of Beef Wellington,' he told her. 'Under orders from the domestic front to bring home something Beth can pass off to the new neighbours tonight as home-cooked. She's up to her eyes checking recipes for World Wide Wendy's new book and the last thing she feels like is cooking for us. I was just wondering if the lamb shanks wouldn't be a tastier option when I saw you. Almost didn't recognize you in winter plumage.'

'Hmm . . . so you announced to half the store! That Wendy woman's never off the telly; last week I watched her doing, what was it? Smothered muskrat! Ugh! Poor Beth, fancy having to cook that one!' Cyn wrinkled her nose and giggled, shoving the pheasants back to their place in the display. She tucked her arm through his and led him away from the crush at the counter. 'Are you on a lunch break? Have you got time for a quick drink and a catch-up? *So* strange seeing you on home ground. It's as if those few Caribbean weeks are real life and this isn't!'

Next thing he knew, Ned was not, as he should have been, on his way back to the office clutching that evening's supper and preparing to sell a Kensington mansion to a balding rock legend. Instead he was perched beside Cynthia on a bar stool at the oyster counter, where they celebrated this coincidental meeting with champagne and a dozen best Whitstables. Followed by another dozen. The beef went completely out of Ned's mind and that evening as he grovelled an apology to a furious Beth, he somehow found himself putting the lapse down to simple forgetfulness, in preference to compounding the offence by admitting to the lavish lunch.

As he rummaged penitently through the freezer in search of enough boeuf bourguignon to feed six, he thought about the day and how Cyn hadn't talked about Bradley and he hadn't talked about Beth. He'd miss Cyn on next November's trip to St George. She'd been, during that same fortnight for the past three years, a lively annual fixture holding court from her lounger beneath the tamarind tree, halfway between the pool and the beachfront jacuzzi. She and Brad had been keen to go for a fourth time, but the dates clashed with a family wedding. A niece of Bradley's was to be married on a tropical beach way out east somewhere: a luxury spa and spiritual retreat where, Cyn had assured him, you got your chakras rebalanced every morning and a rub-down after lunch with smouldering bamboo scented with jojoba. Just about to die for, apparently.

'Of course, I'll miss the old faces,' Cyn had sighed.

'But who knows? The year after we just might be back.'

Ned winced as Beth hurled the frozen block of fancy stew into the microwave and slammed the door shut. Her dark blonde curls flashed this way and that as she zapped between the sink and the cooker, chucking potato peelings inaccurately at the bin and stirring something that bubbled angrily.

'One bloody thing I asked you to do for me today, just *one sodding thing*. I've had a completely hellish day over at Wendy's. Why she thinks anyone outside Saskatchewan is really gagging to serve up braised bear steaks I've no idea. She gets madder by the month.'

Wondering if she'd have thawed out by the time the supper had, Ned went to the fridge to see if he could help her mood along by handing her a glass of Chablis. As he poured it he pictured the way his unexpected lunch date had licked an escape of oyster juice from around her lips and he thought, yes, he might just give Cyn a call, as she'd suggested, just to be friendly, to keep in touch. Where was the harm in that?

# 2

# Pollyanna

3 slices orange
3 slices pineapple
56 ml gin
14 ml sweet vermouth
dash grenadine

It was all going horribly wrong. Beth understood well
enough that the risk of disappointment, hovering like
a big hungry hawk, was always a factor with events
you really, really looked forward to, but after such a
crap few months she'd hoped the mischievous gods
would allow things to go a bit more smoothly.

This November's holiday to St George had 'doomed'
stamped all over it before the tickets had even arrived.
First Delilah had been stricken with glandular fever
and now this. Beth put the kitchen phone down and
went back to the table. What was left of her interrupted
chicken and its fragrant tarragon sauce no longer
looked as appetizing as it had those few pre-phone-call
minutes ago. This was a pity as she'd gone to a lot of
trouble with it, making sure the sauce was just the
right side of piquant and that the cream went in at

the proper time, rather than being sploshed in haphazardly while her attention was on the last blank squares of the *Guardian* crossword.

'How was your mother? Looking forward to her annual punishment duty with the kids?' Ned was picking at bits of the salad from the bowl, licking a drip of the dressing off his thumb. Beth wanted to ask him not to do that, tell him that he'd spread germs around, but she managed to stop herself. Instinctive mumsiness was not attractive. She was careful about that sort of thing these days, since it had all come out about Ned's springtime fling. In spite of what he'd done, she was still pretty fond of him and wasn't going to be careless enough to give him any excuse to bugger off and do it again. Taking a Parisian, rising-above-it attitude towards a mistress might be acceptable, but only *once*.

'Mum's fine . . . but she's not bloody coming,' she told him as she pushed the chicken around her plate with her fork. She really didn't fancy it at all now. Its rather overwhelming tarragon flavour reminded her of the casseroled emu recipe she'd been checking out a few weeks back for World Wide Wendy's next series. Instead she topped her glass up with the last of the Sauvignon. She was in urgent need of calming.

'She's not coming,' Beth repeated after a good gulp of the wine, 'because she's off playing bridge in Madeira or Malta or one of those other elderly winter refuges they all flock to to save on their heating bills.'

Not very fair, that. She felt guiltily disloyal but furious. Helena was entitled to a life, obviously, but not to break long-held arrangements quite so blithely. She'd been coming to take over at the house for that same fortnight for the past three Novembers while Ned and Beth went away on their annual low-season, battery-charging break to St George. Helena, *really, really* loved, she'd always insisted, spending such a good long time catching up with her grandchildren, cooking up the sort of cold-weather comfort meals that she was sure their own mother ought to bother with more, and finding plenty in Beth's domestic chaos to tut about. Except this year. Suddenly, now it was October and with only five weeks to go, Helena had made other plans. It would have to be *this* year, oh thank you so much God, when Delilah would still need the kind of TLC only a close and devoted relative could guarantee, and enough rest to make sure she didn't relapse.

'What do you mean, not coming? I thought it was all fixed up.' Ned pushed the salad bowl away from between them as if he needed a clearer view of her. 'So what will you do now?'

'What will *I* do?' Beth was genuinely puzzled. How come the question of who would take care of Delilah and Nick was suddenly only *her* problem? Did he think you could book teenagers into boarding kennels like dogs? (Not such a bad idea, come to think of it, and not just for holiday times either.) Or did he imagine she would volunteer to stay home and insist he went alone? Perhaps he did, perhaps ticking somewhere in the back of his brain were certain tempting possibilities that might be on offer at a swanky spa to a solitary man. Ned was an attractive sort and always would be. He would age into that slightly dishevelled louche look that gladdened the eye of women of all ages. At Christmas when she watched *The Great Escape*, she could see that he had a hint of the Steve McQueen about him. Even Delilah had mentioned it. Every line and bit of grey just made him look craggy and interesting rather than droopy and drab. This only happened to men, of course – one of life's major injustices. Plenty of carefree holidaying women at the Mango Experience (Sport 'n' Spa) would be eager to take him under their outstretched tricep-toned wings. There was always a good selection of single ones: lone, excitable aunts as part of a wedding party, hyper-energized by the Caribbean heat; defiant divorcées getting the hang of holidaying alone and busy professional women treating themselves to a week of intense pampering prior to the Christmas party season.

Beth evicted such unhelpful thoughts. More useful thinking was in order here. And of course she'd be the one to come up with the answer – wasn't she always? Wasn't she the one would could always be relied on to find a bright side to look on and a solution to every-thing? It was like being bloody Pollyanna – as if they needed a cheerleader to keep them hyped up and fully functioning. Sometimes she wondered what they'd all do in the event of her sudden death. Would any of them have the nous to phone an undertaker? Choose hymns? Would they browse carefully through the coffin catalogue, knowing she would absolutely hate to be sent to the eternal flames in a faux-mahogany box with a relief carving of The Raising of Lazarus tact-lessly etched on its side? Probably not.

'I've no idea.' Her brain raced to sort this hitch, coming up with nothing immediately promising but plenty that *wouldn't* work. 'We can't inflict Delilah on someone else – it wouldn't be fair on her or them.' Beth trailed a limp piece of tepid asparagus around in the remains of her tarragon sauce as she thought aloud. 'And we can't leave her here with just Nick, she'll only get worse again.'

And she'd starve. Delilah's gap-year brother Nick spent every daylight hour taking the bets behind the

16

counter at William Hill and stashing his wages away for the big Australia trip. His night-time hours were spent in ostentatiously noisy sexual activity with a sleek foxy sort called Felicity. If he ate anything at all, it intended to arrive late in the evening by bike, luke-warm and rubbery in flat, square boxes. It was either that or something he'd inadequately defrosted in the microwave between bouts of humping. Not ideal for a convalescing girl in need of building up.

'If we left her behind, she might decide she's feeling much better and have parties,' Ned warned. 'She could fill the place with pissed-up teenagers who'll throw up on the carpets and have sex in our bed. Or the other way round.' He chuckled.

Thank you Ned, so helpful. That didn't get said either. Sarcasm was another item on Beth's new list of don't-dos. Hard work it was turning out to be, this business of Saving Your Marriage. So many times in these months since Ned's heart-stopping revelation she'd kept her mouth clam-shut when her instinct had been to snap something at him, remind him of what a prize pain he'd been. Not that he didn't know, she conceded. No-one could have been more miserably contrite than Ned, the day he'd come clean about the mysterious silent midnight phone calls and the Tiffany key tag (engraved simply, tackily, with the single word 'Darling'. Ugh!) that he'd blushed to unwrap over his birthday breakfast. She'd given it three months now and sometimes she felt *she* was the one on last-chance behaviour, not Ned. How had that come about? Still, like the idea of Ned let loose alone in the Caribbean, it was not to be thought of now. Delilah and the holiday needed to be sorted.

'There is one solution,' Beth considered slowly, reluctantly.

'Hmmm. Bit late to cancel.' Ned second-guessed her. 'I doubt the insurance people would give us a refund on the grounds of a missing granny. And it's only six weeks 'til we go.'

'No, I didn't mean that. I meant we could . . . um . . . take her with us?' The suggestion came out almost as a whisper. Being in charge of a lone teenager at the Mango Experience (Sport 'n' Spa) was not a prospect that could be seen as a bonus to a holiday. Even with Delilah's energy level at its lowest, it would be like taking a loose-pinned hand grenade.

'Take her *with* us?' Ned looked terrified. Beth imagined she did as well.

I must be a very shallow person, Beth mused a week later as she rummaged through the bottom drawer in the spare room wardrobe. It was where she kept her instant holiday kit – swimwear, flip-flops, sunhats (two), sarongs (several), beach bag, snorkel and so on. She was taking out all her swimsuits, lining them up on the bed before trying each one on to decide which were still wearable and which – according to whether she had mysteriously outgrown them or whether the Lycra content was terminally decayed – should be consigned to the bin. This activity, on a dank and miserably dark autumn afternoon, was lifting her spirits enormously. The sight of these gaudy handfuls of patterned cloth, the splashes of unseasonal colour against the slate-blue satin throw on the bed, cheered her far more than, say, looking round an exhibition of worthy art in a pale, cool gallery.

What was so shallow about that, the voice of her supportive inner sister asked. Was anything wrong with the cheap thrill of vivid pattern, or the satisfying certainty that possession of the right swimsuit was an essential (possibly *the* essential) ingredient of a beach holiday? Isn't it OK to relish the deep, perfect pleasure of owning a delicious pink and lilac floral La Perla number with matching wrap-around? And better yet, the pleasure of the thing still fitting flatteringly two years after purchase and a certain amount of midlife weight gain?

Shallow was, Beth replied to the voice as she untangled a couple of sarongs that were caught in the strap of her snorkel mask, shallow was choosing to be up here sorting out swimwear a good month before she needed to pack, when she should have been cooking up a test batch of Endive Flemish-style (*Witloof op Zijn Vlaams*) to Wendy's newly adjusted salt level. Shallow was, in a spirit of anticipatory excitement, already having made that booking at Salon Aphrodite for preliminary vacation groundwork in the form of a Fake Bake tan plus manicure, pedicure, bikini wax and pre-flight de-stress massage. Worst of all, shallow was relishing the prospect of escape from the dank atmosphere of illness that surrounded Delilah downstairs and was somehow making the entire house feel as if it was going slowly mouldy. Unless, as was possible, that was something one of the cats had brought in and secreted in the dark distant reaches under the sink.

'Mum?' You'd think she'd been specially cued up for it, Beth thought, hearing her daughter's virus-enfeebled little voice wafting up the stairs just as she was taking off her knickers to check if the peach striped low-back number had one final sunny fortnight in it.

'What is it, sweetie? I'm a bit tied up.' Pants were hurled into the landing laundry basket, swimsuit was hauled up thighs. Not a seductive sight, she thought, catching a glimpse of squeezed flesh in the full-length mirror.

'Oh . . . nothing. I can't find the remote . . .' The voice trailed away, pathetically. Bloody hell, Beth thought, if the girl's alert enough to be fretting about changing channels . . .

'Have you looked down the back of the sofa?' she yelled down the stairs, pulling the stripy swimsuit over her bottom. It wasn't *too* much of a struggle – which might not all be due to clinging to the right side of size 12. Fabric goes flaccid as well as flesh – when she took it off she'd have a good look to see if the Lycra was starting to perish – if you weren't careful you could end up wearing something dangerously close to see-through and emerge from the sea feeling like Ursula Andress but wondering what everyone was smirking at. She looked in the mirror and tweaked her bottom upwards a bit. 'I'm sure it's sort of dropped,' she murmured to herself. 'Why is gravity suddenly something to be reckoned with? Where will it all have plummeted to, five years from now?'

'Muuum!'

Heavens, now what? Beth took off the swimsuit and folded it back in the drawer. It, and the others, would more or less do for this holiday, though she might run up to Selfridges and treat herself to a new black one – a low V-front would be good, possibly with a halter neck – which would be very flattering to the bustline before that, too, headed irretrievably south. She flung on just enough clothes to be decent and ran down the stairs.

Delilah's glandular fever seemed to have taken over the entire house. It was an affliction that drained not only the sufferer of all energy but also, Beth now knew, those who had to undertake the nursing. Or at least it did in this case; it might just be that the reason the demands of the patient were excessive was that Delilah was sixteen years old and making the most of having the household running round after her with cups of camomile tea and freshly squeezed orange juice and a constantly topped-up biscuit supply.

On the old donkey-grey crackled-leather sofa in the kitchen the elongated skinny form of Delilah lay stretched out beneath a blue fleecy blanket – and a pair of dozy, overfed cats – watching daytime trash TV and alternately flinging herself about, steaming with fever, or huddled up, shivering. It was progress, Ned, Beth and Delilah's brother Nick agreed, that she had made it down the stairs at all. As decreed by the doctor, who warned of long-term, immovable chest infection resulting from staying too long on the horizontal, they encouraged her to try to be up and about now that she was past the worst of it.

'I can't get up Mum! I'm still too ill!' she'd wailed to Beth that morning, turning over and sighing and picking off another shred of wallpaper.

'If you stay in bed much longer, this whole room will need redecorating,' Beth had told her, feeling her sympathy being pushed to its limit as she watched a long slender paper slice (silver stars on purple background, only up two years and Delilah's own choice) being peeled back like an old scab from skin. 'The minute you're better you can strip the whole lot off, seeing as you're so keen to get rid of it.'

'I hate you. You don't care about me,' Delilah grumbled into her squashed old toy panda. 'I might relapse and then it'll be your fault.'

'Sounds to me like you're definitely feeling better,' Beth had said, recognizing the almost-welcome return of her daughter's usual grumbly teenage nature after a couple of weeks of troubling and unfamiliar near-silence.

Beth had often wished that her mother's favourite childhood reading hadn't been the complete works of Louisa M. Alcott. Given that it was, she'd have preferred not to have been named after the feeble runt of the four March girls who had died in her teens. Sharing a name with clever Jo, or glamorous Amy would have been decidedly more inspiring. There had been several teachers in her schooldays who, considering diminutives overfamiliar, bordering on the vulgar, had tried to call her 'Elizabeth'. Every single one, on being put right by Beth, had said, 'Oh I see – Beth as in . . .' and then faltered, recalling the drawn-out, maudlin death of the eponymous girl, a child as sickly with inner goodness as with TB.

Each February, noticing the snowdrops in flower on the bank outside the sitting-room window, Beth's mother Helena used to look wistful and say, 'Look Beth, new life from the old.'

'It's only spring, Mum.' Beth would be dismissive, turning away from the window and from her mother, who, reminded of this fictional anniversary of the Death of Beth, would at any moment start feeling her daughter's forehead and ask her if she was sure she was all right, just as she herself had had to do with the acutely stricken Delilah over the past weeks. Perhaps there was some sort of bizarre karma involved here.

I must have been a huge disappointment, being so robust, Beth thought now as she switched on the kettle and slid a couple of crumpets into the toaster: one for her – the pre-holiday diet could wait a bit, the dour day needed a cheer-up – one for Delilah. But just in case and to ward off the fate of her namesake, at thirteen Beth had been at the front of the queue to have her BCG vaccination. Other girls who were lined up for the school nurse and her dreaded syringe were wide-eyed and weepy with foreboding, claiming they would faint or die from terror. This, after all, was the Big One. They'd all heard horror stories from older pupils about how the vaccine made your skin bubble up into an agonizing, suppurating blister with a scab that must not be touched if you wanted to avoid half an arm's worth of deep-scar tissue. Beth didn't care about all that. With that one simple inoculation she was free of all her Beth March early-death-by-tuberculosis terrors. Better still, she could be sure she had cheated her mother of the chance to have her laid up for months on a daybed in the sitting room, feebly coughing blood into a lace hanky. For this was a fate that Helena considered inevitable, given that Beth spent her weekend nights watching punk rock bands and came home covered in the potentially lethal spit of a thousand strangers. Delilah, on the other hand, had caught what was known as the Kissing Disease. More attractive, surely, than something acquired via anonymous hurtled saliva, but really there were some details of your resident teenager's life that you'd rather not have shoved, as it were, down your throat.

'When's Gran back from Rome?' Delilah asked, now that *Countdown* had finished.

'Some time after the weekend I think. And then she's away again just before we go. Madeira I think. Or possibly Cyprus. I can't remember which. I expect she'll send us a postcard.'

'She's always going off somewhere,' Delilah commented, sounding mildly offended that a woman in her seventies should want to venture further than a WI meeting at the local village hall.

'How true,' Beth murmured, how bloody true. She

slathered a fat layer of butter onto the crumpets and handed one to Delilah.

'She said she'll pop in and see us for a day or so before she leaves.'

'I wanted her to come and stay like she usually does,' Delilah moaned, snuggling into the nearest cat. 'She lets me have Heinz tomato soup and she makes us proper puddings every day. *You* never do.'

'You don't want to come with us then? I thought you'd come round to the idea,' Beth said quickly, wondering, even at this late stage, if there was a magic, unthought-of other solution. It wasn't that she and Ned didn't enjoy holidays with their own children. They did those in summer. This year they'd rented a villa on Fuerteventura and barely seen either Nick or Delilah all fortnight. Perfect. Everybody happy.

' 'S not that.' Delilah hesitated for a telling second, then came clean. 'Well it is. There won't be anyone my age. You and your mates are all, like . . . you know . . .'

'Old?' Beth laughed. 'Is that the word you're groping for? Hardly! We're not even close to ancient; Lesley is younger than me.' Delilah made a face – Beth might as well have offered her a couple of pensioners to play with. She tried again. 'And Gina definitely doesn't count as old. She always travels by herself and makes friends with everyone.' This was true. This was also something of a euphemism. Gina slept on a lounger beneath a palm tree all day, conserving her strength to go out clubbing nightly with the various fitness instructors from the Mango Experience. Like a cat successfully satiated by hunting, she slunk back in the small hours to (they assumed) her single room and yet always managed to be up in time for the Early Stretch class, down at the front, close to the mirror (and to the instructor, especially if it was the gorgeous Sam), as fresh and supple as if she'd had a reviving twelve hours of sleep. If she had a family back home in Connecticut she certainly didn't let on about them.

Delilah gave her mother a look. It said a lot. It said that anyone over twenty, or even, to be on the generous side, twenty-five, absolutely *sooo* didn't count as a person to have a conversation with, let alone spend two weeks keeping close company with.

'Hey – don't be so ageist! I'm sure everyone will be really thrilled to see you. You've met Cynthia, remember? That time she and Bradley called in on their way to Devon back in July? She's one of those people who could be any age – you'll get on well with her. And there are always quite a lot of younger people. It's not just us creaking elderly folks.'

This was almost true. The hotel had an age policy of over-sixteens only, in the hope that by then they could be trusted not to go wild with the price-included alcohol or throw up in the pool in the small hours after hurling all the sun loungers into the sea. Delilah only just scraped in under the wire, plus all the world over it was termtime for schools. There really wasn't likely to be anyone else under mid-twenties at the very least. The youngest guests tended to be in fond loved-up honeymoon couples, practically welded together in a post-coital stupor, holding hands, and, over candlelit dinners, spoon-feeding each other choice bits from their plates. Next up on the age scale were the thirty-something office women on a cheap-season break, smoking on the beach over fat bonkbuster novels or trit-trotting between the Haven Spa's treatment rooms on wedge-heeled ankle-tied espadrilles. They were always up for a giggle, joshing with the bar staff and cackling over just-missed possibilities at the local nightclubs. But they wouldn't want, as they poured into their night-time taxis, a teenager still in need of supervision tagging along with them.

'Plenty of reading matter, that's what you need. We'll go mad at the Gatwick Waterstone's. Or,' Beth suggested slyly, 'you could pack some of your A-level texts . . . get ahead a bit.'

'Yeah, right, whatever.' Delilah yawned and snuggled back down under her blanket. Her hair needed a wash, Beth thought, and a good cut. She would offer to pay for her up at the local Toni & Guy before they went away. Whatever it took, Beth was willing to pay to edge the girl towards a good mood and a positive outlook. Otherwise a dire time would be had by all.

No-one would ever know. Cyn had promised and she meant it. She didn't want her own comfortable domestic boat rocked, let alone Ned's. All the same, sometimes you just had to talk to someone, get your pain shaken out and soothed. So now she confided in her best gym-friend, a sisterly sort (she'd thought), who'd panted and giggled alongside her through their weekly Bodypump contortions for a good two years now, a woman who had very sweetly not laughed at her near-drowning efforts in the Aquasplash class and who was never likely to cross either Bradley or Ned's paths.

It wasn't turning out like the others, Cyn now admitted. (Ned was not, she didn't expect to shock with this, by any means the first). Rather amazed at herself, Cyn then came out with the classic, 'You can't help who you fall in love with,' to this post-Pilates companion in the coffee shop.

There was a bit of a silence and Cyn was starting to wonder if she'd been heard, when, 'Well actually,

Cynthia, you can,' came Gym-friend's tart and un-sympathetic response. 'You can, if you really, really try, exercise a certain amount of moral judgement, unfashionable as that might be.' She was tapping a sharp silver-painted nail on the table, emphasizing her certainty of her words' truth. 'If you can manage to give up carbohydrates, Cynthia, you shouldn't have any problem deciding that some men are no-go areas.'

Cyn looked at her, trusting she'd suddenly break into laughter, say something to let her off the hook such as, 'Cyn! Your face! Like you thought I *meant* it!'

But nothing happened. Gym-friend continued look-ing stern. Friend? Too late, Cyn now questioned this. Surely to qualify as 'friend' you had at least to pretend to agree on issues like this. She *had* meant it – there wasn't so much as a flicker of a smile. Perhaps Cyn should have chosen someone whose sympathies were better known to her, someone who'd be ready with the tissues and hugs if she sobbed, rather than looking down her pert little nose as if Cyn had just admitted to listing 'picking up kerb-crawlers' under hobbies.

'You're judging me!' Cyn rallied. 'You just wait till it happens to you!'

'It *won't* happen to me. I wouldn't let it! And it doesn't just "happen". It was something you did, a route that you chose. And now it's a not-unexpected disaster and it's over. End of story.'

Ooh, said with such feeling. Cyn should have realized: Gym-friend, now she came to think of it, had 'adultery victim' written all over her; those little bitter lines at the corners of her mouth that would challenge any amount of Botox to shift, that glittery hardness in the eyes. Bet she was feeling well smug now – seeing a detested mistress-type crushed and defeated.

Cyn sighed so deeply she thought her lungs would

27

refuse to reflate. She fiddled with the fat diamond on her engagement ring and felt her guilty (but slim, perfectly toned) bottom squirming on the burnt-orange leather banquette.

'But, you know, I truly didn't think it would turn out like that.' She wasn't used to disapproval, it was disturbing, uncomfortable. 'I was so completely sure it was just going to be a bit of fun, nobody getting hurt, both of us able to walk away.'

'Well one of you *did* get hurt, didn't they? And surely *more* than one if you count his family. Not that women like you give *them* any thought.'

Another low shot. Come on, was she supposed to feel responsible for *everybody*? Don't spare the bile, will you? Cyn thought, almost feeling sorry for her. Some people! Had they never done the love-thing? Tasted the forbidden-fruit thrill? No they hadn't. Not if they were the sort of person who considered – and she suddenly remembered a revealing changing-room discussion – that thongs were 'unseemly', and had drawn up dinner-party-menu plans for their silver wedding celebrations ten years hence. What a ridiculous thing to have done, to have chosen this unlikely woman for her confiding, purely on the grounds that she was never going to run into any of the other 'participants'. Where was the support she was pleading for? Gym-ex-friend was gathering up her bag, her *Daily Mail* and her coat and already putting a bit of contamination-free distance between them.

'Yes, they did get hurt,' Cyn agreed, with unaccustomed humility. And worse than that, now that she and Bradley were going east this November, she'd probably never see either Ned or Beth again. Or Len and Lesley, or Gina, or mad old Valerie (though there had been that mishap during the archery session) and her golf-crazed husband Aubrey, or all those lovely, cheery Mango staff. She was now out of that particular comfortable little loop, thanks to Brad's niece picking the Seychelles over St George.

Cyn felt tears of loss and self-pity pricking at the back of her perfect eyelids and hoped they wouldn't overflow and take her mascara cascading down her cheeks. And once tears started flowing, they were so hard to stop – she could be in for a long session of it, possibly all the way to Waitrose and as far as the chilled-goods section. She took a tissue out of her bag and dabbed softly at her eyes. It was horribly, regrettably true: people certainly had got hurt.

'Well, more to the point,' Cyn murmured in the direction of the rigid back of the departing woman who was now well out of range, '*I* got hurt.'

# 3

# Opening Night

**56 ml whisky (Canadian Club)**
**28 ml red vermouth**
**28 ml grenadine**

Beth eased the Audi down the sliproad onto the M26 heading for Gatwick. She counted to ten. Counted to ten *slowly* while remembering to breathe. Often, these last few tense months, she'd been surprised to find she was holding her breath, unconsciously making herself weak and tense. In – hold it for a count of five, then out – all the way down to the last bit of air at the bottom of her lungs. And again, in 'til they were full enough to float her into space. That's better. *Calm.* Everything was going to be fine. Delilah had recovered enough to travel, Ned had not changed his mind and left her for the slender charms (well she wasn't going to be a lardy sort, was she?) of his springtime mistress. The tickets were in her bag, the plane would not (please God) fall out of the sky, the luggage would (fingers crossed) turn up on the baggage carousel at the other end. The car had not run over a fatal nail (and time had been allowed in case it did), nor had Ned left one of the suitcases sitting on the doorstep at home. That last one she'd checked herself, stopping the car in the gateway, getting out and opening the boot to count the carefully labelled bags.

It wasn't as if this was a new and alarming adventure either – as this was their fourth visit to the Mango Experience, the journey should cause her no more stress than a trip on the train to Waterloo. It was only, Beth admitted to herself as she whizzed past a line of lumbering cargo trucks, that she was looking forward to this holiday the way a small child looks forward to Santa. After this tricky year – no, that was an understatement, after this close-to-disastrous year – both she and Ned needed this time away. It was to be a reviver, a renewal – although she had a suspicion that no relationship counsellor worth their fee would have advised anyone with a floundering marriage that having a reluctant sixteen-year-old tagging along was the ideal route to recovery.

Delilah was fidgeting in the seat behind, keeping up a low, complaining growl like a cat in a basket on its way to the vet. How mortifying, at her age, how dire, how just *not* cool was a holiday with her parents and their mad bunch of weird once-a-year friends? Even though it was the fabulous, sunny Caribbean, even though it was an unexpected escape from bleak, dank, late-November England and the too-glittery, too-long, run-up to Christmas, she was a long, long way from suitably grateful.

There wasn't going to be anyone her age. The hotel would be full of star-gazy honeymooners and crinkly-skinned menopausal trouts. She'd be stuck among all these olds, listening to them showing off about their families back home and handing round photos of their kids. They'd want to go out on long, slow trips to look round plantation houses and steamy gardens full of giant plants with big, sweaty leaves. They'd spend their evenings all dressed up for cocktails and sophisticated dinners before getting wrecked and having embarrassing drunken limbo contests in the bar. There'd be no-one to go clubbing with, no-one to smoke spliffs with on the beach in the dark and no-one to mess about with, getting out of it on cheap rum and paddling in the sea in the middle of the night. It could be *sooo* good . . . but it wouldn't be.

Ned dozed in the front passenger seat, oblivious to both his grouchy back-seat daughter and the vapours of pre-travel tension emanating from his wife. He sat silently, as properly penitent and meek as befitted a recovering adulterer who has been forgiven and shriven and generously granted another chance. There was a lot riding on this holiday – it was their first time away together since the awful truth had come out back in August. Fuerteventura hadn't counted. The Cyn-fling had been over for a couple of months by then and he'd assumed that was that, line drawn under and normal domestic service resumed. Certainly he'd had huge and painful twinges of guilt, but in the end he'd come out of it more or less unscathed and been freshly delighted with (and frankly grateful for) Beth's company.

Ned could vividly recall his own deep sigh of relief that the ending with Cyn had been such a civilized one. He'd almost skipped down the Green Park tube steps, like a child on school's last day of term, as he'd left Cyn that final time. They'd had an early evening drink in the bar at the Wolseley on Piccadilly, during which they'd come to an easy agreement that parting was for the best. It had been wonderful, he'd told her, but they must both think of their families. Cyn had nodded brightly, smiled a lot, said oh yes, it was the same for her, back to real life and all that, time to move on.

'No hard feelings,' she'd said and they'd giggled at that. It was entirely painless. Or so he'd thought. It turned out Cyn had thought otherwise. How could he not have read the signs? The overbright glitter in her eyes, that loud clunk as she placed her glass a bit too hard down on the table.

Looking back, it had been a falsely secure lull. After a couple of weeks the phone calls had started: 'Just to see how you are.' Then she'd wanted to meet, 'Just as friends', then, when he'd quietly suggested that a complete break might be best, she had started on the late-night calls with nobody speaking. A quick check with 1471 had shown up her mobile number, as she knew it would, but he hadn't called back. Finally there'd been the birthday fiasco when he'd opened the mystery parcel in front of Beth, who had sat at the table holding her piece of toast halfway to her mouth, suddenly rigid as a statue and her wide, unblinking eyes full of new and painful knowledge she absolutely didn't want.

Beth had shaken the whys (midlife panic: pathetic excuse but there it was) and the whens (during a couple of months, back in spring) out of him. The only lie left was the 'who'. There was nothing to be gained, and a lot of pain to be inflicted, by telling too much truth; so he'd lied, insisted to Beth it had been no-one she knew, a stupid mistake, barely more than a one-off, someone he'd met from work, a colleague on a work exchange who'd gone back to South Africa and wasn't about to reappear. Ever. Cyn and Bradley were off to Mauritius or the Seycelles this year, he couldn't recall which. The opposite direction, anyway – they were probably already there, a safe half a world away. Thank goodness.

The thing that was nagging at Ned now was whether to believe that Cyn hadn't told anyone who *would* be there. She had promised she never would, sworn on her Asprey's emerald earrings that she hadn't e-mailed so much as a hint to Lesley or Gina. But . . . but . . . once, after one of their back-seat sessions in Oxshott woods, rutting like teenagers and challenging the sedate Audi's traumatized suspension, she'd confessed that part of the fun of the naughtiness was whispering hints and confidences to your female circle, just for the thrill of seeing that envious greedy gleam in their eyes.

He'd know, of course, as soon as he set foot in the Sundown bar that night, if she'd let anything drop. His great dread was that she'd told them all, in lurid detail, as some kind of long-distance revenge. There they'd be, the women in their annual party: Lesley, Gina from Connecticut who always came by herself, and the tall bony woman whose husband played golf all day (what was her name? Hilary? No, Valerie) staring at him and appraising curiously, then glancing at Beth with that pity expression that women kept for victims of marital shenanigans.

If he could cross more than his fingers he would – he so wanted this holiday to be all right, although it could be tricky with the small spanner in the works that was Delilah. How was he supposed to rekindle the sparks of romance with Beth across a softly lit table beneath the bougainvillea, with a moody teenager sitting between them playing gooseberry?

'You always say the same thing, Mum. You always say it at least three times,' Delilah was murmuring. 'Such a *paranoia freak*.'

Don't let her get to you, Beth told herself, just *breathe*.

So what if Delilah had a point? So what if Beth always had to come over all head-prefectish and say, 'Now, you have all got your passports, haven't you?' Why couldn't the girl just laugh it off with a trill of jollity, so much better at seven in the morning than this eternal whinge. Whenever, wherever they travelled by plane, Beth always said the passport thing as they were leaving the house, then again at the M25 junction (still just possible to turn back if, after frantic scrabbling through bags, the word 'no' came up) and then once more – as just now – way past the point of no return, on this slip road too close to Gatwick. If this irritated Delilah, then tough. As Delilah herself would say, *get over it.*

Her passport enquiry was as firmly a part of Beth's established holiday ritual as crossing herself and her fingers as the plane took off and having a Bloody Mary nerve-steadier in the departure lounge, regardless of time of day. If these things didn't get said/done, the whole expedition would go horribly wrong. Either the plane would plummet to earth somewhere over the Brecon Beacons, or they'd miss the flight altogether and spend the next two weeks at home, miserably thinking of everyone else on the beach slapping on the lotions against too much sun and guzzling daiquiris at dusk. It was nothing to do with control and paranoia, nothing at all, merely good old-fashioned superstition and nothing wrong with that, if it was all the same to everyone.

'Zone X,' Beth muttered to herself as she followed a heavily laden Volvo estate into the North Terminal's long-term car park. She waited a tense second for Delilah to comment on her talking to herself, but there was at last a welcome silence from behind. She would take this as a good sign. Perhaps, scenting aircraft fuel in the air, Delilah was grudgingly allowing herself to become just a teeny bit excited to be going with them, rather than spoilt-brat crotchety about it. Surely any other girl would have leapt about with delight to be taken on a two-week Caribbean holiday during termtime? A bit of 'Wow! Thanks Mum!' wouldn't go amiss. Beth was willing to concede that the weary aftermath of glandular fever ruled out the leaping bit, but, please God – she put in an ardent request – let her lighten up or she'd personally take Delilah snorkelling a long, long way out to sea and get Carlos to drive the boat back fast to the beach, leaving the girl to see how far sulking got her among the sharks and swordfish.

'Oh. Oh we're here.' Ned shook himself, yawned and stretched, knocking his fingers against the rear-view mirror. He rubbed his hand, yawned again and then clambered out of the car and stood blinking in the chill morning air like a bear fresh out of hibernation.

'Delilah? Do you want to lock your phone in here?' Beth asked as she stashed the house keys in the Audi's glove compartment.

'Er . . . no? Like, I'll need it?' She was doing that irritating thing that teenagers did, talking to her with that 'Are you *completely* mad?' insinuation at the end of every simple sentence. Beth sometimes wondered if she'd been right not to believe in corporal punishment. Obviously she wouldn't ever consider walloping a toddler, but there were certainly times during these mid-teen years of Delilah's when Beth was sure that giving her a hearty slap would do them all some good.

'No you won't.' Ned seemed to have snapped awake at last. 'It won't work on the island.'

'But . . . uh? Texting?'

Her father gave her a look. 'Oh God, *all right*! Delilah handed over her phone and watched with an expression of utter misery as her absolute best friend and lifeline was locked away.

'They've got an Internet room at the hotel,' Beth consoled her as they wheeled their luggage to the shuttle bus stop. 'You won't be completely cut off from the rest of the world.'

What *is* that woman wearing? What does she think she looks like? Delilah sat on the front of the baggage trolley and studied the broad pink velour bottom of the passenger queuing in front of her for the check-in. A prize porker, that's what she looked like. The washed-out pallid back end of a full-grown, overfed Middle White pig, if she remembered rightly from the primary school trip to the Urban Farm. No cute curly tail, of course, but, Jeez, those trousers were so tight you could see individual clods of fat, bagged up like the vacuum-packed meatballs her mum had once (and only once) inflicted on them.

'Delilah? Can you get up please? I need to get this lot moved on a bit.'

Dad and his precision moves. Six inches max, that's all there was space for and what was the point of that? No-one was going anywhere. Checking in was taking for ever. No wonder they said to allow three hours – it was nothing to do with security but all about not enough staff. And no wonder that stroppy teacher-type voice kept coming over the PA with, 'This is the *last* and *final* call for flight whatever. Would *all* remaining passengers *please* . . . etc. They were probably still in the long line-up for the X-ray thingy and had been in the building since dawn.

Delilah turned her head and gave her father a look.

He grinned at her, trying to jolly her along into a good holiday mood. She wasn't joining in, not yet, not 'til some serious sun thawed her out.

'Moved to . . . er . . . where? Exactly?' she challenged. If they moved the trolley any further forward she'd have her nose between the woman's tree-trunk legs. The trolley twitched a warning and Delilah leapt off, aimed a smart kick at the Middle White's left trotter and took swift refuge behind her mother. The pig, awakened from queuing stupor by the kick, turned round and burst into squeals.

Delilah then heard her mother doing a piercing party-screech at the pig and watched her clasp the stout lady to her own comparatively insubstantial front. 'Lesley!'

'Beth!'

'How *are* you?'

'And *Ned*! Oooh giveusakissdarlin'!' The pink piggy wrapped herself round Delilah's dad and planted a shiny slick of Barbie-bright lipstick across his mouth. He didn't, Delilah was staggered to note, seem to mind at all. He was, in fact, hugging this creature and laughing. He so *wasn't* that sort of person. Her mum was now being squashed by a big thing in a sheepskin jacket the colour of Nutella. So far, a pig and a sheep: a farmyard theme was creeping in here. Was this what it was like in the place they were going to? All these people her mad parentals knew, were they teaming up every year for a fortnight with human livestock? Did they have fancy-dress nights where you kitted yourself out as animal of your choice and won prizes? If she'd known she'd have packed some bunny ears and a fluffy tail, like poor Bridget Jones making a tit of herself at the party where no-one had told her it wasn't fancy dress.

'And this must be Delilah!' The Lesley person clutched her hand, crushing her skinny ribcage. The sticky lips collided with Delilah's cheek and she inhaled a whole cosmetic counter's worth of perfume samples. 'Welcome to the party, darling – you'll have a lovely time with us, we have a great laugh, don't we Beth? Hope you've mugged up on your Kinks' classics – did your mum tell you? It's this year's karaoke theme!'

'Er . . . Who?' *Karaoke?* Her *parents*? Should she make a run for the Gatwick Express and head home *right now*?

'Youth of today, eh? What do they know?' Lesley laughed and nudged her sheep-man hard in his middle, then turned back to Delilah. 'Now Delilah my love, *this* is my other half – Len. He'll be after you for the water volleyball. He could do with a bit of young blood on the team!'

He didn't look too dreadful, Delilah conceded, for a sheep. He was chunky and smiley and round-tummied and wearing a zingingly white linen shirt under the jacket. He grinned shyly as if he was terrified of all teenagers (wise man) and looked as if he wasn't sure whether to offer to shake her hand or not. He chose not so Delilah smiled back at him, but promised herself she'd be sure to be miles away from the pool at volleyball time. Flailing about in the water with old gadges like him was so *not* a safe idea. They tended to be heavy-handed and a bit clumsy. Accidents to the bikini fastenings could occur. Surely her mum had told them in some e-mail or other that she'd been ill and needed rest? The only exercise she was planning was climbing onto one of the hotel's spa beds for a gentle aromatherapy massage, followed by a long wallow in the jacuzzi.

'Ooh! Our turn at last! Here we go!' Lesley screeched as the check-in girl drummed her fingers on the desk and waited for someone to bung her their luggage and tickets. 'Cross fingers for an upgrade!'

The steamy evening heat hit Beth as soon as she stepped out of the plane onto the steps. Dusk was falling and she was glad she'd remembered to rub the anti-mosquito wipe over her ankles and arms. It was the worst time of the day, dusk. The first time they'd come to the island she'd gathered a dozen fat, oozy bites on each ankle even before she'd got to the arrivals hall. Ahead of her, a pale, stringy blonde girl was making her slow and careful way down the steps clutching a bulky Pronuptia wedding-dress bag. An older man, who Beth would have assumed was father of the bride (except you could never be sure about these things – the girl might be the younger model for whom some long-suffering, broken-down wife had been traded in), caught up with her as she reached the ground and tried to help, scooping up the unruly package only to be elbowed firmly out of the way by a plump bustling woman.

'We can manage, Michael, thank you *very* much,' the woman said crisply, pushing herself firmly between him and the girl and turning her back on him.

'Ructions there, methinks,' Ned whispered. 'I'm surprised the poor girl didn't elope. She's surely not marrying *him*?'

'Her father, more likely? Divorced, not amicably?'

Briefly, it crossed Beth's mind how a scene like this, a few years on, could have been herself and Ned, squaring up before Delilah's own wedding.

'Perhaps she tried to elope and the parents just tagged along,' Beth suggested, watching the bride's

40

mother swinging half of the cumbersome parcel over her own arm so it swung awkwardly between the two women like a fat beige body bag. It must, Beth considered, be a hell of a dress. 'Michael' trailed behind, alone with his tan leather bag-on-wheels.

'That dress is one big hunk of hand luggage,' she commented to Delilah as they followed the struggling women across the tarmac to the terminal. 'She didn't want to risk it going astray in the baggage, I expect.'

'Why's she got one of those huge meringue frocks?' Delilah looked amazed. 'Why would you come all this way to get married on a beach and still wear something like you'd have in a village church? I wouldn't.'

'What would you wear then, love?' Lesley caught up with them. 'A sequinned bikini? Grass skirt? Ha ha! You'd look luscious in one of those!' Lesley stopped in the middle of the tarmac and did a mock hula shimmy. Delilah groaned, staring at the ground. Would it be like this all the time, she wondered. Was she going to be surrounded by people well old enough to know better, showing off and acting daft like little kids? She hadn't been expecting this, not at all.

'Take no notice, pet, you'll soon get used to Les's funny little ways.' Len, laughing, took Delilah's arm and marched her into the building. 'She's the life and soul, my Lesley,' he told her proudly. 'Life and soul.'

Beth watched her daughter, sympathetic to her embarrassment but determined not to rescue her. She'd have to find her own way of joining in, or of not joining in. She wouldn't be short of things to do at the Mango Experience.

'Can't beat this view, can you?' Ned leaned on the balcony rail and looked down at the beach, out towards the inky sea and across to the dark mound of tiny Dragon Island, a few hundred yards offshore. Leafy fronds waved in the evening breeze each side of his head. 'Even at night you get the sense of where you are in the world, all the scents of the hibiscus and the great palms waving about.'

He resembles David Attenborough on the lookout for a gorilla, peering through the leaves like that, Beth thought as she stowed her underwear into a drawer. This was a good thing, on balance. If this holiday was to rekindle a sex life that had, post-affair, understandably stalled, then it might help if she could think of him in terms of Man She Fancied rather than Bastard Who Cheated. She went to stand beside him and pushed the foliage out of the way.

'It's all going off down at the bar,' she commented, watching shapes moving in the lamplight along past the pool. 'Shame Val and Aubrey won't be here, though I'm not surprised, not after what happened in the archery class last year. And Cyn and Bradley won't be here either. Lesley says they're off somewhere else, for a family wedding. I'll miss them. Cyn was a right old queen bee but I liked her.'

Ned winced. His arm, which had been on its way towards settling comfortably round Beth's shoulders, drooped back to his side. He could feel his blood pressure going up a notch. At the airport, when Lesley had mentioned Cyn and Bradley's defection to the other side of the world he'd been this close to saying, 'Oh I know about that, Cyn told me months ago.' That would have blown it. He'd sat on the plane gulping down a large gin and tonic and almost biting his tongue off at the thought of that particular near miss. He'd have to get the hang of being casual about them – they were likely to be mentioned a fair few times in the next couple of weeks.

'I'll miss Brad, for the diving,' he managed to say now as he and Beth gazed out over the dark beach towards the pale lazy wash of the sleepy shore waves. That was safe enough, as well as true. Bradley had been an excellent dive-buddy, careful and cautious and reliable. Given the chance now, if he had any idea what had happened between Ned and his wife, he'd probably slice though Ned's air supply and leave him, as the Mafia would put it, to sleep with the fishes.

Not a bad room, for a single. Delilah had been half-expecting a sliver of a cell tacked onto the far end of a gloomy corridor and next to a noisy maintenance cupboard or the air-conditioning units. And the bath-room was ace, with a huge walk-in shower with chunky sky-blue tiles and a lush basin that looked like the kind of mad, uneven pottery one of her mum's hairy hippie friends would make. There were plenty of miniature toiletries, shampoo and body lotion and conditioner that smelled of coconut, the bottles handily inscribed 'Cosmic Caribbean'. She'd be able to stash away a load to take home, they'd make great, free Christmas presents for her mates.

She flopped down on the bed – which was a high, four-posted small double and hung with muslin net – and spread her arms and legs out, like a long-limbed X. Above her the roof was sloping to a high point above the door and slatted with dark treacly wood. A brass ceiling fan hung, whirring gently. There wasn't going to be much of a view. Her window and balcony looked out towards the sea but in the way of the beach was the building with the smart seafront rooms, in one of which were her parents. She didn't at all mind being a block away from them. She could be anyone she wanted, up here on her own.

She closed her eyes and drifted off into a fantasy in which she was there as a refugee, to hide, running from . . . what? Oh, of course, yes – the favourite one: running from the world's press, every tabloid on the planet in rabid pursuit of the truth about her and Prince William. How likely was that, the unwelcome sensible part of her brain interrupted her reverie to remind her. She ignored it and dreamed on. No-one knew at school that she secretly considered Prince William seriously buff. If her best friends Sukinder and Kell had even the remotest clue she'd be laughed out of the place. Everyone would know, practically within seconds, right down to the babies in year seven. She'd be pointed at and teased and there'd be hundreds, no *thousands*, of stupid text messages on her phone. Every time she went off to the loo someone would snigger and say, 'Going for the Royal Wee?' *So* not amusing.

Delilah hauled herself up off the bed and looked down at her suitcase. The thought of unpacking her clothes and putting them away made her feel giddy but she also felt travel-grubby and a bit sweaty. She went into the bathroom for a fast and deliciously luke-warm shower, then opened the case and pulled out a sleeveless blue and white jersey dress along with a pair of flip-flops. The rest could wait till morning. Or 'til her mum, remembering she was still a bit feeble, came up to be helpful.

'So who's already here?' Lesley, stunning in a cherry-red silk halter neck and high, gold, ankle-strap shoes, surveyed the pre-dinner drinkers in the beachside bar.

'My round!' Len declared. 'What's everyone's pleasure?' He winked at Delilah and added to Beth, 'Or perhaps I shouldn't say that in front of corruptible young folk!'

'Don't mind her,' Ned said, putting his arm round Delilah and almost daring her to shrug it off. 'She'll have to get used to us as we are.'

'Well you're her dad, she should have got used to you by now!' Len countered. 'OK! Who's on for the opening night? Champagne all round? Grab a table Beth, I'll have a word with young James over there. Oi Jimmy!' he yelled to the barman as he approached through the crush. 'How's those twins of yours?'

'I'd better order you a Coke, Del,' Ned said to Delilah, setting off after Len.

'Oh Dad! You let me have champagne at home!' Delilah wailed.

'It's not the real thing here,' Ned whispered. 'Nothing like as nice, not at all-inclusive rates. You're allowed a bit of wine with dinner but that's all. Hotel rules.'

And a good thing too, Beth thought – the last thing she wanted was for Delilah to show them up by getting ratted every night, courtesy of friendly but over-indulgent bar staff.

'Beth! Hiii!' Delilah sat back and watched, for the second time that day, as her mother was rapturously hugged by another female. American-sounding, this one, older than Lesley and only just squeezed inside a strapless blue dress scattered with diamanté. There was exuberantly applied eyeshadow to match. Delilah, in her flip-flops, was starting to feel seriously under-dressed. Wasn't the Caribbean supposed to be a laid-back sort of place? There were people here (well, women, anyway) togged up almost like they were going to the Oscars. This woman had long, long, white-blonde hair like Donatella Versace, and a tan so deep she must have already been here for weeks. No strap marks either on her bare shoulders, Delilah noticed, just a slight silvery shimmer that looked a bit sweaty but glittered like something cosmetic. She must lie on the beach all day, Delilah imagined, with what looked like double-G-cup breasts out on show, pointed at the sun. She so hoped she wouldn't have to see them.

'Gina! How long have you been here? You look amazing!'

How could her mother *lie* like that? Delilah wondered, astounded. The woman looked like a hooker.

'And you *too*, honey! Had a good year? And who is this sweet young thing? Is she *yours*? Surely not!' Gina took hold of Delilah's hand and, rather curiously, inspected her fingers as if to check whether she bit her nails. Delilah gently extricated her hand and wiped it on the back of her dress, then regretted it. There'd probably be an oily patch of glitter now. Imagine Gina's bed, she thought, by morning it would be like rolling in gravel.

'This is Delilah, our daughter. She's sixteen,' Beth said. Delilah wondered what was the thing with mentioning her age. It was like she was warning the Gina woman off. Was she gay? Like, so what? Delilah had said no to boys (though not to Oliver Willis in the summer holidays, regrettably, and she also wouldn't, of course, to Prince William) and was perfectly capable of saying no to a woman.

'Ah! So sweet, sixteen!' Gina's head tweaked to one side and she gave Delilah a moist-eyed look as if remembering far-off days. Well they would be: what was it her mother had said? 'Gina isn't old?' When did 'not old' finish then? Seventy? Eighty? There was enough Botox in that face to paralyse a whale.

'I've brought someone else too, this time,' Gina said as she accepted a glass of sparkling wine from Ned. 'My aged mother. She says she doesn't want to die in the middle of a Wyoming winter so she insisted on coming with me to do it here. She's up in the block now, waiting for room service and having her evening chat with Our Lady.'

'Your mother has come here to *die*?' Lesley leaned forward to check she'd heard properly. 'What a fabulous idea. And has she brought something to wear for the event?'

'Oh sure! Embroidered-silk designer shroud, new shoes, the whole caboodle. She says she knows it's her time and she's gotten herself ready, every detail. I think, personally, you know, she's got another ten years in her, but hey,' she winked at Delilah, 'parents, what can you tell them?'

Not a lot, Delilah thought, if they're as barking mad as this lot. In fact nothing at all, if you'd got any sense.

# 4

# Morning Glory

**56 ml brandy**
**14 ml dry vermouth**
**dash Pernod, dash Triple Sec**
**2 dashes orange bitters, splash of maraschino**

Lesley sat in a snug hollow on the sand and watched the early-morning waves frilling along the shoreline. There were pelicans out on the rocky reef, lining up as if they were waiting for each other before tackling a communal breakfast. Every few minutes they would plop into the sea, one after another, scooping up fish and filling their deep throat pouches. Not unlike me, she thought morosely, prodding at the fat-pocked flesh that folded itself in hilly ridges across her stomach. Too much food shovelled up, that's what that was. An automatic, unstoppable process that had become too much of a good and comforting thing, with bad results. Middle age was lying in wait but the spread, the midriff bulge had staked its claim first, ready and eager to meet it. What was it that woman had called it, the Spanish girl who'd stayed at their Guernsey guest house last summer? *La Michelina*, that was it. A tyre. Terrific – tell it like it is, why don't you?

It was barely light but several people were up and about, either wide awake with jet lag or eager to make the most of every daylight holiday hour. There were the early golfers, out for a swift round before the sun was strong enough to spoil the experience. Under the trees on the hill, solitary t'ai chi practisers were making their slow, ritual shapes beside the Wellness pavilion. The hard-core boot-camp masochists were already back from a five-mile dawn run and were now grunting through press-ups on the terrace between the Sundown bar and the pool. Even Len was out, over-ambitiously joining the power-walk group, striding up around the headland and across to the hillside plantation where Lesley knew he would pick a hand-ful of barely ripe bananas and munch them down too greedily. Later he'd complain about stomach cramps and blame the airline food from the day before ('Beef or salmon *today*?' the stewardess had offered each and every one of them, as if she'd served these same passengers the day before and would again tomorrow).

Len always did this, overstuffing on something daft, on day one. She always reminded him that he always did it, and then he'd have a go about her nagging and head off for a Bacardi and Coke at ten thirty as soon as the bar opened, claiming she was driving him to drink. He always did that too. She tried not to think about it – it was only once a year, was his mantra, how much could a couple of weeks' overindulgence hurt, out of fifty-two? But she worried about the alcohol intake and the fact that back home he currently considered Pringles (Sour Cream & Onion flavour) to be an essential food group. You could see his clothes were getting tighter by the day. He'd been looking flushed lately and his skin had developed a clammy sheen that

49

was nothing to do with the mild Guernsey climate.

She would talk to Beth about it, see if she'd noticed a difference in Len since last year, and she'd ask her if she had any idea how to go about tackling the problem without Len sussing what she was up to. Beth was a practical sort, one of those nurturing souls who always came on holiday thoroughly equipped with enough Elastoplast, Imodium, after-sun and stuff for insect bites for half the hotel. Last year she'd even brought an umbrella for those instant torrential downpours. People like that weren't likely to leave their common sense at home – she'd definitely ask her.

These early mornings were Lesley's favourite time. Even at home, making a start on the breakfasts in their guest house, she gave herself a moment to have a long look out at the sea and keep an eye on what it was up to. Sometimes it was hurling itself at the shore, furious and threatening, grey and dangerous. At other times it was as sleek as a pussy cat, and as sly, trickling up and down the beach as if its mind was on something else and making you think it was almost safe to trust it. You never could though, not British sea. It was tricky and unpredictable and every day this past summer she'd lived in terror that another guest would go out for an early lone swim and never come back, leaving a stricken family behind, wondering what they could decently do with the lost one's belongings. It had happened that spring, in March as soon as they'd opened for the season. It was worst-nightmare stuff that leaves a fear.

On that awful day, Mr Benson's fidgety wife and pair of plain, bony, grown-up daughters had been sitting in the dining room, waiting politely, unwilling to start breakfast without him. Mrs B. had kept looking at her watch and saying, 'It's not like Bill to keep good food waiting!' Married thirty-five years, she'd told Lesley, and they'd only ever once had breakfast apart – after the night the birth had been going wrong and she'd ended up having her youngest in hospital. That sad Guernsey morning marked the first of Mrs Benson's new lifetime of solitary breakfasts. The police had found his clothes on a rock, neatly folded and safely weighted down by his holiday sandals, a grey sock tied round the strap of each. He'd been a tidy, careful man. It could only have been an accident: he'd left a return air ticket in his wallet and he disapproved of waste, which was to be a clincher later with the inquest verdict and a relief to Mrs Benson, who'd dreaded what she'd called 'the slur of suicide'.

The family had stayed on an extra week just in case, as if he'd been washed away over to Herm on the tide and had been making his slow way back. It had been a harrowing time for them all, with hope seeping away and being replaced with frantic despair. Of course he never turned up. Now, with the season long finished and the victim's room completely refurnished and repainted, Lesley found it hard to go in without fearing that his lonely ghost still hung around, waiting for someone to take it back home to Bromsgrove: a rootless spirit, a corpse unburied and unrested. She knew his presence was still there; she sensed it loitering in the hallway, felt sure that she passed it on the stairs and the garden path.

In a few moments, when the sun had brightened, Lesley would take off her sarong and walk into this gentler, softer sea. She'd swim fast out to the small reef that protected the hotel's foreshore, then along and back, the length of the grounds, parallel to the beach. She wouldn't go any further – beyond the reef was the treacherous ocean. She felt weightless in the water, lithe and elegant and – oooh the bliss of it – thin. Swimming reminded her of how supple she'd been, how in her ballet days she'd been the one whose legs would go the highest, whose pliant body could spin and fold and fly. It was easy for her doctor to tell her that she'd be fine again, that the horrible gnawing anxiety since the Mr Benson episode would go in time and that she might feel better if she could 'just lose a few stone'. Not so easy to do. Not when your life is in dire need of a comfort zone. She wouldn't have any toast today, she decided, just a bit of pawpaw then the crispy irresistible bacon and tomatoes and a couple of those spicy little plantain patties – that would help.

'Hiya. How did you sleep?' Beth flopped down onto the sand beside Lesley.

'Morning, pet. Not bad – woke up at four desperate for a bit of something to nibble, but I got up and made a quick cup of tea and the moment passed. I'm supposed to be dieting.' She pinched a hunk of the ample flesh round her stomach and made a face.

'You said that last year, and the year before.'

If Lesley had a holiday catchphrase it would be 'Ooh, no I mustn't!' faced with any food that was sweet, cream-laden or gooey. Even with drinks she went unerringly for the high-cal option, creamy pina colada, banana daiquiri. She knew the Weight-Watchers points value of each one, the exact number of Slimming World syns, the calorie content and the carbohydrate count. 'Fluent in all diets, that's me!' she joked.

'I know, I know,' she said now. 'It would only be news if I wasn't dieting, wouldn't it?'

'You can't do it here though, not on holiday!' Beth said – as she was expected to. 'Not with all the fab food we get.'

'That's what Len says. He says, "It's paid for, don't waste it." Drowned Mr Benson's sentiments exactly, Lesley suddenly thought – then wished she hadn't; he was the one item from home she definitely hadn't wanted to bring with her.

'Well there you are then. Fancy some breakfast in a bit?'

'Wouldn't mind. Got to have my swim first though. Begin as I mean to go on.'

She stood up and started to untie her sarong and looked down at Beth, all ready for action in her trainers and Lycra shorts and a skimpy sleeveless vest top that any woman conscious of batwing upper arms wouldn't wear. 'You go on and make a start, Beth, I'll not be long behind you.'

Beth hesitated, then recognized an unfamiliar shyness in Lesley. This was new; Lesley might have put on a few pounds (well quite a lot of pounds to be honest, you couldn't help but notice) over the last twelve months but she was still the same woman who'd been the weighty but supple star of last year's yoga class, brash in her turquoise all-in-one and broad bottom up and proud in the air for a perfect Plough.

'Right, er OK, then.' Beth hauled herself up and dusted sand off her shorts. 'I'll just go and see if Delilah fancies joining me for the Wake Up and Stretch class and then I'll see you by the Healthy Options.'

Healthy Options be buggered, Lesley thought, her spirits lifting as she banished hauntings from the late Mr Benson, plunged into the sea and blissfully let the warm salt water take her considerable weight, the day needed a good setting-up with bacon and eggs.

Back in Surrey, Nick and Felicity had heaped up on the hall table the many DVDs that needed to be returned to Blockbuster. There would be a fine, to which, as it wasn't her house, Felicity was unwilling to contribute.

'I'm still at college,' she argued, as she pulled on her coat and prepared to emphasize her non-connection with Nick's debts by going home to her own bed for the night. 'I don't have any spare money at all. And even if I did . . .' She hesitated, realizing it might be prudent not to blurt out that spare money should be shoe money.

'If you did . . . what?' Nick scooped the DVDs into a Sainsbury's bag as he mentally clocked up the expense of having posted each of these movies into the machine in his bedroom only to watch a few short scenes beyond the opening titles. Time after time it had proved too much: no contest, really, on just about every occasion. It was stonking US box-office-record-breaking epic versus the sight of half-dressed Felicity idly scratching her long, creamy, naked thigh as she lay beside him in one of her gorgeous dick-magnet laced-thong knicker numbers. The times he'd started watching a film, then just hadn't been able to resist rolling her across their carton of popcorn and crunching her into the duvet. Surely she wasn't going cold on him now? She always seemed keen enough, made all the sexy noises, went down, on top, backwards, any old way he'd ever dreamed of. It was just . . . the other night, when they were well under way and in the background Johnny Depp was yelling in the face of the storm and doing the thing with the sword, he could have sworn that her eyes, though apparently half-closed and fully concentrating, were actually focused on the Depp action over his shoulder.

'If I did have money,' she said, opening the door and huddling into her furry hood against the vicious wind and rain, 'well, I can think of better things to blow it on than staying home half-watching a bunch of films.'

'You love films!'

'But to go *out* to see them, not to stay *in* every night just to lie on your scuzzy bed watching stuff on your titchy telly. If we went *out* to see movies we might just get to watch them all the way through before you leapt on me and ripped my pants off.'

'But you always seemed . . . You never said. Why didn't you say? We could go out if you want to.' They could if she chipped in a bit anyway, he thought. She might be still doing her A-levels at college but he was in the real world, saving for the big trip. The two of them stood facing each other in moody silence by the open front door. The wind was blowing crinkled leaves in, all over the carpet. That would be more mess to clear up later. Mrs Padgham had already put him on a final warning after throwing a hissy fit about the state of the kitchen. 'I'm not here to pick up after you,' she'd grouched (Nick had wisely managed not to suggest that a certain amount of picking-up-after might be in a cleaner's job description), 'that dishwasher does have an 'On' switch, you know, even for boys.'

'You never fucking asked!' Felicity stamped past him and down the steps. '*Other* people ask.'

*Other people?* Nick chased after her and grabbed her arm as she unlocked her mother's Fiesta. It was only nine o'clock: was she really going home? He'd assumed she was bluffing. It would be a criminal waste of an empty house and the free-sample massage oils he'd picked up in Boots in his lunch hour.

'*What* other people?' he demanded. '*Who?* Just tell me where you want to go and we can go there. And then . . .'

'And then what?' Felicity put her hand on her hip

and raised her eyes heavenward. 'Let me guess, Nick. Umm . . .' She put her finger to her lips, acting annoyingly cute, pensive. 'Oh . . . er, got it! Back here, would that be? For, oh yes of course, more steamy lad's-mag sex? Where do you want me next? Up against the wall? Hanging out of the window while you shag me from behind and make that snuffly noise into the back of my neck?'

Nick put his hands up, surrender style, and backed away, hurt and deeply shaken. He'd got something wrong that he hadn't even begun to suspect. Perhaps he should have, perhaps taking her out to dinner or something would have been a good idea. They could have gone to that little Italian and then afterwards . . . except they couldn't have an 'afterwards' now, could they? Not without her accusing him of rushing her through the zabaglione so he could get his hands up her skirt. It was all spoiled.

There was a breezy rush as Felicity started the car and skidded off fast across the gravel. She didn't even look at him. There had to be more to it than how they spent the evenings. She'd never complained before. She'd got someone else, that was the bottom line, some other bloke. That had to be it. She'd pulled some college sod who smarmed her and flattered her and let her go on about her uni choices and whether the thing in the play was all Lady Macbeth's fault. Over, that's what he and Felicity were. He was dumped, no doubts, no questions.

Lonely, dejected and sorry for himself, Nick mooched back into the house and slammed the door on the cold damp night. Just don't let anyone tell him, he thought as he went to the fridge and pulled out the last can of beer, just don't expect him ever to believe that Felicity really preferred deep, meaningful conversation to the other. Not possible, not Fliss.

And also, he thought as he swigged down the beer straight from the can, what had she meant? *What* snuffly noise?


'Sam! How are you doing?' Beth ran up the polished mahogany steps of the Thai-inspired Wellness pavilion to greet the tall, sheeny-muscled youth who was adjusting the volume of the early-morning ambient music. His hair was finely plaited in shoulder-length cornrows, finished off with clattering beads. She could see that Delilah was admiring them, geeing herself up to deciding to get hers done.

'Beth – hey, good to have you back! Welcome home! I kept your mat warm,' he said, giving her a warm hug as he handed her a spongy exercise pad ready for the floor exercises.

'And this is my daughter, Delilah.' Beth laughed as Sam leapt back a good four feet in mock shock, then got down on his knees to plead with Delilah.

'Whoa! Delilah of the powerful scissors! Don't touch this Samson's hair, beautiful lady, I'll do anything you ask!'

Delilah smiled at him, looking shy. 'You're not really a Samson?' she asked.

'Sure am, sweetie. My mother wanted me to be a big strong guy and thought the name would help. She hates my hair like this but I tell her, hey what d'you want?' Delilah laughed as he tweaked at one of his gleaming black strands, all wound through with red, yellow and green thread. Sam handed her a mat and Beth led her to a cool spot close to the open side of the pavilion, where long white muslin curtains fluttered in a welcome breeze. Other guests were assembling for the class and standing around flexing their hamstrings and choosing spaces for their mats. Among them was the bride who'd carried her dress from the plane the day before, trailing sullenly behind her mother. Both of them looked pale and pasty and extremely grumpy, as if they'd started the day with an argument. There was no sign of 'Michael'.

'Haven't seen the happy bridegroom yet, have we?' Beth whispered to Delilah. 'I wonder what he's like?'

'Gone, probably,' Delilah giggled. 'Run off with someone who's more fun, which would be, like, *anyone*.'

Beth, obscured in the pavilion's mirrored wall by the bride's mother in front of her, watched the bits of herself that were visible as the exercises started. She could see her left leg pointing forward as Sam settled the class into a slow calf-stretch. Without being able to see the rest of her body, she felt as if the leg didn't belong to her and she could look at it objectively. It wasn't too bad, fairly curvy and not flabby. The base of fake tan helped. Delilah's leg was the next one along in the line. By comparison it looked almost tragically thin, a mixed result of both her youth and her illness. Delilah had certainly proved it was true that staying in bed made you grow. There must be at least another two inches of her – all length, no width – since the beginning of the glandular fever. No wonder she'd been so exhausted.

'Don't overdo it, Del. Just lie on your mat if you get tired,' Beth whispered as they slowly rolled their heads down in the direction of the floor and she trailed her fingertips across the top of her feet.

'Don't fuss!' Delilah hissed back, then looked towards the main entrance as someone clattered up the steps.

'Sorry I'm late everyone! Hi Sam, sweetie!' Gina

arrived, whizzing into the room wafting a scent of something expensive. She wore tiny tight white jersey shorts and a matching cropped-off sports top, very cut-away at the shoulders. She grabbed a mat from the pile and settled herself quickly right at the front by the mirror and only inches from Sam. The bride's mother, ousted backwards, huffed and shifted crossly, but Gina simply gave her a broad and innocent smile and a cheery, all-American 'Good morning!'

'OK, to the floor now everyone – feet straight out in front and *stretch* down, head towards knees.' Sam looked around the room. 'No, it's bending from the hips I want, not your shoulders, honey,' he called to Delilah, crossing the floor to take hold of her arms and pull them gently forward towards her toes.

'That's as far as I go,' she complained, though obediently wrapping her hands round her feet and wriggling her hips down for more leverage.

'That's fine, much better, give it time and relax down now.' Sam grinned at her, returning to the front of the class where Gina, supple as a cat, had parted her legs in order to nestle her chin all the way to the floor. Beth glanced up, watching Gina effortlessly fold herself in half like a Marmite sandwich.

'Hey look now folks, this is what you're aiming at!' Sam told the rest of them, as one by one the group raised their heads to admire Gina's suppleness.

'She always does this,' Beth muttered to Delilah. 'You wait, at the end she'll be staying behind to practise her splits and getting Sam to "help" her.'

'Gross,' Delilah said, rolling back flat to the floor for the next exercise.

Beth pulled her knees up towards her chin, wrapped her arms round her legs and rocked gently as instructed. Her spine snuggled itself into the mat and the floor beneath as she languorously uncurled, sent her right leg to lie on the floor and raised the left one high, grabbing hold of the back of her calf and pulling down. She felt as if her blood was coursing fast into every sinew, and that muscles were loosening properly for the first time in months. In front of her, she caught sight of Gina's left leg, rising high then going all the way on down till it lay against Gina's ear. How did she get to be so bendy? Had she been a child star gymnast – did she represent the USA in some long-ago Olympics? Or was it from years of highly adventurous sex? Impossible not to think about that, what with Gina so obviously taunting poor Sam, and her crotch practically pushed into his face.

Unwelcome thoughts about Ned and his mystery woman came to mind, however much Beth tried to stop them by concentrating on getting her hands over the baby-pink soles of her feet. She was doing her best; she honestly believed Ned when he promised it was all over months back, and she'd promised herself, after the initial fury and a cool spell of only the crispest communication between them, that she wouldn't rake it all up again. What would be the point? Delilah and Nick would be bound to pick up the atmosphere and worry they were about to become maintenance children. She especially didn't want to drag it into this holiday – the one where everything was supposed to fall back into place. So no pressure there.

All the same, as she watched Gina effortlessly change legs and haul her other foot down so far she could kiss it, if she, Beth, was able to do physical tricks like that, would he have felt the need to go off and experiment with someone else? Or was the urge to copulate on extra-mural premises so very much more basic than a matter of having fantastic sex: some thrill sparked off by a different perfume, different shape, different conversation? And if it was conversation, was it down to the fact that much of Beth's evening chat repertoire involved sharing with Ned World Wide Wendy's unpalatable plans for buffalo fricassee, or wondering if they should opt for *Newsnight* or *Satan's Supermarkets*?

'And . . . relax now, legs down together on the floor. Lying flat out and still, close your eyes, just concentrate on breathing and feeling the peace. *Melt* that body into the ground.'

'Mmmm,' Gina moaned voluptuously. Sam switched off the music and everyone adjusted their limbs into flat relaxation. There was no sound but the gentle swoosh of the drapes, the soft splash as the stream from the hillside met the water of the ornamental lake over which part of the pavilion was built, and the deep, even breathing of at least six different nationalities gathered together to doze on this dark wooden floor. Then came a loud snort like a huffing horse and the bride's mother shook herself awake with a start, sitting up abruptly and staring around, wide-eyed.

'Yo, we have a sleeper!' Gina sat up and pointed at the woman. 'Here's the snorer, everybody!' No-one, Beth thought, could ever describe Gina as quietly spoken.

The bride tittered and her mother glared around her as everyone turned to stare.

'You're *supposed* to be totally relaxed,' she hissed at Gina. 'That's if you're doing it properly and not just here to *show off* and flex your muscles at the hunky instructor.'

'Hey, sorry and all!' Gina pulled her hair free of her elastic band and shook it out, flicking her head right back so the hair cascaded prettily across her shoulders. 'No big deal, lady – don't wreck the chill vibes!' But she was talking to a broad hunched back as the bride hustled her decidedly un-chilled mother out of the building and in the direction of breakfast at the poolside restaurant.

Beth could feel Delilah giggling beside her, and Gina came over to the two of them. 'Come on you guys, let's get breakfast,' she murmured. 'We'll take a seat close beside that uptight witch and I'll give her the bad girl's guide to eating a weenie.'

Oh God, please don't, Delilah prayed silently, hoping and hoping that a weenie was only a sausage.

# 5

# Beachcomber

42 ml light rum
14 ml Triple Sec
14 ml each of lemon and lime
dash of sugar syrup
14 ml grenadine

Oh the bliss of being so idle. Beth lay stretched out on her lounger with her eyes shut, her book face down on her tummy. The huge cream canvas parasol shaded her face against the ageing ravages of the sun and factor fifteen was slicked all over her body and limbs. She could hear the nearby slap-slap of flip-flops on concrete, a hard, rhythmic splash as someone being sporty in the pool swam up and down, and the rise-and-fall ripples of chatter from the tables by the Sundown bar. She could smell the sweet coconut tang of suntan lotion and taste a hint of sea salt on the breeze.

Better than work, this, definitely, she thought. Far, far better than spending the morning experimenting with herbal seasonings for Savoy Cabbage Flemish

63

Style (*Savooikool op Z'n Vlaans*) to a background chirruping of Wendy detailing how effectively HRT was boosting her libido. Why was it, Beth wondered, that whenever Wendy stirred a gloopy, steaming sauce, she felt compelled to discuss bodily fluids of some kind? From a past medieval existence, was she missing the arcane visceral contents of a cauldron? Ned had a theory that she'd hit on her winning formula for international extreme cuisine after casseroling her own babies' placentas. If that was the case, Beth fervently prayed she wouldn't return to her original inspiration and expect her to help testing out concoctions such as caul pâté or umbilical soup. Surely there was only so much the nation's couch cooks could take?

'Hot, isn't it?' Lesley, alongside with a Jilly Cooper and sipping a glass of iced water, wafted air in front of her face with her sunhat. 'Think of all the poor souls back home, bundled up against the cold and the day getting dark before the afternoon's half gone. Hee hee!' she chortled gleefully.

'I'd rather not think about home,' Beth told her. 'We've left Nick and his Felicity floozy in charge of the house. I hope they're OK.'

Would they be? Suppose there was a sudden wintry freeze-up and all the pipes burst, sending water from the loft tanks cascading through the ceilings? Suppose a gang of vicious burglars followed Nick home late at night and beat him to a pulp for the plasma-screen telly?

'They'll be all right. Don't you worry about it.' Lesley waved away her concerns. 'Anyway, there's not a lot you can do about anything from here, is there, even if they have trashed everything you own. Just relax and forget about home. That's what you're paying for.'

'I'm trying, I'm trying!' Beth insisted, wishing domestic arrangements hadn't crossed her mind. That was the problem with the one-in-charge role, it was so hard to switch off. 'But I can't help imagining Nick making a late-night bacon sandwich and forgetting to turn the grill off. We could be going home to a pile of cinders and an insurance company wriggling out of paying, on grounds of leaving an irresponsible teenager in place of me.'

'Well you can stop that right now or you'll worry the whole fortnight away. Beats working, this, though, doesn't it?' Lesley echoed Beth's earlier thoughts, stretching her arms into the breeze and yawning. 'It's just after lunch, home time. If I was back in Guernsey I'd be ironing a whopping great pile of pillowcases. What about you? You're still working for World Wide Wendy, aren't you? What's she up to?'

'Oh the usual,' Beth told her. 'Wendy's now working on the cuisine of Belgium. There's a new book on its way, with a TV one-off called *Horses for Courses*.'

'You're joking!' Lesley spluttered. 'The woman gets worse!'

'I wish I was joking,' Beth sighed. 'But it seems the more crazily off-putting the title, the more people rush to buy it. I think we're only doing one horse recipe though; the Belgians seem keener on endless endive and vegetable soups.'

'I'd always had Belgium down as chips and chocolate. I watched Wendy's last TV series. Len wanted to see it because he thought *Eating about the Bush* sounded rude. How typical is that?'

'Ha! And what he got was how to cook curried kangaroo tail and emu carpaccio!' Beth laughed. 'Poor Len, how very disappointing for him!'

'And you actually had to cook that, the kangaroo

thing?' Lesley sat up and swung her legs down from the lounger to the ground. 'Wasn't it just gross?'

'It was a bit – the tails arrived frozen but they were still whole and furry. The viewing public didn't get to see that bit. The producer deemed it a preparation stage too far.'

'Yuck! I couldn't even touch it.' Lesley shuddered. 'I like my meat skinned and plucked and cling-filmed, me.'

'Wendy prefers to get to grips with the essential animal aspect. Like a sort of international Hugh Fearnley-Whittingstall. We had at least twelve goes at it 'til she was happy. To be honest it tasted like any other strong red meat; venison's about the closest. You just try not to think about Skippy. Roo steak is on every bar-food menu in Oz, apparently.'

Beth wished they hadn't started on this track. Work, domestic routine, these were the things she'd come here to escape. Now her head was full of wondering about Nick, about how he was getting on all by himself back at home. She pictured him slumped on the sofa, the crumpled, slightly greasy, nineteen-year-old length of him, fast asleep in the middle of the afternoon in front of the Disney Channel and surrounded by beer cans and pizza boxes. One could also, she thought as she crossed her fingers, if masochistically inclined, pull the mental camera back from the sofa scenario to include thirty hung-over, post-party teenagers, many broken windows, something stinking and indelible drying all over the stair carpet and the police forcing an entry. Do not, she told herself, go there. As long as Nick fed the cats and remembered to get up for work, that was the main thing. She should *not* worry about him, for in that direction lay mollycoddling and the formation of one of those helpless, bleating men who ask where their clean socks are. He was past voting age, for heaven's sake, and only a few final saving-up weeks from flying off to spend months fending for himself in Australia. He'd have to survive well enough there without someone reminding him that tee shirts didn't wash themselves.

'Mum! Mum, I need money!' The long skinny shadow of Delilah fell across Beth's face and she opened her eyes.

'What do you need money for? You don't have to pay for anything here, it's all included.'

'For on the beach. There's someone selling sarongs and I really *need* a blue one. She's got the exact right thing to go with my spotty bikini. I've got money, but it's English. And it's miles away up in my room.' Those two clinchers should do it. Beth could almost see her brain ticking along on a mother-manipulation track, holding out the promise that: a) it was only a loan and b) Delilah was being careful not to overtire herself.

'OK, how much? A tenner's-worth?'

Delilah's lip curled up sideways in her best 'I think *not*' expression.

'*Muuum!* Twenty, at least! She's got lots of stuff, shell bracelets and coral necklaces and that.'

'Twenty then, but I want it back and there'll be loads of chances to buy things . . .' But Delilah had gone, flip-flopping fast down the short path towards the shopping opportunity, stopping only for a second to stroke one of the hotel's many cats.

Lesley watched her go. 'Gorgeous, isn't she? What I'd give to be sixteen again.'

'Would you really though?' Beth settled herself back on the lounger. The sun was now blazing under the parasol at chest level, and she'd have to put something over that stretch of thin, delicate skin or it would burn and shrivel. 'Would you really want all those exams and the worry about which university and all that peer-pressure competitiveness?'

'Well since you put it that way ... no. And I wouldn't want to lose my virginity again either.' Lesley shuddered. 'Or if I did, I'd want something classier than the school thug and the back of his dad's Ford Escort in the Arndale multi-storey. Somewhere like here would be just perfect, sixteen or whenever.'

That was another train of thought Beth wasn't over-keen to pursue. If Nick's sex life was something she was forced, by way of his bedroom sound effects, to know about, it was quite the opposite with Delilah, who kept her fancies and fantasies firmly between her mobile phone and her circle of mates, and thank goodness for that, in Beth's opinion. There were times when she understood exactly what teens meant when they put their hands over their ears and yelled 'Too much information!'

The sun had sneaked further under the parasol and was now searing her legs. What next for maximum enjoyment of the moment? Another dollop of lotion? An icy lime cordial? Or a spot of exercise?

'Have you been into the Haven and booked any treatments yet?' Beth asked Lesley.

'Not yet. Shall we go now? The early rush will be over. I'm trying to persuade Len to go for the Lovers' Massage. Dead romantic, I reckon. You and Ned should try it.'

Beth tried to imagine herself and Ned under the tutelage of big Dolores, the chief masseuse, learning how to smooth each other's sinews with oils, by the light of scented candles and with the inevitable Enya soundtrack wafting from the crackly old speakers.

'I dunno, I think we're a bit too English to get the most out of it. We'd probably giggle,' she said.

Lesley looked stern. 'You've got to keep that fire stoked,' she warned. 'Or you'll find it hard to get it restarted. That's what my mum always told me. And she wasn't talking about the one in the sitting room.' Then she laughed. 'Though of course she might have been. She always kept a very warm house.'

Delilah sat cross-legged in the sand, carefully folded her lovely new sarong, placed it down in front of her and put the pair of bracelets side by side on top of it. Which one to keep, which one to give to Kelly? Perhaps she'd wear both of them during the holiday and make a decision when she got home. Kelly wouldn't know, and she'd only have been trying it out. She picked up the one with the tiny blue spiral shells and held it up towards the sun. You could almost see through the shells and the light glinted off the pearly insides. Was it Kelly's sort of thing? Or, back in wintry Surrey, would she just give her that sneery look and say it reminded her of garden snails?

'That's pretty. Did you get it off the woman with the sarongs?' The sand beside Delilah scuffed up as the pale bride-girl sat down beside her. 'You don't mind if I sit here, do you? I thought, like, I could see you're on your own with just your family and I'm on my own with mine.' The girl grinned at her. 'I'm Sadie.'

'Um, I'm Delilah. And no, I don't mind.' Don't mind, she thought, understatement or what? She'd assumed she'd be condemned to talk only to people with eyebags and elephant skin for the entire fortnight. 'I thought you were getting married though,' she added, as if this made Sadie the enemy. 'Wasn't it you carrying a big dress off the plane?'

The girl's grin disappeared. 'Oh, well yeah. I am. Well that's the plan, but it's been going a bit pear-shaped. We shouldn't even *be* here.'

'Huh? Like you've come to the wrong *place*?'

Sadie laughed. 'No! Well yeah actually, but not like that. It was going to be in the Seychelles. And it was supposed to be just me and Mark on this sort of deserted island, no-one else, dead romantic. We had it all planned ages ago. We'd made all the arrangements.' She stabbed a stick in the sand and impaled a bit of palm leaf on top of it.

'So, like how did you end up here?' No-one could be that bad at geography, Delilah thought, that they'd go the wrong way across the world for their own wedding. And wouldn't someone point it out at the airport when they checked in?

'The hotel we were going to suddenly closed. "Refurbishing" they told us, which really means they've gone bust. The tour operator was all apologies and offered us this instead. My uncle said he'd been here a few times and that it was OK so we went for it. But then,' Sadie sighed, 'Mum decided *she* wanted to come. And then Dad found out about that which meant *he* didn't want to be left out so he's here as well, even though they're divorced and hate each other and barely even speak.'

Delilah hardly dared ask but out it came. 'And Mark?'

'Couldn't get on the same flight. Don't even ask how that cock-up happened. He's supposed to get here tonight. He'd bloody better, that's all I can say.'

'Yeah. Um, right.'

Close up, under the harsh sun, Sadie didn't look much older than Delilah. Young to be in charge of a whole wedding, anyway. Delilah gazed out to sea, past the reef towards the yachts moored over on Dragon Island, and tried to imagine the hassle of planning her own wedding. It would be all right if it was to Prince William, because presumably the royal flunkeys would take care of all the arrangements and she'd just have to roll up to the Abbey (the gold coach? Like Princess Di or Cinderella?) in a fabulous frock with her hair (Nicky Clarke) and make-up (Jemma Kidd) looking brilliant. She somehow doubted William would be allowed to sneak off alone with her for a quick Caribbean beachfront ceremony with a steel band and rum punch. But suppose she met someone in the next couple of years who she couldn't imagine living without? So far in her short life she hadn't had to plan anything more complicated than Suki's surprise sixteenth a few months ago. It had been a vodka and Red Bull extravaganza down the local rec, that had had very messy consequences all over the see-saw and some old Neighbourhood Watch colonel-type threatening to set his fat Labrador on them. Her own wedding, without serious and responsible grown-ups in charge, would probably be the same sort of fiasco.

'Aren't you a bit young?' Delilah asked bluntly.

'Twenny-one.' Sadie sounded gloomy again. 'And me and Mark, we're solid. Well we would be if they'd just effin' leave us alone to get on with it. My uncle and aunt are coming on the same plane as him, so that's even *more* people. We've got nearly two weeks 'til the wedding, plus a week after for, like, the honeymoon, so they thought, well hey, might as well turn up for a holiday. They'd even planned to tag along to the Seychelles, can you believe? To "surprise us"!' She held up her fingers in little quote signs and looked furious, then she delved into her straw beach bag and pulled out some cigarettes. 'Want one?' Delilah shook her head.

'Why are they coming then if they're not invited?' Funny people, Delilah thought, gatecrashing a wedding thousands of miles from home.

'Because they think of us like we're their extra kids. They've got a son of their own but he's gone to live in Sydney with his friend, if you get my drift.' Sadie nudged her in the side and grinned.

'Huh?' Delilah felt confused. 'Oh, you mean he's gay.' She hadn't come across many gay boys yet – at least she didn't think so. The ones at school used to call each other 'gay' all the time, whenever someone knew the answer to a question in Eng. Lit. or actually did their maths coursework, or admitted to liking cricket. They'd calmed down a bit since GCSEs – now it was more like a term of affection. Pretty hard going for them if they really *were* gay though, and statistically some of them not only must be, but should know it perfectly well by now. Oliver Willis wasn't, she knew that for sure. Delilah was at least the fourth girl in their year that he'd managed to persuade out of her pants. Unless . . . well he might just have been trying out what it was like with girls, so he could make what her mother would call an informed choice. She hoped she hadn't been so crap at sex that she'd been the one to sway the balance. By next term he might be going out with Pink Paul in year eleven and it could all be down to her.

'Yeah – he was a trolley dolly on Quantas for a while,' Sadie went on, sounding, to Delilah, impressively breezy. 'But now he and his mate run a bar in Darling Harbour.'

'Right.' Delilah was lost, though flattered to be assumed to be following Sadie's worldly-wise trail. What the buggery was Darling Harbour? Was that an exclusively gay hang-out? She'd have to e-mail Nick and find out.

'We're getting married over there.' Sadie pointed her cigarette out to sea, towards Dragon Island. 'Classic innit? So even though we're here and not in the Seychelles we still get our little desert island, all palm trees and white sand.'

'And snorkellers. They go out there by the boatload, from the water-sports hut. I've just seen them.'

'Not on my wedding day they won't, not on that afternoon anyway. We've been promised,' Sadie growled, then turned to Delilah with a big bright smile. 'You can come if you want! Why don't you? Be my best woman! You'll look really pretty in the photos.'

Glad to be of use, Delilah thought. And what exactly, she wondered, was a best woman supposed to do? She hoped it wasn't the same as being a bridesmaid. She'd been one of those twice before, and if you did it three times it meant you weren't ever going to be a bride. Glad as she was to have made a new friend, there was no way she was going to muck up her chance of being Princess Delilah.

They'd picked the wrong moment. As Beth and Lesley walked into the air-cooled, jojoba-scented reception area of the Haven spa, a piercingly raised voice was splintering the calm.

'There's nothing wrong with my blood pressure!' The mother of the bride was slapping her hand on the desk. Miriam, cool and calm and in charge of taking the bookings, continued to smile at her, refusing to fuel the fury.

'For Christ's sake, look, it says "Seaweed and Scented Oil Head Wrap". It's only a hair-conditioning treatment! There's nothing to get my blood boiling about! I've never heard of anything so absurd!'

Bride's mother stabbed her finger hard against the spa treatment brochure she was waving at the still unruffled and smiling Miriam, who must have been through this a hundred times.

'Lordy, how that woman rants and raves!' Lesley murmured to Beth. 'Shall we come back later?'

'No way,' Beth hissed back, 'I want to see the outcome.' She pulled Lesley over to the big squashy sofa and the two of them sat down, watching the action from comparative safety through a conveniently placed arrangement of bird of paradise flowers on the table beside them.

'I'm afraid it's in the rules,' Miriam explained quietly as she gently tapped the end of her pen on the desk. 'Where any heat treatments are involved, we have to exclude all risks. That is why all guests have a health check with the nurse first, if there are any "yes" answers on the medical questionnaire. It's for your safety, Mrs Morrison, your blood pressure was slightly on the high side.'

'My safety! It's to cover your arses, you mean.' The voice of Mrs Morrison went up another decibel. Automatically, Lesley and Beth leaned further back against the sofa. 'In the brochure it gives a list of treatments included, and the hair wrap is one of them. It doesn't say anywhere, does it . . .' And here she looked round at Beth and Lesley, inviting some back-up. 'It doesn't say you can have anything you want as long as you haven't got a broken nail or a slight headache.'

'Do you have headaches? Because we don't recommend . . .' Miriam interrupted.

'Nowhere does it say anything about bloody . . . blood pressure!' Mrs Morrison stamped her foot like a toddler having a supermarket tantrum.

'If she doesn't calm down we'll be seeing exactly

where blood pressure gets you,' Beth whispered.

'You're right. Let's go.' Lesley and Beth left the sofa, inching slowly and stealthily past the flower vase in case of anger fallout, and backed silently towards the door, but it opened suddenly, almost sending the two of them crashing forward into Mrs Morrison. Beth, off balance, clutched Lesley, fearful that tripping against the furious woman might result in a smack in the mouth.

'Hey you guys, what's the fight about? We can hear the racket from out there on the deck!' Gina, accompanied by the presumed father of the bride, Michael, joined Beth and Lesley, staring at the source of the din.

'Oh I should have guessed! It's Angela picking a fight!' Michael laughed loudly. 'Now there's a surprise. Nice to see you being so consistent, *darling*!'

'Get lost, Michael,' Angela hissed at him. 'And what the hell are you doing in here? Are you following me?'

'I'd imagine he's doing the same thing as you are, honey; just booking some nice, relaxing massages.' Gina placed herself squarely between Angela and Michael as if, Beth thought, she was preventing a full-blown punch-up breaking out. Perhaps she was. Brave woman, standing in the line of fire like that.

'I'd be booking a nice simple hair-conditioning treatment if they didn't insist on a note from your GP before they'll even file your nails in this place.'

We don't actually . . .' Miriam cut in.

'Hey listen, Angela is it?' Gina pointed to the treatment list. 'Forget the hair stuff, it'll only turn your highlights green. Let me recommend the Muscle-Melt Stress-Away Massage with soothing frangipani. It's to die for, isn't it Beth?'

'Definitely. It's bliss – you'll come out feeling just *so* calm,' Beth agreed.

'Are you saying I'm stressed?' Angela glowered at them both. Beth held her breath as Michael let out a sudden barking laugh.

'Is Angela stressed? Is a banana yellow?'

'We're only saying you might *seem* to be a little stressed, Angela honey.' Gina spoke quietly, holding the woman's wrist lightly like a nurse checking a pulse. 'But you don't have to be. You can let it go. That is what this place is for. Trust me,' she smiled. 'Start your vacation with the Muscle-Melt, like I said,' and Beth saw her wink at Angela. 'And ask for Fabian. He has *the* touch.'

Calmed at last, Angela booked herself enough treatments to cover the first week of her stay, while the others waited patiently on the cream sofas.

'Thank you so much,' Angela eventually said to Gina and Beth as she was about to leave. 'That was sweet of you, I do get a teensy bit overanxious at times, especially now. We're here for our daughter's wedding you see, so you can imagine . . .'

'Oh sure! I so hope it goes well.' Gina gave her her best, broadest smile and Angela left the spa, heading back to catch some sun before lunch.

'And now honey,' Gina turned to Michael and treated him to a sexy pout, at the same time stroking his bare arm with a soft finger. 'This two-together sensual massage I was telling you about, shall we see if they've got a slot this afternoon?'

# 6

# Headless Horseman

56 ml vodka
3 dashes Angostura bitters
ginger ale

Bloody hell. Sod it. So that was why the radiators were
stone cold. Nick had woken up alone and shivering
with an arctic gale blowing outside and the wind
doing its best to get inside the house through every
rattling window and door frame. Exactly what had he
done, he'd asked any available deities, to deserve
parents so mean and so uncaring about his comfort
and welfare that they'd deprive their first-born child of
heating when they weren't in residence? Bad enough,
he'd considered as he'd lain with the duvet huddled
round his ears, that Felicity was now enjoying the free-
spending favours of some suck-up tosser who
smarmed his way through *nice dinners* in order to get
into her underwear; the well and truly last crumb in
the biscuit tin was existing in a house where you
had to bribe the cats into your bed with KiteKat
Munchies to keep warm.

Now, out by the shed, Nick stared hopelessly at the

gauge beside the oil tank, willing it to register more than zero. He tapped at it with a stick, but with no expectation of results. Why hadn't anyone (i.e. parents) checked it before they went away? How was he supposed to know the oil was going to run out and screw up the boiler and that it was down to him to order some more? Did they really think he would actually *read* every last word of the instructions they'd left? There were pages of them. Well, two – but very close-typed. Most of it was blah-di-blah about not smoking in bed, making sure it was diesel he put in Beth's car and clearing enough floor space for Mrs Padgham to get the Dyson round. He was nineteen not nine, for buggery's sake. He could survive alone in his own home for a couple of weeks. Except it turned out he couldn't.

He stomped back into the house, chilled right through to his bones from the sleety rain that had joined forces with the ice-cold wind.

'Bit of a rush on. That'll be due to the inclement weather,' the oil-supplier receptionist told him down the phone, in a manner that suggested a bit of a chill was highly unusual in late November. She didn't seem to get the idea about the word 'urgent' and couldn't promise anything before Thursday – three glacial days away. He should have lied – said there were small babies in the house, that the boiler ran the only means of cooking. That would have been the smart thing to do. Why wasn't he smart?

Nick found Beth's pashmina hanging on the hook by the back door. He wrapped the soft pink fabric Lawrence of Arabia-style round his head and wandered out to the log pile under the lean-to at the back of the garage. This was more promising; he'd keep a blazing fire going with this lot and sleep on a sofa in the sitting room. Pity Felicity wouldn't be around – she'd have looked perfect lying on the blue rug, her creamy naked body softly lit by the flickering flames. They could have toasted marshmallows, drunk hot chocolate with a tot of warming brandy in it and cuddled up together snugly. But it didn't do to think of her – that way lay regret and a sense of failure.

On closer inspection, the logs seemed on the big side: huge slabs of tree trunk, in fact. Come to think of it, there'd been a heading on page two of his mum's instructions. He'd only read as far as 'Logs', assuming he wouldn't need any further information. He could now, looking at these hefty boles, guess what followed. The gist of it would be: 'Cut logs with useless blunt axe provided and stack into a pile artistically worthy of a long-ago North-West Frontier cabin-dweller.' While she was at it, his mum would have taken the opportunity to add: 'Chop big enough supply for entire winter, seeing as you're young and fit and your dad's knocking on a bit and has better things to do like earn enough to feed, clothe and educate you lot.' Depressing. Plus the way things were going at the moment, he'd probably hack his foot off.

Nick went into the house and switched on the kettle and the immersion heater. At least he could have a good long soak and a hot cup of tea. There'd be a hot-water bottle somewhere that he could take to bed that night and he'd let the cats get under the duvet. Hardly up to the standard of Felicity, but hey, beggars couldn't be choosers. What he'd give to be like the rest of his so-lucky, holidaying family, lazing around in a climate where the only tricky thing was how to stay cool enough. What he'd give ... A small wild thought crossed his mind. Maybe it wouldn't cost that much, not a massive dent in his Australia fund. It was the cheap pre-Christmas season and according to the ads, airlines could barely give the seats away. He wasn't busy at work — even hardened horse-fanciers were putting their cash into their kids' Christmas presents rather than gambling it all on slow nags. Maybe (when he'd thawed out) he'd make a few phone calls, check out the cost of a cheap ticket to St George and a room with a brick-wall view at the Mango and then just turn up. Wouldn't they all be surprised?

The Mango Experience wasn't so vast as to be coldly impersonal. Beth and Ned had once stayed at a complex on Lanzarote that had catered — frenziedly but inadequately — for a thousand guests. Here, with no more than a hundred guest rooms, you would never have to share beach space with a party of sixty Swiss hi-fi dealers having their annual sales conference, or watch them yodel their way through nightly limbo contests. On the other hand, it wasn't so small that you couldn't avoid those guests that you'd prefer to keep at a comfortable distance. At the other extreme, in a sleek, minimal boutique hotel with only a dozen rooms, it could be tricky avoiding getting trapped in the Thai-theme ocean-view bar with someone who wanted to show you photos of their daughter's graduation, or tell you how world peace could easily be achieved by a spot of nuclear zapping in strategic areas. Here at the Mango, Beth considered, was just about the perfect balance. Ned, on the other hand, was more wary.

'Not sure I want to spend too much time around Gina's mad mother, but I wouldn't mind having a chat with her, see what all this death stuff is about,' he murmured to Beth as they approached the Sundown bar for a pre-lunch drink.

'Why?' Beth was curious. 'Do you honestly think she's likely to have inside knowledge about the great hereafter?'

'No idea. I just wonder what makes her think it's imminent. Suppose she's right? Suppose she can give us all a clue what to look out for?'

He was joking, wasn't he? Oh please, she prayed, don't let his next midlife hobby be a morbid obsession with death. Even a never-ending parade of other women might be better than that. At least they'd keep him cheerful.

'What, the sort of clue like "look out for a hooded skeletal chap who carries a big scythe"? Not sure I'd want to know.' Beth shuddered. 'Especially if I still felt well enough to prop up a bar and hold court.'

Ned gave her a look, one that smacked of 'you cynical cow'. Perhaps she was being a bit harsh, Beth conceded, taking his hand and giving it a squeeze. He squeezed hers back and kept hold of it, as if trusting her to save him from the pursuing Grim Reaper. Tough one, that: a far more formidable enemy than some silly slapper sending Tiffany trinkets.

Gina's mother could be seen sitting bolt upright on a high stool beneath the fringed shade of the bar's over-hanging palm-thatched roof, gazing around her through very dark, gold-rimmed sunglasses. Her hair was wrapped in sombre black cloth, turban-style a toque – Beth remembered her grandmother had been keen on them – secured at the front with a jet comb. She was wearing a loose black silky kaftan that flapped lightly in the wind like big wings and reminded Beth, in view of the circumstances of her visit, of a vulture waiting to pick at a corpse. Not a comfortable thought, really, given that the woman was the one apparently about to *be* the corpse.

'She's very certain of her imminent demise, according to Gina. She's quite determined that she won't need a return ticket, so she didn't even buy one. What if she's wrong? Or worse, what if she's right?' Ned asked, glancing nervously at the woman by the bar as if suspecting she might be looking to take someone along with her on the ultimate mystery trip.

'I expect Gina will throttle her if she's still here by going-home time,' Beth said. 'She seems quite keen for her mother to have her own way on this one. If I get Gina by herself in the sauna I know she'll tell me all about it.'

'Whether you want her to or not?'

'Oh, I want her to! Well, I do as long as she doesn't confide that she's planning murder. We only see each other once a year, what would be the point of holding back on the gossip?'

Oooh – possibly something that would have been better unsaid, that one. Beth was pretty sure she saw Ned actually wince. Or perhaps a passing mosquito had flicked against his face. The one thing the Mango Experience didn't provide in terms of 'wellness' was a full-on counselling service. Maybe she'd put it forward on one of the Visitors' Suggestion forms that the management were confident enough to risk placing in every room. Maybe there was a potential niche market here, providing away-from-home therapy complete with after-session stress-relief class and meditation. Tattered marriages could be patched up, work anxieties soothed, perspectives redrawn. And on the guests' return, the luggage carousels of Gatwick (or Frankfurt, New York, Montreal) would be surrounded by beatific, patient, smiling folks who couldn't give a flying one if their matching Louis Vuitton bags had disappeared for ever to the world's lost-luggage cave.

'Don't panic,' she laughed, 'I won't be telling her anything about you and your fancy piece! We women have better things to talk about than midlife men and their meanderings, you know.'

This time he definitely *did* flinch. How sensitive he was, she thought. Anyone would imagine he was the one who had been cheated on. At what point, exactly, had this infidelity business changed from something he'd got himself into quite deliberately, to something deeply traumatic that had happened to him by accident, purely at random?

Beth sat down at a vacant table beneath a sunshade and privately admitted that what she'd said hadn't been strictly true. She and her women friends joked about midlife men quite often in casual passing, although generally in an abstract rather than a personal kind of way: discussing yet another ageing star being caught by the tabloids leaning on a gloriously fine-skinned twenty-something babe for ego support. She'd always assumed it must be quite disappointing for the traded-in wife, this lack of imagination on the husband's part. Bad enough that he'd left her, worse to find he was merely another of life's clichés, resorting to the predictable leeching-from-the-young approach to reassuring himself that he could just be immortal after all. For all that she *didn't* know about Ned's extramarital activity, she'd at least gathered it had been with a grown-up.

'Where's your beautiful daughter? She gone out and met some hunky guy already?' Gina joined Beth at the table and plonked her drink down in front of her. It was the burstingly exuberant Caribbean caboodle: fruit-filled, sparkly, bright pink and complete with three paper umbrellas and a couple of swizzlers. Beth thought of Cyn and the midday rum punches she used to have, with their extra coconut chunks crammed onto the cherry stick. It helped strengthen the gums, Cyn had claimed, though for what Cyn would need Olympic-power jaws, Beth could only speculate.

Gina pulled her chair round closer to Beth in the shade and lit up a cigarette which she placed in a long onyx holder.

'She's gone to book in for some sailing with a girl she's met,' Beth told her. 'I've hardly seen her since breakfast.'

'Aha, so she's making friends already. That's great!'

'Very Princess Margaret!' Ned commented, indicating the cigarette holder as he returned from the bar with a beer and Beth's fruit punch.

'You kidding? Isn't she dead?' Gina looked alarmed.

'Oh yes, very dead,' Beth agreed.

'Unlike my mom,' Gina muttered, shooting a daggered glance at her mother, who was now sipping a glass of sparkling wine and informing the bartender that she could drink all she liked, whenever she liked, now she knew how long she'd got. Or hadn't got. 'No call to hold back!' Beth heard her bellow to anyone in range, followed by a harsh cackle and a volley of barking coughs.

'We haven't been introduced yet, and Ned's dying to meet her, if you'll excuse the pun.' Beth nudged Gina. 'Are you so ashamed of your holiday pals that we can't meet your mama?'

'You really wanna meet her? She's one scary lady – are you sure?' Gina gave Ned a warning look.

'Oh absolutely, ' Ned agreed. 'Of course we do.'

'OK then, but remember it was your choice. Don't you go blaming me for any consequences.' Gina sighed and pushed back her chair and went and firmly manhandled her mother off her bar stool. The barman seemed relieved: he'd begun to look close to tearfully defeated under the non-stop monologue, and an impatient queue was building up.

'Mom! Come sit with us. I want you to meet my friends.' Gina led her mother across to the table and pushed her gently into a shaded seat. 'Mom, these are Ned and Beth – they come here at the same time each year, just like me. Ned and Beth, this is my mother, Dolly.'

'Hi Dolly, good to meet you.' Beth shook an emaciated brown-speckled hand and was surprised that the returning grip was as hard and fast as a parrot claw.

'*Is* it good?' Dolly asked her with a grin that dazzled with incongruously bleached-white teeth. 'Not that it matters nohow if it isn't. It won't be for long, you know. I have a date to keep with the next world.'

'Oh Mom, please don't keep on . . .'

'Don't keep on what? I don't want to get these folks thinking I'm their new best friend and then have them spoil their holiday with mourning.' Dolly glared at her daughter. 'In fact you better just stop with the introducing and friend-making, Gina, it isn't fair on anyone. Hand me a cigarette, girl, and you can put yours out *right now*. Are you trying to be the only American in the world who still smokes?' She turned away and leaned confidingly towards Ned. 'It's only when you got no health left that you can risk playing chicken with it. Isn't that right Ned?'

Beth remembered questions like this from Latin at school: questions framed in such a way that the expected answer had to be 'yes'. Of course it would have been impossible to disagree, however mad a proposition Dolly had come up with. With an air of nothing-to-lose lack of inhibition she wasn't likely to let day-to-day conversational etiquette get in the way of her opinions.

'I'm not sure it's OK to tempt fate about your health at any age,' Ned told her, bravely, in Beth's view, for this was one autocratic, opinionated lady: very Bette Davis at her peak. Then Ned added, 'I always try not to, anyway.' Beth felt her eyebrows raising themselves at this: from where, exactly, had come this po-faced factor?

'Piffle,' Dolly snorted, pointing to his beer. 'You're doing it right now. You drink alcohol, don't you? You drive and you cross roads and travel by plane? You do as you choose and to hell with the consequences. The difference is that at my time of life – or death – you can take risks that are as crazy as you like. I wish I'd taken more over the last year or two.' She inhaled deeply on her cigarette and coughed. 'I should have slept around and tried heroin and pulled off a bank heist just for the hell of it.'

Beside Beth, Gina groaned quietly and drummed her fingers up and down on the table. Something told Beth that Gina had heard her mother performing this particular party piece many, many times before. Possibly this 'I'm going to die, any minute' scenario had been going on for years, a sure-fire emotional blackmail into getting your own way. Poor old Gina if that was the case – no wonder she went over the top, putting it about a bit on holiday. She tried to imagine Dolly disguised in a joke-shop George Dubya mask and wielding a sawn-off shotgun, ordering the customers of the Guildford Barclays to lie on the floor and freeze. Not easy, but not impossible. Dolly would make a formidable bank robber; keen as she was on a risk-filled life, you wouldn't want to argue with her, armed or not.

\* \* \*

'It's called "doing things as a family",' Ned explained to Delilah as the three of them waited beneath the reception archway for their taxi, 'and besides, you're the one who wants the new snorkel mask. You'll need to try it on.'

'Yes but . . . Carlos told me he'd take me and Sadie out on a boat this afternoon,' Delilah complained.

'We won't be out long,' Beth told her. 'I need to be back by three – Lesley and I want to give the t'ai chi class a go.'

'Ugh, how can you? It's right on the beach in front of everyone! You've never done it before – everyone will laugh!' Delilah put her hands over her face as if she was already being forced to be a spectator at the world's most mortifying event: her mother in gym kit, making slow, strange body shapes and looking mad in front of a crowd.

'Of course they won't!' Beth laughed. 'Why would anyone be watching us? They've better things to do; you for one, you'll be sailing.'

Lordy it was hot. Beth fanned herself with her hand as she waited. A tiny hummingbird flitted past, then hovered beside them as it sucked nectar from the pink hibiscus flowers.

'Amazing little things, aren't they?' Beth turned round at the sound of a non-family voice. It was Michael, father of the bride, ex-husband of the feisty, fraught Angela. Amazing how much you could know about people in this place, she thought, in only twenty-four hours. He was dressed for town rather than beach, in cream linen and carrying a beaten-up panama hat.

'The speed of those tiny wings,' he went on. 'You wonder how they get enough food going in to turn it into so much power.'

'Doesn't take much to keep a titchy bird in the air,' Delilah chipped in. 'I mean it's only like a big dragon-fly, no-one thinks that's much of a miracle.'

'Delilah!' Ned warned.

Delilah shrugged. 'Sorry. Didn't mean to sound rude, I just thought, well you know . . . I suppose they've got bigger bodies than dragonflies though.'

'Conceded generously.' Michael was laughing at her, something that Beth felt she should warn him was like playing chase-the-string with a tiger.

'We're going down into Teignmouth for a snorkel mask,' Ned told him. 'Would you like to share our cab, if you're going that way?'

'Oh. Are you sure? How kind – yes I would. No point in taking two, is there?'

The cab was a minibus, which was just as well, as at the last minute they were joined by Angela.

'You won't mind me tagging along,' she announced, hauling herself awkwardly into the seat beside the driver just as they'd all got settled. 'Sadie wants me to get her some Dream Curl lotion and then I thought I'd go to meet my brother at the airport. I know they've got transfers included but it might be a coach and they go all round the houses, don't they? He and his wife are arriving for Sadie's wedding.' She beamed round at Beth and Ned in the row behind her, her smile fading to something close to a snarl as she looked at Michael, who sat with Delilah in the back seats.

'And Mark's,' Michael added.

'What?'

'Mark's wedding. Chap our daughter's marrying. Remember him?'

'I know who he is,' Angela said.

'I could have got the hair stuff for Sadie,' Michael told her.

'No you couldn't,' Angela snapped. 'You've never come back from the shops with the right thing before, why should I trust you to start now?'

Delilah caught Michael's eye and the two of them started giggling like small infants, covering their mouths in fear of being heard.

'Naughty me,' he whispered into her hair. 'Never get anything right. Just as well I'm already sitting at the back of the class or she'd stop the cab and send me there.'

'I can hear you, you know,' Angela said.

'And we can all hear you too, my one true ex-love,' Michael said. Delilah shook with squashed-down laughter and a sense of having learned something new: grown-ups could be the most absurdly childish beings. Peculiar, that. How come they were the ones always telling you to grow up?

Much later, Ned wasn't quite sure how it came about that he was on his way to the airport, alone in another eight-seater taxi with the fearsome Angela. It had happened entirely by chance. There he was having a beer outside a gallery on the road beside the marina after pottering contentedly by himself in the town. Beth and Delilah had stayed only until the snorkel mask (Delilah) and a pair of bead-trimmed espadrilles (Beth) had been bought, and then they'd returned to the Mango for their various appointments with sport. Ned had stayed on alone to go to the bank and mooch around the harbour, having a look on the board outside the chandlery at the photos and details of boats for sale. Who knew? One day when (if ever) the kids had flown the coop he might cash in the pension fund, buy a yacht and spend a few years sailing around the Windward Islands with Beth, joining the ever-growing throng of middle-aged ocean-dwelling dropouts. Michael had gone for a wander round the town and said he'd take a local bus back later, after a look at the museum and cathedral.

'You make sure you get to see all the island while you're here,' he'd said to Delilah just before setting off in his battered old hat. 'Make the most of the trip, get to know how the place works.'

'You sound like my geography teacher,' she'd teased. Ned had been surprised, she'd said it almost fondly – quite unusual when mentioning anything to do with school.

'Good,' Michael had replied. 'That means I can set you a test on what you've learned.'

If he, Ned, her own father, had said that, how would she have reacted, he wondered as the cab containing himself and Angela sped eastward to the airport; would she have thought it just about the funniest thing she'd ever heard? No. Of course she wouldn't. It took a stranger to drag hilarity out of a teenager. He'd be willing to bet that Michael's daughter Sadie would have given her father the classic teenage 'you think you're *so* funny' look that Delilah would have given him. Perhaps all parents of the young should swap round now and then, get themselves a quick fix of that feeling they can still amuse.

Angela had pounced while Ned had been dreaming away, watching a couple of about the same age as him and Beth, loading supplies onto their catamaran. They had cases of Carib beer, a box of bananas, basics like loo rolls and groceries. He found himself envying the string of pennants hanging from the mast – small flags of countries they must have visited. He recognized Grenada, Barbados and Antigua among them. This was a lot more than one up, it seemed, on being a caravanner, trundling down the A30, your stickered back window boasting trips to Woolacombe and Bridlington.

And then suddenly Angela had landed, bang-flop in the seat opposite him, as if she'd been there all the time, waiting till his thinking was done to accost him with her suggestion.

'I mean it makes sense, doesn't it,' Angela was now saying, as she'd already said twice during this journey. 'No point forking out for two taxis when you're both going in roughly the same direction.'

He nodded vaguely. There really wasn't anything to add to the last time he'd replied to the same comment, apart from something obviously rather impolite such as that actually, it was only in the direction of the Mango Sport 'n' Spa if you didn't mind a six-mile detour to the east. Still, what was to race back for? He'd only feel obliged to join in the 5 p.m. beach-volleyball game. Len would insist on him being in his team and then trample all over him. Bulky sort, Len, bigger than ever this year but still a swift, if clumsy, demon on the sand.

'Nearly there now,' Angela said. 'Can't wait to see them. And Mark of course.'

Ned had gathered from the earlier ride into town that this was the bridegroom, a young man who might well have been happier to travel to the hotel in the tour company's minibus rather than, exhausted by a long flight in the back of the plane, have to make polite chit-chat with his scary future mother-in-law.

'Oooh look, the plane's in! They've landed!' Angela was practically bouncing in her seat now as the cab drew in alongside the runway where a British Airways 777 was parked, all doors and hatches gaping open like a huge gutted fish.

They pulled up outside the arrivals terminal and Ned climbed quickly out of the cab, just to savour the humid air after the taxi's fierce air conditioning. He'd never felt cold before on the island. For much of the time on these holidays he was close to gasping in the damp heat. Presumably drivers here considered motoring in a near-frost something of a treat.

'Oh look! Here they are! Over here!' Angela was on the pavement, shrieking in the direction of the open-air arrivals hall, causing at least thirty bemused-looking newly landed passengers to turn and stare at her.

And so here they were. Ned stared at Angela's approaching brother and his wife and blinked, then blinked again, hoping and hoping they'd change into someone, anyone else. Posh and Becks, Tony and Cherie Blair, the late Kray twins, anybody. But now Angela was hugging her sister-in-law fondly, while Ned stood beside her digging his nails into his messily sweating palms, wishing he was back home – even working would be better than this, possibly even searching the Horsham B&Q for Rawlplugs would be, on a frantic Bank Holiday morning.

'Cyn!' Angela's voice, who would have thought it possible, notched up yet another decibel. 'Lovely to see you! Good flight?'

Ned remembered his manners and shook Bradley's hand. 'Great to see you!' Brad said. 'Are you still up for the diving? Cyn was saying on the way over that she hoped you and Beth would be back this year.'

Like she didn't know. Ned wished *he* had. What kind of trick was this to pull? Whatever happened to 'somewhere out east'?

And then there she was with her body against his and her arms around his neck, still deliciously scented with that slight vanilla tang, giving him a social little hug and whispering close into his ear, 'Ned darling! How *sweet* of you to come and meet me! It was going to be a surprise!'

Oh it was, Cynthia, it was.

# 7

# Black Velvet

3 measures Guinness
3 measures champagne

Beth very much admired the colour of the paint on the walls of the Haven's treatment room no. 6 (Rosemary). The pale reddish-oxide was, and she filed this away for future useful reference, almost exactly the shade of a newly ploughed field she'd noticed the summer before on the borders of Devon and Cornwall while driving Nick down to look at Falmouth art college. Of course it wasn't quite the same now that Petallia had turned off the overhead lamps and lit the three chunky scented candles in their individual cube alcoves high on the wall, but even in the half-gloom Beth could appreciate its earthy, restful quality.

The colour was definitely a contender for the spare bedroom back home that was so dismal and dated (hydrangea pattern curtains, walls painted a chilly Diamond Blue) that it would qualify perfectly as a 'before' room for any extreme makeover show. Perhaps she could ring Nick and have him pop down to Homebase for sample pots of Farrow and Ball's range of historic russets. The old silver-grey carpet in there could go as well; it was decidedly moth-eaten around the edges and beneath it lurked an old but possibly decent quality woodblock floor. Or would that, combined with the terracotta walls, result in too much of a cardboard-box effect, colour-wise? Decisions, decisions. And they shouldn't be made now; Beth was in the middle of her Sensuous Aromatherapy Experience and was supposed to be paying attention to her inner serenity, not to the interior décor of her guest room. By this stage – front almost done – her brain should be barely functioning. In mind and body alike, she should be as floppy and malleable as a jelly.

Beth tried hard to clear her head of all mundane thoughts, the better to absorb the benefits of an hour and a half of being deliciously slathered with aromatherapeutic gunk (the Tranquillity Option: lavender, camomile, melissa, geranium – to soothe and relax). Petallia was doing her highly competent best, working her way limb by limb round Beth's supine body. Every now and then, sensing tension, Petallia would smile and murmur, 'Relax,' in a soft, soothing tone.

This was, after all, a key element of a stay at the Mango Sport 'n' Spa. You were supposed to leave all domestic dross behind and forget all the niggling concerns of day-to-day home routine. If there were problems to return to, you were supposed to face them mentally and physically equipped, invigorated and empowered. At least, that was what Louella, the hotel's yoga guru, had informed her class while Beth, Delilah, Lesley, Gina and Cyn had been crouched and hunched like a row of Sainsbury's chickens down in Child's Pose in the Wellness Pavilion that morning, trying not to giggle.

And what a surprise *that* had been, Cyn and Bradley arriving. Ned hadn't seemed particularly thrilled about it when he'd got back from the town the day before and told her. In fact he'd been downright abrupt, catching up with her as she and Lesley had a glass of fizz at sunset with a grumpy 'Cyn and Bradley have turned up.' But then who *would* be in a good mood after sharing a long cab ride (plus airport detour) with the dreadful Angela?

Beth now tried deep, even breathing and concentrated instead on trying to shut out the background soundtrack of communicating marine life. Why, she then found herself wondering as Petallia deftly smoothed scented oil up and down her right arm, why (and how) exactly had someone first concluded that this whale-song stuff was calming and gentle? Suppose the whales were not actually wallowing joyously in the ocean, beatifically cooing sweet notes of love to each other, but shouting furious things to their young, a sort of sea-life equivalent of 'You're not going out dressed like that!' Maybe the one that was now going 'Wwhooo wwhooop' in this scented darkened room was actually bellowing to its teenage whale calf, 'If you don't eat that plankton, you'll get it served up at every mealtime 'til it's gone.' And why whales? Sensitively recorded and with a bit of suitable accompanying harpsichord perhaps, the sound of cats purring could be just as rhythmically soothing as this.

Slip slap went Petallia's expert fingers on Beth's right thigh, denting deeply into all the places that Beth would identify as chubby. She imagined the honey-combed pockets of fat beneath the skin, constructed like one of those cross-sections of a quality mattress that appear in ads in the Saturday newspapers. She was depressingly convinced that whatever creams and lotions were rubbed in, however many volts of electronic toning were applied, these pockets were constructed with a semi-permeable membrane allowing flab to percolate in but never out. Except with Cynthia – something in her had obviously unstoppered and let any last trace of surplus fat out of her. Far too thin, that's how she was looking this year. Lovely as it was to see her, it had been a shock to realize how very slender Cyn had become when she'd appeared in the yoga class that morning. Losing a bit of weight was one thing; having successfully stuck to a diet called for congratulations to be offered in an obligatory, sisterly woman-to-woman gesture, albeit through envious, gritted teeth. But Cyn looked somehow shrunken and drawn, so that her head seemed a bit too big for her body. Her fine-boned face was etched with the tiniest creases, and the overbright glitter in her eyes told Beth (and Lesley, who had made a comment when Cyn went off to the loo) that something was deeply amiss. Perhaps she was ill.

'I expect she'll tell you,' Lesley had teased as they poured freshly juiced mango at the breakfast buffet that morning. 'You've got that Agony Aunt appeal.'

'People do tell me stuff,' Beth had sighed, thinking of Worldwide Wendy and her intimate discussions of internal secretions. 'I must have been given a confiding face.'

'Oh you have,' Lesley had agreed. 'And you always seem to be so calm and relaxed. I envy you. I might look like a big, fat good-time sort but I'm all a bundle of worry inside.'

Petallia held up a big ochre towel to screen her eyes from the dire sight of exposed flesh as Beth turned herself over with extreme care (for how easy but how undignified it would be to crash to the floor from this plank-narrow bench) and settled herself on her front. Perhaps, Beth thought, she'd have more chance of escaping her own thoughts in this face-down position. Perhaps at last she'd start to feel nothing about anything, think nothing about anyone and actually feel the benefit of all this me-me-me attention at last. Beth sighed as she lay beneath the firmly kneading hands of Petallia, annoyed at herself for wasting the benefits of this session, intended to smooth away her own inner troubles, by worrying about someone else's. Cut it out, she told her brain, just leave it. Enjoy the moment; don't waste it. But it was too late. Just as she was beginning to sink into a near stupor as Petallia kneaded her back, she felt the masseuse's fingers doing the pit-pat raindrop thing up and down her spine. A few moments of utter silence followed and then a tiny bell tinkled. All over.

Delilah padded along the shore, knee-deep in the sea, feeding chunks of breakfast bread to the shoals of minute greedy fishes that flowed around her ankles like a silky drift of patterned fabric. She could see Michael further up the beach, mooching along by himself past the early morning t'ai chi group. He had a look of that artist, the blond gay one who lived in California, Delilah thought as she watched him coming nearer. David Hockney, that was the dude, all floppy yellow hair and quite cool glasses. They'd studied him in art at school and in one of the photos she'd seen of him he'd been wearing a cream outfit and a beaten-up straw hat like Michael's.

She liked Michael, she decided, as she watched him stop to pick up a shell from the sand and stand looking at it for a few moments, turning it over and then putting it in his pocket. He was really brave to have come here with that horrible always-cross ex-wife and his selfish Sadie daughter who'd wanted to cut her whole family right out of her wedding. How mean was that? Michael was all right. He'd definitely be OK at a wedding; he was the sort you could have a laugh with about the bridesmaids' dresses and he was also someone who, like Delilah, had tagged along on this trip without being properly attached to anyone.

What had gone wrong with him and the wife, she wondered? He'd certainly pissed off the Angela woman big-time for her to be so horrible to him. Perhaps there'd been an issue over sense-of-humour failure with her. *Not* a woman you could ever rip the piss out of and then say 'Joke!' She'd probably hit you with a brick.

'Good morning, Delilah!' Michael called as he approached her. 'Tell me why you're paddling around throwing food into the sea. Is this a variant on anorexia? Have you also chucked in a plateful of bacon and eggs that you'll swear to your mother you've eaten?'

Delilah laughed. 'No! How rude is that! If I *was* anorexic that would be a terrible thing to say – it could set my recovery back by months!'

'Oh I know, I know.' Michael shrugged. 'It's one of the many subjects you're not allowed to mention to teenage girls, isn't it? Even the porky ones.'

'Especially the porky ones. They might have bulimia or binge-eating issues,' Delilah agreed. 'What I'm doing is I'm feeding the fish. You only have to wade in a few inches and they're all round your legs. Look! Aren't they brilliant?' She pointed down at the sparkling clear sea.

Michael peered into the shallows. 'Ugh, slimy swimming things. The teeming life of the ocean is best viewed from a safe dry vantage point, I think. Do you fancy a trip out in one of those glass-bottomed-boat things later? I'd ask Sadie, but now Mark's arrived she's all wrapped up with him. Literally, I should think at this early-morning moment. Or is that something else I shouldn't mention to a teenage girl?'

'No you shouldn't,' Delilah advised him solemnly. 'A teenage girl could decide you're being gross and disgusting.'

'Apologies. Yet again,' Michael offered, then delved into his pocket. 'Here, have this very pretty shell as a token of my contrition. Or are you now going to tell me I'm upsetting nature's balance by picking it up from the sand?'

'Thanks. I don't know much about the nature-balance thing. We haven't done seashore. For GCSE it was mostly oilfields and hill farms and the traffic system in Swanage.' Delilah looped up a corner of her sarong into a pocket and tied the shell safely into place. 'And yes, I would like to go out on a boat with you, as long as . . .'

'As long as I promise to keep off forbidden topics?'

'No!' she laughed, 'I like forbidden topics. It makes a change from people who are always so careful to talk to me as if I might explode any minute. All I get here is safe, dull suck-up stuff like, "That Rachel Stevens song's really good isn't it?" and, "I expect you've got that new Busted album" when they haven't a clue, I mean like I'd care about crap pop? What I meant was, I'd like to come as long as the boat doesn't fill up with people you've already picked fights with.' Delilah bit her lip. 'That's probably something *I* shouldn't have said too.'

Michael laughed. 'No you're all right, and you're dead right. We'll sneak off when none of them are looking. About mid-morning suit you when they're kippering on the loungers or doing beginners' snake-charming or whatever?'

'Snake-charming! I wish! Yeah I'll come. I hope we see turtles.'

'Me too, and a big shark. I shall tow it back and set it on my beloved ex-wife. They'd be pretty evenly matched. See you later.'

This was where it could all start to go horribly wrong, Ned thought as he checked his regulator and picked up the air tank ready to walk down the beach to the dive-boat. There was a good-sized crowd going out on the first dive today – sixteen or so. They had three instructors among them, but there was still potential for accidents if anyone was determined to get careless.

'I've been really looking forward to this,' Bradley said, hauling up the zip at the back of his wetsuit. 'You can't beat a good wreck dive.'

Well, you could interpret that in one of two ways. Ned prayed silently that Bradley was referring to the magic of underwater sea-life. He could, on the other hand, be looking forward to a cuckold's watery revenge – making sure that Ned got the ultimate punishment for messing with his wife and somehow got 'lost' inside the rusted cargo hold of the old sunken Marylla ferry boat. He could just see him, surfacing in a pretend panic, devastated to have let down his dive-buddy, swearing he'd never dive again, how was he to face Beth, all that. The perfect murder. They'd never even find his body; he'd be shark meat by the time they sent a search boat out.

'Do you think that big old grouper is still living in the hole in the hull?' Bradley went on as he adjusted his mask strap. 'You wonder if it's the same one, don't you? Year after year, it's there. I wouldn't have thought they'd live that long. Maybe it's a thriving fishy family business: the senior member gets to occupy that hole and pop its head out every hour to entertain the daily divers.'

What a good bloke Bradley was, Ned thought, feeling sly and unworthy. Bradley wasn't going to kill him – he couldn't be that good an actor; he was too damn nice. He obviously knew nothing about his wife and her latest extra-marital adventure (if Ned *was* her latest; possibly there'd already been time since spring for another brief dalliance or two). If he – Ned – had expected to meet up with Brad again this year, would he have taken it as far as it went with Cynthia? Impossible to come up with an answer. He liked to think it would be a resounding 'no'. If it wasn't, if it was even a shady 'maybe', then what kind of bastard did that make him? And did it make any difference? Surely he was a bastard anyway for cheating on Beth, a woman he saw every day and completely loved. Why was he getting all chewed up about behaving dishonestly to Brad? It was because he felt the dishonesty was still going on, that was why. It was because they weren't being equal here: Brad took it for granted that Ned was a Good Bloke. Beth, of course, knew different. But by not bagging up all his possessions for Oxfam, scratching 'Bastard' on the car roof or blowing their joint savings on a slow racehorse, she was choosing to believe that the better side to him was redeemable.

Ned knew only two things for certain at this moment. One was that he wished he'd persuaded Beth that Mexico might be fun this year, and the second was that he very much hoped he'd return from his dive without Bradley having stuck his diving knife through his windpipe.

* * *

Beth lay on her lounger in the gently wafting shadow of the big date palm, some way along the beach from the main pool, the bar, the jacuzzi and all busy activity. In keeping with the earth theme of the massage room, she'd had an urge to lie in the sand at the sea's edge, immersing herself in the elements, but had resisted. With sand gluing itself to all the oils on her body she would end up looking like a fish finger. At least, and at last, she was now relaxed completely, and emptying her head of all thought. Her eyes were closed, her breathing calm and even, and her book lay abandoned on the sand. A bit late, but Petallia would approve. The sea was all she could hear, plus now and then the faint buzz of light chatter as a group of people nearby bobbed idly in the water, discussing their mosquito bites and the many muscles that ached from the power yoga class they'd over-ambitiously joined the evening before.

Petallia had given Beth a list of what not to do in the couple of hours following her aromatherapy session, and Beth was busily and obediently not indulging in sex, cigarettes, food, alcohol, caffeine, sun exposure or sporting activity. Nor, at last, was she thinking about paint colours, Nick and his domestic arrangements, whether Wendy would fire her for refusing to pluck a puffin, what was quietly bugging Lesley or why Cynthia had become so skinny. Perhaps it was this final non-thought that had a talk-of-the-devil effect for, while Beth was drifting to a geranium-scented nirvana, along came Cynthia herself, noisily dragging a lounger to the spot beside Beth and plonking herself down on it with a gusty sigh.

'So what's new with you this year, Beth?' Cyn tapped Beth's left knee with a sharp silver fingernail, jolting her out of her perfect blankness. 'Beth? Wake up and tell me who's still here and who's not. I gather Valerie and Aubrey aren't, but I'm not surprised, not after what happened with the arrow. And why's Lesley's old man looking so red and porky? If that man was a car, you'd say he was long overdue for a service. And I don't mean,' and here Cyn giggled and nudged Beth hard in the side, '*that* kind of servicing. I mean the full-on BUPA check-up. He looks like a walking heart attack if you ask me. Mind you, Lesley's no Kate Moss herself. Perhaps it's something in the Guernsey water.'

'Beth sat up and put her sunglasses on, sad that this glorious moment of peace had passed. Cyn couldn't have got any closer – the loungers were almost touching. Had the woman never heard of the concept of personal space?

'Perhaps the walking-heart-attack thing is more true than we know,' Beth told her. 'Lesley's not as jolly as she usually is. Something's worrying her, perhaps it's Len's health.'

'If something's worrying women there's usually a man at the bottom of it. You'll get it out of her,' Cyn laughed. 'She'll tell *you*.'

'Funny, that's almost exactly . . .' Beth began, then stopped. Not really fair, that, she thought, letting Cyn know that she and Lesley had been discussing her in a similar way.

'Anyway, talking of weight,' Beth then said, glancing at Cynthia's tiny, shrunken body. The fast loss of weight had left the skin on her arms and legs looking as if it needed ironing. Cyn seemed a couple of sizes too small for what Beth recognized as one of her last year's bikinis, a velvety black one, printed with tiny white birds. Where her breasts used to sit pert above the low-cut cup, the bikini top sagged emptily. The matching sarong was edged with white marabou and Beth found herself imagining that Cyn only needed a sequinned and beaked mast to complete a fancy-dress magpie effect. 'Have you been on a diet?' she asked, in the way that women who wished to compliment each other did. 'You're looking very trim yourself. Which one was it? South Beach, GI, Atkins or Hay?'

Cyn didn't answer immediately, but bent down to fish about in her bag and pulled out a silver cigarette case. Eventually she said, 'Oh, you know, it's partly the gym, a spot of highly fashionable wheat intolerance, this and that.' She busied herself with her lighter and the fierce, fast inhalation of hot nicotine. How, Beth wondered, could she do that in this heat? She waved the smoke away from her own face, mentally apologizing to Petallia for inadvertently breaching one of the post-massage instructions. Perhaps it didn't count if breathing in the fumes was accidental.

'Sorry!' Cyn noticed Beth's gesture and immediately hurled the barely touched cigarette into the sand. 'Horrible habit! I had given up. Just been a bit uptight lately, that's all.' She smiled, but looked tense. Then she stood up abruptly as if sitting still for more than a few seconds was painful, her bag falling to the ground and tipping sun lotion, keys and a clutch of make-up items into the sand. 'Hey, why don't we go for an early drink?' I've been looking forward to one of Jim's rum punches.' Cyn nervously scrabbled around in the sand, collecting her belongings together. Her bony fingers were spread out like a child's drawing of a crab, all skinny long sinew. Beth watched, wanting to tell her to calm down, that it was all all right.

'OK, I quite fancy one of the fruit cocktails,' she agreed instead, stuffing her unread book back into her beach bag. The two women set off along the shore, walking close to the sea's edge. Cyn at first skipped out of reach of the waves, then took off her spangly sandals and waded up to her thighs in the water.

'Was it a big disappointment, coming here after all instead of the Seychelles?' Beth asked. 'Your niece Sadie told Delilah about the change of venue for the wedding. It was clever of you to suggest they all came here instead. Funny that we'd already met Angela, and her being Brad's sister! We had no idea!'

'Ghastly isn't she? The woman's a dreadful witch! No, I didn't mind – I was delighted to be back here in fact. Hanging out with people that we already know means the Angela effect is somewhat diluted!' Cynthia giggled, splashing along, not bothering to keep the feathered sarong out of the water. The salt water would ruin it. The Cynthia of previous years wouldn't have risked that, Beth realized. She'd have taken it off, folded it carefully and made someone on the sand look after it for her while she frolicked about in the sea. Frolicking in the sea at all wasn't like her, either. She had now flung her bag onto the sand and was fully immersed, plunging down into the small waves and bobbing up again like a child who's just learned to swim and can't quite believe that it works. Cyn usually did typical lady-swimming: earrings up out of the water, head craned back for minimum submersion of the hair. It was not like her, either, to go in search of a drink at eleven in the morning.

The lure of the turquoise sea was too much. Beth chucked her own bag down on a vacant lounger, picked up Cyn's belongings and put them beside her own, then joined her in the warm water. The two of them floated together on their backs, relaxing in the gentle up-and-down movement of the waves.

'Would you look at that? Is that a half woman, half seal?' Cynthia indicated a woman in a black neoprene hood, the sort surfers wear in winter, fifty yards out by the reef, swimming a fast, competition-level crawl and carving her purposeful way right through a group of casual snorklers.

'What's she got on?' Beth peered through the blazing sunlight, seeing strange black paddle-shaped hands coming out of the water.

'Special go-faster gloves. And goggles. And a peculiar belt thing, and look . . . one of those weird Olympic-type racing swimsuits! Mad!'

'Well the Mango is called *Sport* 'n' Spa,' Beth laughed. 'You've got to have *some* overactive types to balance out the lazy spa bunnies like us!'

'Why can't she chill and just *swim*?' Cynthia sounded almost angry. 'Where does she think she is, an Olympic training camp?'

Beth watched as Cyn floated flat and closed her eyes against the sun. '*This* is what it's all about,' she murmured, as if consciously offloading a year's worth of hassle. 'Just doing nothing. Letting it all wash over you.'

Beth tried not to be conscious of ninety minutes' worth of diligently applied aromatherapy oils seeping away into the Caribbean sea, and instead willed herself to savour the delight of the moment. Beyond the end of the reef, she could see a pair of boats pass each other. On the incoming one she could just make out Ned, standing among a group of neoprene shapes at the back of the dive-boat and adjusting something on one of the air tanks. And on the other, the purple and pink glass-bottomed boat that plied its trade each morning from the water-sports hut, she could see Delilah's long hair streaming out behind her in the sea breeze as she leaned over the side of the boat beside Michael, their two blond heads peering down into the water.

Pity Nick isn't here too, she thought suddenly, with a sharp, regretful sense of missing him; they could all have been together for a proper seaside holiday like they used to be when the children were little. With so much to occupy them on the premises they'd see a lot more of each other than they did on the holidays in summer, when the teenagers vanished along the beach strip to party with their peers in the nearest bars. The whole family could be here, floating in the warm ocean doing absolutely nothing, but doing it together.

Nick was well pleased with the sunglasses. He took them out of the box and put them on, turning this way and that to admire the look. He assumed they were a bargain, being duty free. He bloody hoped they were anyway – there hadn't been time to do the price research, the way he usually did for a major purchase, but then it had been something of an impulse buy. Anyway they looked cool enough and he'd need them for Australia, if he ever managed to get there.

Nick took the sunglasses off and returned them to their soft pouchy case, pulled back the bolt on the lavatory door and walked down the aisle towards his seat. Time for lunch. The trolley was rattling about just behind him and he could smell the metallic tang of microwaved foil and oversoft vegetables. He unscrewed the top of the travel-issue bottle of champagne and decided he'd be needing another one, possibly two. After all, it was a long way, and thanks to Felicity and her Blockbuster choices, the movie on offer was one he'd already seen.

Felicity. The thought of her made him smile and feel

both world-weary and worldly-wise. She could, if she'd played it right, be with him now. If she'd been a girl of more experienced negotiating skills instead of a greedy little two-timing slapper, she could have steered him into taking her along with him for the ride. And what a ride it could have been. He wouldn't have been on his own trying on sunglasses in that lavatory: he'd have had her hitched up against the titchy basin, one foot (hers, that is, not his) balanced on the loo seat, the other braced against the wall. No problem. Instead, here he was on his own: not a scuzzy backpacker but a grown-up smart-guy world traveller.

And wouldn't they all be surprised? Oh they would, they would. And it served them right. They should have ordered the fucking heating oil. They were the ones who'd brought him up in a certain amount of lavish comfort – they could only expect him to go in search of alternative means of staying warm, even, and he smiled to himself, if it meant a three-thousand-mile trip and a bit of a dent in the Oz budget.

The trolley clattered alongside, bringing with it a breeze of strong perfume, a spicy mix of aftershave and deodorant, and the super-smooth voice of the steward cooed in Nick's ear, 'Now sir, what's your fancy? Beef or salmon *today*?'

# 8

# Screwdriver

56 ml vodka
112 ml orange juice
slice of orange

'I think the ball's got stuck in one of those trees over
there,' Ned called to Len as he peered across the fair-
way and waved his club in the direction of a clump of
banana plants. Ned hadn't played golf since the same
time the year before, when Aubrey had beaten him
soundly in the first round of the Mango's weekly
tournament. Len had gone on to win it, as he always
did, and at the manager's Cocktail Party he had been
presented with a pink Mango Good Sport tee shirt to
join his Channel Island hoteliers' tournament trophies.

Ned was not a natural golfer. He found the finicky
precision of the swing and the grip entirely pointless.
What did it matter how you clouted the stupid ball as
long as you actually hit it? The allure of the many
swanky courses surrounding his Surrey home had
passed him by, but here at the Mango's nine-holer he
had an annual go at the game, because here you had a
go at everything. Later in the day, he foresaw rather

dispiritedly as he prodded the banana tree, Len would probably be beating him at badminton just as he was now beating him at golf.

Still, it wasn't all hopeless. He would thrash Len in the sailing regatta on Thursday, especially now he'd got Nick here to act as crew. (Nick who had so casually swanned in in time for dinner last night, as if St George was just down the road, like Brighton.) He was looking forward to that – Len was always swaggering about in sports kit and trainers, looking for the next opportunity for competition. He was even worse this year, bouncing around doing ostentatious cool-down stretches every time he got back from his morning run, trotting up and down on the spot in front of the early risers who were quietly having cups of tea by the Sundown bar. Who was he being? Bloody Linford Christie *sans* impressive lunchbox? Who'd think it, though, that was the thing, in someone so bulky and boozy? No wonder Lesley was always nagging him to drink more water and 'accidentally' adding plenty of Diet Coke to his rum. He was starting to look like ambulance material. If he didn't watch it, Gina's mad mother would have someone to go hand in hand to her maker with.

'Are you sure it's there?' Len was now openly laughing at him. 'Maybe an iguana's run off with it!'

It was a possibility, it was that sort of course – nine rather short holes surrounded by brilliant flora, alarming fauna (big blue-black lizards, iguanas the size of small dragons, the odd mongoose, all being stalked by the hotel's half-feral cats) and wonderfully free of Surrey's beige leisurewear, antiquated rules and prissily manicured landscape.

'No, I'm sure it's up there.' Ned poked harder at the plant with his club, knocking its rudely bulbous

111

purple flower to the ground. 'Sorry,' he heard himself say. Why was he talking to a tree? It must be the heat. It was confusing him and addling his brain. Worse than talking to plants, why was he playing golf with a man whose handicap would have St Andrews begging him to become a member? Because it was what you did on a holiday, that's why. Because it was what you did when you needed a fast excuse when your ex-mistress crept up behind you when you'd just seen your wife and daughter off to their daily early-morning Wake Up and Stretch class, and whispered, 'Ned, let's just you and me go out on a bike ride round the headland and back.' Adding in a purring sort of way, as if he didn't quite get it, 'Just the two of us. We could talk.'

Talk. What was to talk about? Talk had never featured that highly between them, even at the time they'd been . . . well, at the time. She could be lurking right now on the far side of the lake by the Wellness pavilion where Beth and Delilah were, at this moment, being exhorted by Sam to stretch their hamstrings and flex their quads. Or the other way round. She could be hiding behind the big mahogany tree, waiting to pounce on him as he triumphantly birdied (so likely!) the ninth and graciously split the game 50-50 with Len.

Ned found the ball at last, sitting like a sad, abandoned egg in a clump of spiny aloes. He quickly bashed away at it without even looking at where it should be going. Who cared? What kind of grown-up game was this where you patted a small sphere of stuffed plastic at a hole in the ground?

'Shot!' Len was standing with his hands on his hips, staring at him in amused amazement. 'You been practising, mate?'

'Eh?' Ned scratched his head. He should have worn

a hat – the day was already blazing and he hadn't had breakfast yet.

'You've only gone and holed it, you plonker! Didn't you realize?' Len was pointing at the flag. It looked an awful long way away, tiny like the sort of thing that should be on top of a child's sandcastle.

'Are you sure?' Ned didn't believe him and squinted into the distance.

'Sure I'm sure!' Len came over and thumped him hard on the back, right in the middle of the sun-seared painful patch on his right shoulder blade. 'Come on – we've earned our breakfast. Let's go. I fancy some of that fried plantain and bacon with a bit of scrambled egg. All on toast. Loooverly!'

Ned flinched at the very idea. His appetite seemed to have gone on the blink along with a large chunk of holiday spirit, missing and presumed dead since the moment he clapped eyes on Cyn at the airport. On the whole he hadn't proved very adept at this adultery business and would certainly not be going in for it again. Maybe that was why so many men of his age took up golf. It was a far safer displacement activity than midlife carnal thoughts and deeds. Maybe, he considered as he retrieved his ball from the hole and acknowledged he felt rather chuffed with his fluke shot, he should give the daft, dull game another go after all.

An excellent idea this, Beth thought as the taxi-driver picked his route very carefully down a steep and deeply pitted track, a visit to the Water's Edge restaurant along the coast for a family lunch. The Mango's communal buffet (today's theme: Mexican) was all very good and tasty, but today Beth wanted to touch base with her family without the presence of the others. She didn't want to be surrounded by the Angel of Death in the form of Gina's mother, Len and his constant 'Anyone fancy a top-up?' and Lesley picking over the afternoon activity schedule and calculating whether Intermediate Fencing or the Lithe 'n' Limbo class would use up more calories.

She also wanted to get Nick away from an audience and find out what he was up to. He'd stage-managed his arrival unseen for maximum surprise impact. Having checked in and unpacked, he'd sauntered casually up to their usual table in the Sundown bar the night before, beer already in hand, and pulled out a chair between Delilah and Lesley without having so much as phoned from the airport to let them know he was on his way. His typically laconic, student-type excuse for joining them, 'Because I was cold', had made everyone laugh but there must be more to it than that, and he wasn't going to tell them with Lesley and Len and Cyn and her warring wedding-party in-laws in the vicinity.

Beth climbed out of the taxi and followed Ned into the restaurant, which was a low-built, palm-thatched wooden pavilion open to the sea and painted in bright Caribbean shades of turquoise. A fat brown Labrador dozed in the shade of the beachfront verandah, and three young children in maroon and white school uniforms swung on a rope hung from a bent palm. She could see sand between the rough treacle-dark floorboards and, as she sat at a table overlooking the water, she watched a pair of small pink crabs scuttle beneath her feet and disappear, corkscrewing into sand holes beneath the slats.

'Beers all round? Coke for you, Delilah?' Beth asked, opening the menu.

'No thanks, I'd like a Virgin Mary please,' Delilah said. 'With lots of Tabasco.'

114

'I suppose that's seasonal, anyway,' Ned commented, nodding in the direction of two more children twining tinsel round a pillar. 'It's always a bit of a jolt to see Christmas decorations going up in this place. By the time we go home the island airport will have a Santa centrepiece and piped music about sleighbells ringing.'

'Please! I've only just got here!' Nick groaned. 'Do you have to mention the "going home" word?'

'*Words*,' Delilah cut in. 'There's two of them.'

'There *are* two of them, dumbo,' Nick flashed back. 'Anyway, whatever, don't mention them. I want to forget about home.'

'Hmm. And perhaps you'd like to give us a clue what you were running away from?' Ned opened the case for the prosecution. 'Women? Hitmen? Did you get fired?'

'I wasn't running away!' Nick was on the defensive. 'I just felt like a break. And the job was . . . well it was coming to a natural end anyway – the maternity-leave woman was coming back, so I just thought . . . you know, come and join the folks.'

'And what about Felicity?' Beth asked. Well, someone had to. After all, the girl had been in and out of their home (mostly in) for the past year. It was only polite to ask after someone whose underwear you'd discovered more than once among the family laundry.

Nick shrugged and gazed out towards a vast cruise ship making its way across the horizon. 'I expect we'll still see each other as friends.'

'Hah! You mean she dumped you!' Delilah could, Beth decided, be brutal on occasion.

'Del, it doesn't necessarily follow.'

'No, she's right.' Nick nodded. 'Felicity wanted . . . more. Different. Something else anyway. So I'm single now and it's great. Glad I came. And such a great view.'

As he said this, he was actually, Beth noticed, grinning at the waitress, a tall and curvy early-twenties girl with her hair piled up in a complicated arrangement of tiny plaits. Beth hoped he wasn't going to be trouble. He had clearly left England in a frame of mind geared up for spontaneous and possibly reckless behaviour, and was likely to be on a go-for-it kind of high. For someone who usually needed a good three days of preparatory nagging to change his bedlinen in time for the laundry man's weekly visit, he'd quit his job, got the cats into kennels, and himself over to St George in record time.

But really, all in all, what could be better? Beth sipped her beer and felt a wave of something like utter contentment wash over her. Her family was all here just as she'd been silently wishing, in this beautiful place. Her mother had always said you had to be careful what you wished for, which was a bit much coming from a woman who'd named her daughter after a child-mortality statistic, but Beth refused to let any fears of a celestial payback spoil this moment. Not every silver lining had a corresponding cloud. She reached across the table and took Ned's hand and he smiled back at her, a smile full of seductive suggestion, as he laced his fingers between hers. Later that afternoon, between her t'ai chi and Ned's Salt Loofah Rub, she might suggest they go back to their room for a bit of a siesta.

'Mum, Dad, you're like, holding *hands*?' Delilah fanned her hand in front of her face in teen disgust.

'Yes, stop that at once. No PDAs in front of the children,' Nick added.

'PDAs? Interpret please?' Beth asked.

'Public Displays of Affection. Unseemly in anyone over eighteen,' Nick explained.

'Oh, I get it,' Ned said. 'So it's all right for teenagers to grope and snog and shove their tongues down each other's throats, but we oldies . . .'

'Dad! No! Stop right there!' Delilah giggled. She'd gone scarlet and covered her outraged face with her hands.

'They know nothing, do they, the youth of today,' Ned teased, stroking the palm of Beth's right hand with his thumb.

'I do,' Nick declared.

'Yes we all know what *you* know. We've heard the sound effects, don't forget,' Ned laughed.

'Dad! *No!* This is so *wrong*!' Poor Delilah was bouncing in her chair with mortification.

'OK, enough now. Let's get some food.' Ned relented as the waitress returned.

Delilah ordered spare ribs and a jacket potato, Beth and Ned went for the spiced crab cakes and Nick ordered a burger with fries. His eyes followed the slinkily swaying rear end of the waitress as she returned to the kitchen.

Was Nick attractive? Beth tried to look at her son objectively – not easy, as his highly biased mother. She decided that on balance, he probably was, very. He seemed to be entirely comfortable in his body and neither stooped around with the apologetic, awkward stance that some boys took years to grow out of, nor strutted cockily or sprawled when he sat, open-thighed and crass. He was quite tall, built for cricket rather than rugby, she'd say if asked to pick a field sport to suit him, and his skin was not disastrous. He had hair like Ned's – light brown and rather flat like an Ancient Roman – though in Nick's case the front was

117

gelled up into a bit of a lift as if a rill of wind had caught it. Why did boys do that, she wondered. Was it a cuteness thing, something to do with adding height or just a lazy lad's touch of texture? She could ask Delilah, who would be sure to have an opinion.

Felicity had obviously found Nick highly attractive, even if she had now abandoned him. He didn't seem too cut up about it. Beth wondered if he'd confide in her if he was – probably not. Probably already he had that male thing about shying away from discussing feelings, especially with women. Ned was the same: after the affair he'd had in the spring, she'd made attempts to find out how he'd felt about the woman and he'd practically raced out of the room in panic. 'It wasn't a *feelings* sort of thing,' he'd managed to mumble before, in a desperate change of subject, asking her if she'd seen the black-handled screwdriver as the door handle in the downstairs loo was coming loose.

Their food arrived at the same time as a large party of smart island women dressed in business suits and high heels, each one clutching an elegantly wrapped Christmas gift.

'Office Christmas party,' Ned commented, as the women took their seats at a long table on the other side of the restaurant.

'No escape,' Beth sighed. 'There won't be much time to organize presents when we get home. It'll be all last minute, as usual. Not that I'm complaining. I'd much rather be here than fighting my way round Kingston in the crowds and the cold.'

'I'm going to buy Christmas things here in the town,' Delilah said. 'Fun tacky stuff like mugs with "A Present from St George" on them.'

Presents. The sight of the women passing around

their gifts started Beth thinking, and there was something she needed to know. As soon as they'd finished eating, Delilah and Nick went outside to sit on the sand and Beth had Ned to herself.

'Ned, I know we're long over this but I'm just curious about one small thing.'

'What thing?' He looked nervous, sitting back in his chair and crossing his arms defensively. His eyes were hostile and she now wished she hadn't said anything. Talk about spoiling the moment. She tried to lighten the mood. 'Hey, no big deal. I just wondered, you know that Tiffany key ring thing that arrived in the mail on your birthday? Have you still got it?'

He grinned. 'Why? Have *you* got a secret someone you want to send it to?'

She clouted him hard on the arm. 'No! Definitely not. I couldn't cope with the hassle! No, I suppose it was just idle curiosity. Am I likely to come across it at the back of the kitchen-dresser drawer?'

'Actually I mailed it straight back. It seemed the only thing to do.' He took hold of Beth's hand again. 'The whole thing had been over for ages by then. Really over. You do believe me, don't you?' He looked almost as anxious as he had all those months ago. She shouldn't have brought it up again, it was messy, like an exhumation.

'Well, I believed you back then,' she reassured him. 'So why wouldn't I now?'

'Um . . . no reason. Just don't change your mind. There's absolutely no cause to. No reason at all.'

Lesley had finished with Jilly Cooper and donated her to the hotel's library shelves, then picked up Bill Bryson from the pile of books she'd hauled along from Guernsey. There was a good hour's reading time 'til her Indian Head Massage appointment over in the Haven, and it was also time for tea, which was laid out far too temptingly for guests to help themselves on lace-covered tables in the Sundown bar. She wandered over to collect a cup of camomile tea and to check out the cakes and sandwiches, lining up behind the super-sized American family that she'd overheard Nick and Delilah talking about. The Flintstones, they'd nick-named them. She wouldn't actually eat anything, she decided, not today; her own decision, nothing to do with the presence of the massive Mr Flintstone as a dire warning. She'd just have a look at what was on offer. She would feast her eyes rather than her body.

And where, she wondered was Len? Right on cue there was a loud burst of laugher and she saw him, over in the big jacuzzi where the pool terrace met the beach. From where she stood he looked the complete Brit-on-holiday lardy slob, lying back in the steaming bubbles and laughing his head off at some joke she wasn't in on. And oh yes, she noted, there was the inevitable drink in his hand. It might be the colour of Coke but there'd be a whopping great triple measure of rum in there too, you could count on it. He'd got the young folk with him: Sadie and her boyfriend Mark and Beth's young Delilah and Nick, all lying back in the sploshing bubbles sipping lurid-coloured drinks.

What was Len doing with that lot? She'd be willing to bet he thought he was being the bloody life and soul. If he went on like this much longer, all that drinking and overdoing the sport, 'soul' would be all that was left. She'd be stuck there at the Mango wondering, like poor Mr Benson's widow back in the Guernsey spring, what to do with his golf clubs and baggage and should she take them home or find a charity shop and save the bother. And everyone would feel sorry for her but not want to talk to her, in case her misery contaminated their holiday.

Would the travel company fly her back home early if the worst happened? It wouldn't be easy, not when you'd got to arrange for a body as well. There weren't exactly daily flights to Britain and of those there were, some were sure to be to Manchester and Glasgow. Just so long as he didn't go off swimming by himself, it might be all right. When she got him home he was going straight to the doctor, no question. He needed telling. She'd take him a cup of tea now, she decided, show him an example.

'They don't let you starve here, do they?' Michael appeared beside her and looked at the tempting array of cakes. He lifted a gauze cover from a plate and, deftly manipulating the tongs provided, took a small square of almond slice and a miniature chocolate éclair which he laid beside a pile of crustless triangular sandwiches on his plate. Lesley's taste buds prickled agonizingly. 'Are you having some?' he asked, still holding the plate cover.

'Er . . . no, not today, ta. Got a figure to watch,' Lesley told him, patting the tyre that she could swear had expanded since the holiday began. Must be the heat. Liquid expanded in high temperatures, she recalled from school. Every drop of wet stuff that her body contained, all the blood, lymph, digestive fluids, pee, must have plumped up and doubled in quantity. And weight.

'And it's worth watching,' Michael said, 'if you don't mind me saying.'

Lesley wasn't sure whether she minded or not. It depended on what he'd meant, exactly. Did he mean it was a good thing she was keeping an eye on it, seeing as it was so clearly running way out of control, or did he, and how very unlikely this seemed, mean that she was worth looking at? She knew she was starting to blush and felt flustered.

'Um . . . I might just get a small sandwich. For Len, not for me,' she said, turning away to the plates on the adjacent table. She wouldn't eat them, she reminded herself as she picked out a couple of tuna and cucumber and added a ham and tomato one to go with them, she really wouldn't. She spotted a plateful of egg and cress on wholemeal and took three of those, plus a miniature sausage roll, then walked across towards the jacuzzi, conscious that Michael, should he choose, could watch her large backside showing it had a life of its own beneath her sundress.

'Len, you coming out of there for tea? I've got you some.'

'Tea?' he called, waving his glass at her. 'Only if it's eighty per cent proof, darling!'

'A sandwich then?' she tried again, looking at what seemed to be, mysteriously, rather a large plateful. Well he could do with it, mop up some of that alcohol.

'No thanks, you go ahead. Indulge yourself – that's what we're here for!'

Oh well, she supposed he'd saved himself a few calories there, by not eating. No way was she going to the bar to get him a boozy refill, though. The amount he got through – he was the sort of guest who must make the management think twice about their all-inclusive policy.

Lesley climbed back onto her lounger with the tea and put the food on the table beside her. The hotel's ancient, scruffy, white cat sauntered up and sat next to her chair, gazing up at her with its cool blue eyes. 'OK puss, you can help me out with this little lot. We'll go sharesies.' She put a tuna sandwich on the ground and the cat wolfed it down almost in one, not even hesitating over the crusts.

'You'll make yourself sick. Slow down,' she told him, reaching out to stroke his grubby ears. The cat tolerated the attention, but all the time with his eyes keenly focused on the plate, so she gave him the rest of the tuna and the ham. 'And the egg ones are mine,' she said. 'It's only a bit of protein, isn't it, cat? It'll do me good.' The cat ignored her and started washing his paws. Quite likely, Lesley thought, he heard plump women from all round the world whingeing versions of the same weight issues, week in week out. If he heard anything at all, that is. From some bizarre memory of that sad week back in March, she recalled poor Mrs Benson talking about her husband's own beloved white cat, and saying that the blue-eyed ones were all stone deaf.

'I'm starving. Shall we get some tea? Or are we too late?' Beth asked Ned as the two of them went back to the pool terrace from their room.

Beth felt quite deliciously elated and energized as well as hungry – afternoon passion sessions didn't often feature in their Surrey life. Perhaps they should, although where the necessary element of spontaneity would come into it she didn't know. She'd have to make sure it wasn't a day when the window cleaner was due, when Delilah wasn't likely to bunk off games and come home early, when she hadn't got one of Wendy's weirder experiments bubbling unpredictably on the hob.

'We could have stayed in the room and had a bottle of fizz sent up. Let's go back.' Ned tugged her hand, pulling her towards him. 'I don't much want to see anyone else right now.'

'Too late — Delilah's waving at us.'

'Where've you two been?' she called from the jacuzzi. 'Ugh! You're looking all loved up.'

'Ah, look at Ned and Beth, everyone! How sweet!' Len waved his glass at them. 'And they say romance is dead.'

Cyn, lying face down on a nearby lounger, raised her head and smiled at Beth. Conspiratorial. The word leapt straight into Beth's head as she met Cynthia's cool eye. Ned's grip tightened on her hand.

'Listen, I just need to go to the dive shop and talk to Ellis about my regulator. See you later for a drink?'

Beth nodded. 'No problem. I might go and have a quick splash in the sea. It'll wake me up.'

Ned hugged her close to him quickly. 'Love you, don't forget that.' And paced off fast towards the dive shop. Cyn sat up on her lounger, and grinned at Beth. 'You two look very lovey-dovey,' she said as Beth came to sit on the seat beside her.

'It's just the sea air and enforced relaxation.' Beth yawned. 'We had a short siesta.' She felt faintly embarrassed. The expression on Cynthia's face was a determinedly inquisitive one. Any minute now she half-expected her to blurt out, 'Had a good shag, did you?' loudly enough to render everyone in the jacuzzi silent and to have Nick and Delilah disappearing under the water in mortification. No wonder Ned had beaten a canny retreat. She wished she'd gone with him.

'A *siesta*?' Cyn snorted. 'Is that what you call it?'

A burst of raucous laughter came from the occupants of the jacuzzi.

'They're having fun, aren't they?' Beth said, in a feeble bid to distract Cynthia. 'Lovely to see all the young ones getting together. I was worried Delilah might be bored.'

'Your Nick certainly doesn't look bored,' Cyn commented wryly, glancing at the noisy party in the bubbling water.

Beth watched her son. His right arm was draped round Sadie's shoulder and he was using that hand to pour, very carefully, sparkling wine into Sadie's glass, a difficult manoeuvre that seemed to require her to giggle a lot as she leaned in very close to him, squashing her breasts against his chest. Nick, trying to steady the bottle so it lined up with the plastic glass, kept spilling wine into the water.

'He'd have better luck using the other hand,' Beth commented, hoping he wasn't stirring up trouble. Mark seemed pretty much oblivious at the moment, chatting amiably to Len about football, but things could easily turn nasty if he was the jealous type.

'From where I'm sitting he looks as if he's having all the luck he wants,' Cynthia said, giving Beth a sly glance. 'Must run in your family, that.'

# 9

# Rum Punch

One of sour (lime juice)
Two of sweet (sugar syrup)
Three of strong (dark rum)
Four of weak (pineapple juice or water)

On each Tuesday at 6.30 p.m. at the Mango Experience (Sport 'n' Spa), come rain, wind, thunderbolt or mosquito swarm, the Manager's Cocktail Party was held. Every guest was invited, by way of a stiff white gold-edged card pushed under their room door, to the pool terrace at dusk for syrup-sweet punch and spicy savouries guzzled down to the sound of an energetic steel band. The event, was, to most, a welcome opportunity to dress up in something smarter than average in order to mingle with fellow guests, along with members of the hotel staff chosen for their sociable savoir faire with clients and an ability to fend off potential complainers. Ned, on the other hand, considered the whole palaver irritatingly anachronistic and entirely pointless.

'We do our own perfectly good mingling all day – hanging out by the pool and in the bar, getting stuck into the various sports,' he grumbled to Beth as he came out of the bathroom wearing only a towel and dripping water across the tiled floor. 'This is just more of the same but in poncier clothes. You stand around feeling daft, trying to balance a drink you don't like and a plate of deep-fried plantain nibbles, and you end up talking to people you've just spent the entire day with.'

'You said that last year,' Beth reminded him. 'And then you met that bloke from Somerset who was in the market for a big white house in Notting Hill. Paid off, didn't it, that bit of social chit-chat?'

'OK, in *that* case I suppose it did,' he conceded. 'But I didn't come all the way here to talk house sales. Nobody in real life actually has cocktail parties any more, do they?' Ned said, 'except in hotels like this one. I wonder why they still call it cocktails? It sounds so 1950s. They could just have put "Drinks" on the invitation.'

'I expect it's to make people think they're staying somewhere tremendously elegant, and it's an excuse for women to wear something over-glittery which didn't look so OTT at home. Something they'd otherwise only wear if they're invited to some Masonic event.'

'And that's another bloody hangover from bygone days. Bloody Masons – just don't get me started on those.'

Beth smiled at Ned by way of the mirror where she was doing her make-up. He required no more than quiet humouring in this kind of mood. It wasn't a bad one, more a state of enjoying a bout of grouching. No question, he was, with middle age, turning into a grumpy old man. It was close to qualifying as a new hobby. The minute they got home he'd start moaning about the mail containing endless invitations to link the electricity bill to Nectar Points, how badly thought-out was the five-year roadworks plan for the M25, and the fact that, due to global warming, the grass would need cutting all through January. By the time he hit pension age he would be one of those growly old buggers who carried a walking stick entirely for the purpose of shoving teenagers out of his way off the pavements and into fast traffic.

On the plus side, just now Ned looked very tanned and fit. Having something good to look at was always a help if you'd got to converse with a fault-finding misery-guts, in Beth's opinion. The ripples across his stomach even seemed close to that male Holy Grail of a six-pack. He was diving every morning and then something sporty – sailing, volleyball or tennis – in the afternoons. Back home, he ticked over physically on one not particularly strenuous visit to the gym per week. It was highly unfair, Beth reflected, that a mere couple of weeks' holiday activity could make so much difference to a man's physique, but with women it took months and months of exhausting, constant effort to stop gravity and excess poundage in their inexorable tracks.

'So do we have to go?' Ned asked her now, sounding like a child reluctant to go to a birthday party. 'Why don't we give it a miss and just grab a drink in the Frangipani bar instead? It's always the same – shake hands with the management, reassure them that, yes, we're having an excellent holiday thank you, then drink enough vile sweet punch to put us off dinner.'

'But what about *my* over-glittery frock?' Beth protested. 'I've put it on now. It's looking forward to its outing. And anyway, there's Nick and Delilah to consider. Some new younger people might have arrived and it could be a chance for them to meet someone to hang out with.'

'OK, OK, if it helps get them off our hands. Though why they can't just go on their own . . .' Ned pulled on a sky-blue linen shirt. 'It's just that it makes me think of cruise ships, all this glad-handing and small talk.'

'Heavens, you're so unsociable!' she laughed. 'If you're not out diving, all silent under the sea, you're away with the fairies in a world of your own. Another time, perhaps we should rent a villa miles from any-where, then you can be as moody and isolated as you want. Now . . .' She fluffed out her hair and did a twirl. 'Do I look all right?'

'All right? You look gorgeous!' Ned told her, coming over to her and kissing the side of her neck.

And so I should, Beth thought as she fastened her lilac strappy kitten-heeled shoes. The dress was a silk Matthew Williamson number, blue drifting through purple to hibiscus pink. It might have been from Harvey Nick's sale but still represented a meteorite-wallop dent in her bank account. She'd bought it back in August, as an 'I deserve this' gesture to get the last of the Other Woman Blues out of her head. She looked terrific in it, even according to her own overcritical gaze. The fabric seemed to know exactly which places on her body to cling to and which to drift around in a tactful and sensitive manner. Now all she had to do to live up to it was to forget about why she'd bought it in the first place.

'Mum?' Delilah knocked on the door. 'Can I come in?'

'Of course you can.' Ned opened the door. 'Oh and don't you look like a princess!'

'Dad! Pur-lease, I'm sixteen, not *six*!' Delilah slunk into the room wearing a short scarlet skirt slung almost criminally low on her hips and comprising no more than ten inches of a double row of frills, no bigger than would be needed to trim a cushion. On her top half, or rather, Beth calculated, her *quarter*, she wore a very much cropped-off matching sleeveless vest. It crossed Beth's mind that the chunky silver necklace and bracelets she was wearing made up about as much in square inches as her skimpy outfit, but the girl did look fabulous. Just so long as she hadn't got plans to go out on the town, dressed like that.

'You look lovely darling,' Beth told her. 'But aren't you . . . shouldn't you . . .'

'*What?* Am I what?' Delilah challenged. 'Cold? Isn't that what you usually say when you think I'm showing too much body? Er, like no? It's about ninety degrees out there?'

'OK, fine.' Beth backed away a step, her hands up in surrender. She didn't want to drag a cloud over the evening. Whatever Delilah was wearing, there'd be others wearing less – Gina for one, she was willing to bet. And they wouldn't look anything like as good as Delilah. You needed to be under twenty, for your skin to be at its show-off, glowing best, if you planned to reveal that much acreage of it.

'You look fantastic,' Beth laughed. 'There's just this clucky habit you get when you're a mum – something to do with keeping your baby chicks safe from preying foxes. You wait till it's your turn. Come on then, let's go and grab some of that horrible sticky punch.'

And talking of preying foxes, she thought . . . 'Where's Nick? Did you knock on his door on your way, Del?' she asked.

Delilah slip-slopped out of the door in her wedge-heeled shoes, calling back, 'I did but he wasn't there. He's probably gone on ahead. He played badminton with Sadie after you'd gone for your bath.'

'What about Mark?' Beth asked, quickly, hoping her son wasn't up to no good. 'Didn't he feel like joining them?'

'Oh, Sadie told Nick that Mark didn't do ball games and that he'd gone off to have a sauna. I think he was a bit . . .'

'Bit what?' Beth asked as Delilah's voice trailed away and she started walking faster, getting well ahead of her parents.

'A bit *what*, Delilah? You didn't finish the sentence!'

'Nothing!' Delilah called, now a good ten yards in front of Beth and Ned. 'Mark's fine! You're walking really slowly and it drives me nuts so I'll see you there!'

Beth watched Delilah disappear round the corner of the Haven spa, towards the pool and the bar terrace. The dark path was lit by festive flares every few feet, brought in for the occasion. The trees were now decorated with swirls of tiny white lights, ready for the Christmas visitors a few weeks away. The festive season was creeping up on them. By the end of the week a Christmas tree would have appeared overnight in the Frangipani restaurant, gold baubles and glittering stars would be hanging from the rafters in the Sundown bar. A pale, skinny cat slunk by, carrying a wriggling rodent in its mouth, and vanished into a clump of hibiscus, and she could hear the steel band strike up a bouncy version of Bob Marley's 'One Love'.

'OK, unto the breach we go,' Ned muttered as they approached the terrace, which was crowded already with party-dressed women and clean-scrubbed linen-clad men. 'Looks like a Home Counties cricket club social,' he added as his last-ditch attempt to persuade Beth into the comparative peace of the Frangipani bar, so handily placed beside the restaurant.

'Except that in December they wouldn't be outside under palm trees by the sea and wearing strappy little dresses or have gorgeous gleaming tans,' she said through gritted teeth, as she approached the outstretched hand of the Mango Manager.

'Or reek of mosquito repellent,' he countered in a feeble bid for game, set and match.

Ned caught sight of Cynthia just along the pool terrace by the diving board, chatting to Sam, the dreadlocked fitness instructor, and Miriam, the receptionist from the Haven. You could hardly miss Cyn: she was in shocking pink with something beaded and feathery in her loosely piled-up hair. She wasn't concentrating. Ned could see that she was looking for someone from the way her head darted from side to side and her eyes checked out new arrivals. He more than suspected he was the quarry, but luckily the Mango's Manager was a very bulky man so Ned attempted, awkwardly, to place himself so that he wasn't directly in Cyn's eyeline.

Keeping his head low and feeling like a schoolboy playing at spies, he accepted a cherry-pink drink, lavishly bedecked with fruit, from a tray offered by a waitress, and then exchanged, as he'd predicted, a few words about enjoying the holiday and confirming that yes, he was making the most of the lavish facilities. He even found himself agreeing that they could definitely put him down for the staff versus guests volleyball game, a brutal, no-holds-barred event he'd sworn he'd never take part in again after collecting too many bruises to the ribs from sharp elbows.

'Hey Ned, Beth, come over and sit with us!' Bradley was with his sister Angela, who seemed to have bagged a large table and an entire trayful of various savoury nibbles for herself. She was chomping busily and another delicious-looking morsel was in her hand, already on its way to her mouth. 'Try one of these mini-kebabs,' she encouraged Beth, 'they'll blast your head off.'

'Thanks, I will in a minute. I was just wondering where our daughter had vanished to.' Beth peered through the crowd as she sipped her gluey drink. It was pretty strong – she hoped that Delilah, if she'd taken one of these instead of the alternative fruit punch, would decide she didn't like it and swap it for something else. There was no immediate sign of her, or of Nick. Nick had probably lain down on his bed for a few minutes and fallen fast asleep. She'd give him a call from the bar phone, as soon as she'd located Delilah. She didn't want to fuss, but in an outfit that minuscule the girl ought to be kept within parental viewing distance. She didn't remember it being so tiny when Delilah had worn it in Fuerteventura that summer – another sign of a growth spurt during her illness.

'Oh you don't want to worry about your Delilah,' Angela shouted across the table, even though Beth was only a few feet away. 'She can take care of herself!'

Oh really? And you know that for sure do you? Beth thought but managed not to say. What an irritating woman.

'She's gone down to the beach with my ex,' Angela went on, waving her glass in the direction of the shore and splashing much of her drink across the table. She didn't seem to have noticed. 'Gone to look at the stars, they said. Stars my arse!'

'Sorry, what are you talking about?' Ned joined in. 'Who is Delilah with?'

'She's with *Michael*.' Angela leaned forward and beckoned him closer, breathing fierce rum fumes at him. 'Michael is taking *care* of her. On the *beach* over there.' She pointed a fuchsia-pink fingernail, adding, 'In the *dark*.'

'Ned, perhaps I should go and find her.' Beth started to move away from the table and peered out towards the sea. She wasn't at all concerned now she knew Delilah was with Michael, but she didn't want to stay at this table with Angela. The woman was at the mean-and-feisty stage of drunk.

Several people had overflowed from the terrace to the beach. Some were perched on loungers, chatting, some wandering about, drinks in hand, enjoying the sultry warmth. There was a full moon and a clear sky and the stars were well worth a viewing. Whatever Angela had hinted, it was barely even what you'd call *dark*.

'Don't take any notice of Angie.' Cynthia caught up with Beth as she peered towards the sea from the edge of the terrace. 'I heard what she was saying – half the hotel did! She's an evil old bat, loves to stir. Michael had a fling with somebody not much older than Sadie, and Angela thinks he's on the permanent lookout for young blood. It's warped her.'

'Something certainly has,' Beth agreed. 'I didn't like what she was getting at. Delilah is only sixteen.' And not, she added to herself, wearing much in the way of clothes.

'Well, sixteen, lucky her! What a fabulous age!' Cyn laughed. 'I had a *ball* at sixteen. I kept several boys on the go at once. I could get any of them I wanted.' She clicked her fingers. 'Just like that. They'd come running.'

Beth gathered that she was supposed to be impressed, although she thought she detected a small note of sourness in Cyn's triumph. At sixteen Beth had been more interested in clothes and music than boys, though she had fantasized that Adam Ant would ask her to apply his warpaint for him.

'Of course I was just a trophy,' Cyn continued. The bitterness was definitely there this time. She sounded like a let-down teenager, albeit rather a conceited one. They just wanted me for how I looked,' she went on, 'so they could brag to their mates. Men, huh? Do they ever change?'

Beth wasn't sure what to say, other than that she rather thought they did. 'But Bradley's not like that, is he? You got lucky there.'

'Oh Bradley's a sweetie. But you can't expect fireworks after all these years, can you? You have to make your own.' She opened her bag, pulled out her cigarettes and lighter and inhaled deeply on a duty-free Marlboro Light.

'Is that what you've been doing? Making fireworks?' Beth asked. Cyn nodded, looking serious. Beth wasn't surprised. It wasn't rocket science to work out that a woman who'd been used to having men fall at her feet might want to recapture that heady power. Perhaps it had been the same sort of thing for Ned.

'Well you're not the only one,' Beth told her. 'There's a lot of it about.'

Cyn's eyes widened. In the dark they looked as if they belonged to a tiger with its lunch in sight, rather than a human. 'What, *you*? *When?*'

Beth laughed. 'You sound as if it's the most impossible thing you could imagine! Well thanks a lot!'

'Oh I didn't mean . . . oh you know, it's just you and Ned, you seem so *secure*.' Her hands shook as she put her cigarette to her lips again and her eyes were sharp and glittery. 'It just shows, I mean you never can tell, can you?'

Beth suddenly twigged that very much the wrong

end of a stick had been grasped. 'No, no, Cyn, you've got it wrong. I didn't mean that I'd . . .' she started, then abruptly stopped as she heard a shriek and a crash from the far side of the terrace. Through the crush of party guests she could just make out Angela standing up, wiping the front of her dress with a napkin. Bradley was trying to help her but was being pushed away impatiently.

'Bit of accidental spillage over there by the look of it. Again.' Beth pointed across the pool. 'Your dear sister-in-law looks like she's dropped her drink down herself.'

'Pissed old bat. She never could take more than a glass or two.' Cynthia dropped her cigarette and pushed it into the sand with the toe of her elegant gold sandal. 'I'd better go and rescue Brad. She's one of those who is a fighter when she's drunk. God knows what she'll start saying. I'll see you later.'

Beth watched Cynthia walk around the pool, conscious that she'd taken away with her entirely the wrong impression. The chance would have to come up later to put her right. Or maybe she'd just let it go. It didn't much matter, and, although she'd been about to, she really didn't want to tell her all about Ned. It had just been one of those woman-to-woman moments, and now it had passed.

She turned to go back to the party. She could see Gina and her mother talking to Lesley and decided to go and join them. Glancing back towards the shore she could also see Delilah now, wandering along the edge of the sea carrying her shoes and talking to Michael. The two of them stopped and pointed at the stars. It was one of those nights that was so clear you think you must be seeing every single one in the universe. The more you stared, the more of them came into sight.

Delilah and Michael were coming towards her now, so she waited. Delilah lost her footing and slid sideways on the loose sand and Michael grabbed her arm to steady her. Beth hoped Delilah's unsteadiness wasn't because of that punch. It was strong, heavy stuff. Delilah would be OK with a glass or two of wine, but this potion was something else. She'd probably be horribly sick on just one glass of it. As, she imagined, would Angela.

'So spliff's really, like, easy to get here?' Nick asked Sadie as he accepted the expertly rolled joint she offered him.

'Course it is,' she replied with suitable scorn. 'It's like *tradition*.' She watched him take a couple of drags, then he handed the joint back and she inhaled greedily, narrowing her eyes. What a very pale face she'd got, Nick observed. She must be one of those who took all that government advice on skin cancer to heart. Not the info about smoking though. Or perhaps she just burned easily and didn't want to look blotchy on her wedding photos.

'It's excellent. Top quality,' he commented. 'I've got a mate whose mum grows it in her greenhouse. That's not bad either, but there's nothing like a smoke on a beach.'

'Nah — and how often in England can you do this? Even in the middle of summer it's never quite warm enough.'

Nick giggled, a childlike splutter that made him think of drains gushing in the rain. 'We're talking about the weather! How *Brit*!' He couldn't seem to stop chortling. Suppose he never did? He'd be chortle-man. Giggle-boy. No matter, it would wear off by morning. Unless it didn't.

They'd made themselves a comfortable and private little enclave there on the beach, safe from over-inquisitive eyes. They weren't far from the pool terrace where the party was fading as guests wandered up to the restaurant for dinner, but all the same, they didn't want members of the management catching pungent drifts of what they were smoking. Mark had pulled together four loungers and shoved a couple of open beach umbrellas deep down into the sand so that they now formed a low roof over the seats.

'Keeps the smoke in,' he'd explained to Nick before ambling off back towards the bar without another word.

'He doesn't do smoke,' Sadie said, as Nick was wondering what had made him leave. 'He's more a pint and a whisky-chaser sort.'

'He doesn't say a lot either, does he?' Nick wasn't sure how comfortable he was with this – it had felt like Mark was tucking the two of them in for the night. All they needed was a couple of blankets and a bedtime story . . . or a DVD, some popcorn and . . . no, no use thinking that way – the Felicity days were long gone.

Sadie laughed. 'No, you're right there. Mark's more of an all-action type.'

Nick picked up more than a hint of nudge-nudge in that reply.

'That'll be a good thing then, seeing as you're marrying him in a few days' time,' he said. He nodded his head and it seemed not to want to stop. Giggle-man, noddy-man. He could see, beneath the low rim of the umbrella, the white foam of the sea's edge trickling up the sand and back again. Scary stuff, sea. Why did it do that going-in-and-out stuff? There must be a reason. That was the thing with dope – sometimes you got just this close to working out the meaning of everything, and then it slipped away.

'Yep. We're getting married.' Sadie was nodding too. Nick watched her, wondering if she was getting the nodding-too-long thing as well.

'*Why* are you getting married?' Nick had to ask. He was genuinely puzzled; they weren't much older than him. Sadie wasn't pregnant; at least he assumed not, she was all flat and smooth down the front. Girls didn't drink rum punch and smoke dope when they were pregnant either, did they? Even if they were stupid and didn't care and were completely selfish cows, wouldn't it make them feel sick?

'Dunno. We just planned it all and then suddenly it was happening.' Sadie turned and glared at him. 'We do love each other, you know.'

'Hey, I never said you didn't. It's just, all that "forsaking all others" or whatever it is in the contract.'

Sadie was silent for a moment, then, inhaling a bit more of the joint, said quietly, 'Well that depends if there's been any others to forsake.'

'Huh? Whoa! What, like it's just been you and Mark? Like, you've never . . . not with anyone else . . . ?'

'Yeah. So? What's wrong with that? Though I only meant me. I know Mark'd been around a bit before we got together.'

'Ah!' Nick whispered to her. 'So you don't know what you're missing. You know what, Sadie?' He moved closer across the lounger towards her. 'You know, you're going to wonder about that for evermore. You're going to be asking yourself, and I promise you this, you're always going to be asking yourself if there's something you're missing out on.'

Sadie shifted towards him and chucked the roach down in the sand between the lounger's slats. 'You know what, Nick?' she whispered, so close now he could smell her perfume. It was Ghost, the same as Felicity's. It was causing some serious stirring.

'You're, like, *so* wrong,' Sadie murmured, so close now he'd barely have to move a centimetre to kiss her. 'I won't be wondering *at all*.'

Oh God, old people dancing. Her own parents. How could they do this to her? Delilah sat on a stool at the bar beside Nick and felt utterly mortified. Her toes literally curled in horror. It wasn't that they looked worse than anyone else – in fact they weren't too dire for people who should be old enough to know better. At least they didn't clear acres of space around them by waving their arms over their heads like Len. Looks like a sheep, dances like a sheep – that was Len, with whoopy sound effects thrown in now and then in case it hadn't been noticed that he was enjoying himself. It was just that, really, there were some sights that a vulnerable teenage girl shouldn't be compelled to witness.

'Did you think it would be like this?' she yelled into Nick's ear over the blaring of the Rolling Stones.

'Yes. Especially when they got all tanked up with that punch earlier,' he shouted back. 'And it's always the same when "Honky Tonk Women" gets played. There's something in those opening notes that gets the oldies remembering their down-and-dirty days.'

'Ugh.' Delilah shuddered. 'They should have forgotten all that years ago!' She was beginning to appreciate her bridge-playing grandmother. That was what grown-ups should be doing: sitting around quietly in places like Madeira playing calm card games, not jumping around like they were in the

Glastonbury mosh pit and embarrassing themselves and everyone else.

'You're right there. Or possibly not . . .'

What did he mean by that? Delilah looked at where her brother was looking. Gina seemed to be the one on the sharp end of his focus. You couldn't miss her in the shiny, tiny white halter-necked dress and with that long pale sheet of hair. In the half-dark with the disco lights flashing (disco lights! Another weird old-people thing!) you could hardly see her hypertanned flesh, just her teeth now and then as she smiled, so the dress gave the impression it was slinking around as if by itself.

Delilah watched her brother watching Gina. Gina was dancing with Sam, quite competently too, Delilah would have to admit, which was pretty agonizing for her. Such a fit bod, he had, that Sam. She seemed to be sliding herself up and down his body – it must be an American thing – either that or she was a pole dancer back home. How to compete with that? Beside her, Nick inhaled hard on his cigarette while Delilah planned making a move on Sam.

'You could grab her for the next one – but if it's a slowy, be warned – she slicks glitter all over her skin and it'll come off all over you,' Delilah suggested, nudging him. 'But get me a drink first, won't you? I fancy some of that fake champagne.'

'How many have you had?' Nick asked, his eyes still on Gina.

'Only one. I like it. Go on Nick, please, the barman knows I'm not eighteen and he keeps offering me lime soda.'

'Aah, poor baby! OK, just the one. Go and sit over there where he can't see you.' Nick indicated a group of vacant sofas and went to the far end of the crowded

141

bar, returning a few minutes later with an opened bottle of Cava. Delilah perched on the arm of a sofa, fearing she'd disappear from Sam's view if she was low down in the seat.

'This should keep us going for a while,' he said, pouring a glass for each of them.

'God, look at them all,' Delilah said, watching Michael now as he was doing what he'd probably call 'groovin' on down' with her mother. 'You know what, Nick? These holidays where they all get together every year, I reckon they're all a bunch of swingers.'

'Swingers! That's a good one Del, excellent thinking!' he laughed. 'Do you think that us being here is cramping their style?'

'God I hope so,' she groaned. 'But I can't speak for the others. I mean look at Angela.' Angela, whose dress had been soaked by drink earlier in the evening, was now wearing what looked like a huge silk sarong. She must, Delilah decided, have believed all those magazine articles about how a large square of fabric, carefully folded and tied, can make a Stylish Dress. Perhaps she hadn't read the instructions properly – it seemed to be working its way loose as she flailed about to 'Ride a White Swan'.

When the music slowed, the inevitable 'Lady in Red' almost had Delilah, in spite of her Sam quest, heading for the door, but, oh joy, he and Gina were suddenly there by her sofa.

'Are you two available for dancing?' Gina asked, grabbing Nick's hand and tugging him to his feet.

'Oh go on then, twist my arm.' Nick gave in, though not unwillingly. His hand, Delilah noticed, instantly slid down on Gina's naked shimmery back to where her tiny dress ended. She wouldn't be surprised if more than just his hand ended up covered in glitter. What a schmoozer.

Sam expertly moved Delilah across the floor and slid his arms round to the small of her back, making her tingle. She looked around, to check her parents weren't watching, and gave herself up to being clamped deliciously close against Sam's body. Oh perfect, she thought – if it could just go on like this the whole night. Could he tell how she was feeling? She must be giving off stacks of hormonal messages. He definitely was. As his mouth brushed softly against her ear, she could feel something that was a lot more scarily impressive than the contents of Oliver Willis's boxers being pressed against her.

Across the floor, she watched Angela attempting to crush Ellis the dive master to her ample front. When the music stopped and he pulled away, her dress finally gave up the fight and fell to the floor, revealing a full-on-frilled and laced black basque and matching French knickers. Cheers and whistles broke out and Angela gave a plump and gracious curtsey to her audience.

Oh Jeeze, and I joked about swingers, Delilah thought, I really wish I hadn't.

# 10

# Splash and Crash

56 ml amaretto
168 ml cranberry juice
56 ml orange juice
14 ml strong rum

What a horrible dream. Delilah woke with an aching head and a dread of opening her eyes and facing what she'd seen in her sleep: hordes of ancient, *truly* ancient people going crazy on an Ibiza club dance floor. What a collection of creased, flecked skin, sparse grey hair and wizened limbs all flailing around through her sleep hours. One of them had been Gina's mother Dolly, only with a pale, hollow skull instead of a face: a dancing skull, wrapped in sparkly black stuff, whirling thin, glittery arms in the air.

It wasn't light yet; the clock told her it was only 5.30. So she wasn't over the jet lag then. By the time she was, it would be time to go back home. She snuggled down into the bed and closed her eyes, trying to give herself something to think about that would send her back to sleep. Thoughts of Prince William usually worked but she'd now discovered a rival for him. Tricky one for Delilah, this. Who would she rather wake up next to? Prince William or hunky Sam the Mango-fitness-man? They were such opposites: fair William with his baby-pink, puddingy English features and his innate gawkiness, contrasted with brown-skinned, gleaming Sam with his super-toned body and utter elegance. She loved the way he moved – kind of lazy but certain. Simply watching him walk across a room made her feel quite limp and heated. William she now pictured as something of a clumsy puppy, appealing and sweet but a bit annoying. Sam was more like a lean, lithe cat. It was no contest – she'd never been a dog person. She would be sad to see William go, but it seemed to be time. He'd been up there at the front of her wish list for so long she felt as if she was losing a much-treasured childhood friend. She thought of his big, eager smile and tried to get back the feeling she'd had for him, but it just wasn't there any more.

She supposed, as she lay stretched out on her back staring at the treacle-coloured roof slats, that this was a growing-up moment. It was goodbye to juvenile fantasy and bring on the real-life experience. There was just one small niggly thing that got in the way. Sam was fit, buff, desirable, no question, but it was totally stupid that as a couple they'd be Samson and Delilah. What had her parents been thinking of when they named her? Were they being completely loopy? Were they *on* something? Didn't they *think*? How come Nick got a perfectly normal – even boring – name, chosen after an ancient uncle, yet she got the biblical nutcase? Surely there'd been women in the family that they'd admired, or whose names they liked a tiny bit? Helena would have done perfectly well, after Grandma, or even just Helen to avoid confusion, but *Delilah*. She could just see the wedding, hear the splutters of laughter echoing all round the church as the stupid words came out: 'Do you, Samson, take thee, Delilah . . .'

Delilah now came to the really big question, the one that was about reality this time. If she got the chance, say she was on the beach late at night all by herself with Samson, bit of a moon shining but not too much, no-one around, they'd had a couple of drinks, would she go with him to that big old sofa she'd seen at the back of the water-sports hut and actually *do it*? She might. She just might. Thank goodness for that fumbled practice run with Oliver Willis back in the summer. She'd never imagined, the day it all went off in his scuzzy bedroom with the curtains closed against the dusty August daylight, that she'd be really glad they'd had that quick and slightly disappointing non-event. After the great build-up (two months of going out, loads of intense snogging, some quite exciting groping) all she'd got out of it had been glandular fever and a certainty that sex would have to get better than that. This could just be the chance to give it another go.

'OK so who's coming over to Dragon Island this afternoon for a snorkelling session?' Ned was in the dining room, where those who could face it after a surfeit of rum punch the night before were tucking into breakfast. Beth sipped her pineapple juice, spread a dollop of guava jam on her toast and watched him ambling from table to table, rounding up a boatload, looking like a scout leader in determined search of volunteers. He started with Gina, fresh from the early stretch class (and where had she disappeared to the night before? One minute slinking about on the dance floor and the

146

next, simply vanished – no goodnights, nothing) and did the rounds by way of Len and Lesley and on towards Bradley and Cyn.

There was no sign of Angela. Beth guessed that a vicious headache was being nursed in a room darkened by firmly closed blinds. Amazing underwear that woman had been wearing – had she meant it to be displayed to the entire Frangipani bar like that? It seemed she had – it was hardly the sort of thing you wore with simple personal comfort in mind. Strange.

Sadie the bride sat by herself in a corner, reading a magazine and munching toast. She was looking decidedly sulky and her choice of a faraway corner table had 'Do Not Disturb' written all over it. Beth hoped fervently the sulk was entirely to do with her mother's drunken near-strip and nothing to do with Nick. She'd seen the two of them emerge from their snug nest of beach loungers, giggling and too close to each other. Being dumped by Felicity was no excuse to go making free with other people's fiancées: that way lay a well-deserved thumping from the prospective bridegroom.

'We don't have to go out to the island in one big party,' Beth reminded Ned, when he eventually returned to the table carrying a hangover-blasting plate of bacon and eggs. 'Carlos will run the boat over to the island and back whenever anyone puts up the blue flag.'

'Oh. Have I got it all wrong?' He frowned. 'Didn't you say Lesley would only go snorkelling if there were other people with her? I thought if we made up a big enough party and she changed her mind, there'd be someone for her to sit on the beach with.'

'She said she was nervous swimming in deeper water. But it isn't so very deep out there and there's all of us to be with her – Delilah and Nick want to come too. We didn't need to round up Gina and Cyn as well.'

Ned gave her a sharp look. 'Why? What's Cynthia done?'

Beth laughed nervously. 'Cyn? No, why? Has she said something to you?'

'What would she say to me?'

'Who knows? What *could* she say to you?'

Ned shrugged and concentrated on his bacon. They made it very crisp at the Mango. He cut into it rather too hard and shards scattered all over his plate and onto the tablecloth. 'Nothing to tell,' he said to Beth, as he collected up the bits. 'Do you think Gina's mother will want to come?'

'She might just for the boat trip, though I can't see her being up for the snorkelling bit. But if she is, we mustn't let her drown. I can imagine her ghost hovering over the Sundown bar saying "I told you so".'

It was the tricky thing about holidaying as a group, however loosely assembled they were. You didn't want to do absolutely everything together, but at the same time you didn't want to offend anyone by leaving them out if there was anything going on. Beth would prefer not to spend the afternoon with Cynthia – not until she'd got her on her own and made it clear that she wasn't the one who'd been enjoying extra-marital larks. Cyn kept looking at her now from across the restaurant, waving her fingers and smiling in a gleeful 'your secret is safe with me' sort of way which told Beth exactly the opposite.

Cyn adored gossip and intrigue. The year before when Gina had been seen late at night getting into a taxi with the Frangipani restaurant's maître d', it had been all round the hotel by the time the breakfast chef had fried the first egg the next morning. Beth would have to put Cyn right, and soon, but she intended to do it without telling her about Ned. That had been a near thing, brought on by the rum punch, but if she'd managed not to talk about it to close friends at home she certainly didn't want to drag it all up again to entertain Cyn. She'd make something up – say she was talking about a friend of hers maybe, or just say she was generalizing and mention footballers or some silly young tabloid soap star.

'What's the matter with Cynthia?' Lesley, on her way to claim a lounger, slid into a vacant chair beside Beth. 'She keeps staring over here and grinning like a loon. She's practically wriggling in her seat like a toddler needing a pee.'

'Is she?' Ned's voice registered at least two octaves in as many words. 'Is she still doing it? If I turn round now it'll look obvious.'

'So turn round! What's wrong with obvious?' Lesley laughed and prodded him in the ribs. He winced, pained.

'Perhaps she knows where Gina disappeared to so suddenly last night,' Beth ventured, deflecting gossip.

'Or perhaps she got on the right side of Brad, if you get my drift! He's not a bad looker, that Brad. And you're not so bad yourself, darling, even on a morning after.' Lesley winked at Ned and would have nudged him again, but he had managed to be out of his chair and halfway to the door in one swift avoiding movement.

'Must go – got to check equipment at the dive shop. See you later!' he called as he vanished into the searing sunlight.

'Something I said?' Lesley asked. 'You know me, I was only messing about!'

'Oh he's fine. The divers are off to see the sharks this

morning. I expect he's a bit nervous, wondering if he's going to be fish food.'

'Ugh!' Lesley shuddered. 'Sharks! They eat anything, sharks. Dead bodies, dolphins, gulls, you name it.'

'The goats of the ocean,' Beth said. 'I must admit I always feel a bit nervous when Ned goes on that particular dive. I wonder what would happen if . . .'

'No don't.' Lesley put her hand on Beth's wrist and gripped it tight. 'Stop right there. Don't think about it, don't talk about it. Just . . . give him a specially nice goodbye kiss before he gets in the dive-boat.'

'Would that be a just-in-case type of thing? It's hard to get close to him when he's got all the kit on!'

'Just do it. Do it for me, OK?' Lesley gripped Beth even tighter.

'OK, OK. I'll do it for you. I'll give him one for you.'

'Oooh naughty, yes I'll have one of those as well!'

'A goodbye kiss, I meant! Does no-one round here think about anything but sex?' Beth laughed as she started gathering her book and her bag together, preparing for an hour in the early sun before seeing whether Nick and Delilah (when they finally emerged from sleep) fancied a trip into the town or to the wildlife park.

'What are you two laughing about? Can we all share the joke?' Cynthia, carrying a tennis racquet and a white visor, appeared across the table.

'Oh it's just sex! Always plenty to laugh at there!' Lesley told her.

'Ah well, sex. That age-old hobby.' Cynthia gave them a weary smile. 'Beth been regaling you with her adventures? You must share them with the rest of us, Beth. Let's all have a giggle!'

Without waiting for a reply, Cynthia turned and

stalked off, swinging her tennis racket. Beth watched her back view as she strode towards the tennis courts. She was wearing a demure little tennis outfit – such a cute white dress with pert pleats from her skinny hips, towelling wristbands and her hair pulled back with a white scrunchie. She looked like a sixth-former about to win the inter-schools challenge cup. Beth could imagine Cynthia regretted the passing of frilled tennis knickers. How dull and sexless she must think the current fashion for wearing plain Lycra shorts instead.

'What's up with her?' Lesley asked. 'She's a bit antsy this morning, isn't she?'

'I've no idea. Maybe Angela's getting on her nerves. I wouldn't be too thrilled to have her as a sister-in-law myself. She must be a hoot at family parties. Do you think she often drops her clothes like she did last night?'

'Horrible thought! It was Cyn who wanted to come to Sadie's wedding, though. You can't say she didn't know what she was letting herself in for.'

'True – maybe she thought things would be different away from home.'

'Never is though, not really, is it?' Lesley sighed. 'So much for getting away from it all.'

Ned was the first one on the dive-boat. He waded out from the shore as fast as he could, hauled himself up the boat's stern ladder and carried his oxygen tank to the front so he could sit under the canopy in the shade and out of view from the shore. He looked back at the hotel, feeling safe from Cynthia at last, although who knew where she might be watching from? Was she still on the tennis court (if that was where she'd gone – maybe she'd just fancied slinking about in front of him in her tennis kit and had now gone to change)?

She was everywhere he went except out here, on and under the sea.

The night before, after she'd grabbed him for a dance in the Frangipani bar when Beth had gone off to the loo, she'd run her hands so thoroughly over his body it had only been just this side of decency. She'd then crushed herself close against him, checking to see if the hand-running had had its intended effect. And of course it had. No good explaining to her that it was virtually nothing but reflex. He'd defy any man's penis to stay 100 per cent limp against such a skilful mauling. And where had Bradley been then? Oh, only a few metres away at the bar, that's where, chatting to Len and all oblivious. If he'd bothered to turn round and distract himself from cricket talk, he'd have had a prime view of his wife desperately attempting to relight the cold dead embers of her affair. Cyn was one woman who just didn't give up, even when Ned had actually been quite rude, telling her that the words 'flogging' and 'dead horse' were appropriate. Except she'd been able to point out that the horse was clearly not quite as dead as he'd claimed. Which bit of 'it's over' did she not understand? But then she always did like the risk factor.

What had she really expected last night? That he'd agree to meet her round the back of the Haven spa and give her a fast seeing-to against the bougainvillea-covered wall? The dire truth, he thought, as half a dozen more divers climbed aboard and Carlos began carefully steering the boat out beyond the reef towards the south of the island, the truth was that she'd expected exactly that. The thrill of the unplanned, that was what she'd adored, except that during those few short springtime months there came a point where he realized that Cynthia's 'unplanned' escapades were about as spontaneous as a US military invasion.

One of Cyn's favourite tricks had involved catching the train into London on the slightest whim – a libido-raising sultry day perhaps, or a quest for non-rural shoes – and 'surprising' Ned outside the office, usually just as he was about to get into his car to show a client of potentially stonking profitability around a Holland Park mansion. Regardless of colleagues or clients, Cyn would purr erotic suggestions down her mobile phone and promise to wait in Starbucks round the corner till he was free. It was too distracting as well as being mildly terrifying, and he was unnervingly guilty of giving less than full attention to the job in hand. Sometimes she would have to hang about waiting for him for hours, yet he'd race back from his meeting to find her slowly turning the pages of a glossy gossip mag and sipping a skinny latte as if she was having a quick reviver mid-shopping. She must have got through countless cups of coffee. He suspected it was what made her so hyper. That or the slimming pills that she'd bought in bulk over the Internet and was considering selling on to the stout dowager ladies of her village.

'I don't need diet help any more,' she'd gushed into his ear one torrid afternoon as he rolled off her snaky naked body in the starkly (and Starckly) minimalist third-floor room at Chelsea's latest hip hotel shag venue.

'I'm achieving corporeal perfection by more natural means. Sheer sleekness through sex,' she breathed as she twirled herself into the crisp linen (2,000 thread count) sheet.

It had been the tiny but dangerous fireworks she'd lit that had led to the end of the affair. Only a couple of weeks in and she'd softly thrown the odd post-coital sizzler: 'Bradley and I, well it's almost dead, our marriage. And the house echoes and rattles now that Simon's grown up and left home.'

A little more scorching had been: 'That first meeting in Harrods, don't you feel it was more than coincidence, more *meant* to *be*?'

And then the almighty rocket explosion: 'You and I, Ned, we're at that all or nothing stage. We must pack our bags, slam the doors and run from our old dull lives before it's too late!'

This last had been on a very warm May night. Ned had lain with Cyn on a picnic rug on a patch of scrappy grass close to the perimeter fence at Fairford airbase. Ned was uncomfortable, feeling conscious that he was getting too old for all this. Back home, Beth had been testing an unseasonal Canadian recipe for goose stuffed with prunes and apples. The house was filled with a deliciously warm celebratory scent and he'd hated leaving it, lying all the way out of the door to keep a date for something he could get far more comfortably – and perfectly happily – at home. The ground beneath the rug was stonier than he had expected, and he feared there could be airbase security lights that would catch the two of them in eerie greenish brilliance. Cyn, giving it her all on top of him, might well trigger it off by sheer exuberance and she wouldn't, he knew, be in the least put off by the spotlight effect. She'd probably love it, play up to it and suggest a repeat performance to entertain the troops. This all had to stop, Ned had decided there and then. He had no intention of leaving Beth. It had never crossed his mind that he would run out on her and Nick and Delilah for the sake of Cyn's energetic flesh.

Now, as the boat sped past the end of Dragon Island, the hotel grounds were far behind, and even if she was watching through binoculars, Cyn would find it hard to pick Ned out among the various bodies in wetsuits. Perhaps she would, from a safe distance, select some-one else to be her plaything. Just a pity it didn't seem likely to be her easy-going, good-natured husband Bradley.

It would be only too easy never to venture outside the hotel grounds. Beth wanted Nick and Delilah to see as much as possible of the island – its rain forest, magical hidden waterfalls, the bustling, colourful capital with its twice-weekly spice market and east-coast beaches with the mountainous rolling surf, but she had to admit that the Mango's facilities were stiff competition for outside attractions. From the Wake Up and Stretch class, you could start after breakfast with a reviving lie-down on a lounger with a book, then when the sun took a hold for the morning you could join an archery lesson, join the Aquasplash workout in the pool or wander off to the Peace pavilion for the yoga class, meditation or the stress-release session. Beth liked this one – it required no more effort than the letting-go of inner turmoil under the guidance of Louella. She lay there now, drifting away into dreamland, stretched out on a mat staring up at the pale green painted roof slats with their overhanging thatch of plaited palm leaves, and feeling the gentle wind wafting in between the balcony railings. It was like being on a giant Balinese bed, open to the sea breeze and scented with the surrounding jasmine and tamarind.

'And ... release.' Louella almost whispered her instructions. Beth was sure she'd been recruited entirely for the calming tones of her voice. Deep exhalations followed from her twenty class members. Beth had let go so deeply she could barely feel her limbs. It would be a huge effort simply to lift a hand. Her body was as limp as a sleeping kitten and she was only vaguely conscious of the floor supporting every ounce of her weight.

The only disturbance from outside, other than the distant swoosh of waves on sand, was the rhythmic thwack-thwack from the tennis court, where Cynthia was playing for a place in the Mango's weekly challenge final. By the sound of it, Beth realized, as Louella gradually restored her charges to full awareness of their surroundings and relaunched them at the day's activities, Cynthia (and it had to be her, Beth could hear her shrieking curses with every muffed shot) was making Wimbledon-level efforts to demolish her opponent. As her faculties returned to normal, Beth could hear a fierce, deep grunt with every serve, all this signalling a furious determination to win no matter what. Cynthia should come to the stress-release class, Beth thought. Whatever pain she was working out against her unlucky tennis opponent, surely a simple bout of lying flat out, breathing deeply and rhythmically and just letting it all go hang couldn't fail to unwind her.

'AAAAAQUAAAAEERO*BICCCS*!' Delilah heard the rallying call from Sam as he approached the pool through the Sundown bar and summoned the mainly female sunbathers for an hour of water aerobics. Sam did the poolside rounds, joshing and cajoling as many idle bodies off their loungers as he could, with the seductive promise that he'd go easy on them but at the same time revive their essential vigour. Most of the men looked doubtful at his lavish promises regarding their virility, but many women were charmed and allowed Sam to lead them by his elegant brown hands to join the pool class. Only the plump American stalwarts in their habitual spot on the higher terrace completely failed to respond.

'I think their only exercise is moving hands to mouths,' Nick commented to Delilah.

'You're so harsh on people,' she snapped back at her brother. 'You don't know how they feel. They might have medical reasons for keeping still or they might be really embarrassed at the idea of being seen flobbing around in the pool in public.'

'Huh! Doesn't stop them stripping off in the sun, does it?' he countered, nodding towards the vast tattooed artwork that was Fred Flintstone's corpulent stomach.

'Enough sizeist prejudice, Nick. I'm out of here.' Delilah flung down her book and climbed off the lounger.

'Are you doing this class?' Nick sounded surprised, watching her unfasten her sarong and hang it over the sunshade's struts. 'Wouldn't have thought it was your sort of thing. At school you usually skive off games.'

'You're my brother. You haven't a clue what's my sort of thing!' Delilah tweaked the bottom of her bikini into place. Why did it happen, the pants riding-up-your-bum? She was forever sorting a wedgie like a little ballet girl tugging at a leotard. It must be since the glandular fever – her body had shrunk. She wasn't filling the bikini top as well as she had in the summer. She'd never exactly been voluptuous but she did long to have her pre-illness shape back.

'You joining us, Delilah darling?' Sam was setting up his sound system as Delilah dropped down into the water in front of him. He looked down at her and smiled. Devastating, she thought, oh just *so* fit.

'Hooowf!' was all she managed to gasp, taken by

surprise by the sudden chill of the water on her sun-warmed skin. 'Um, I mean, yes.'

Bugger, she thought, that went wrong. If Kelly and Sukinder were watching they'd be in fits at her hopelessness. She'd intended to slide gracefully into the pool. Now she felt a total twit, covered in sudden goose pimples and a certainty that her instantly chilled skin had gone a horrible rice-like shade of dull pale.

'Hey come and hang out by me at the front, sweetie!' Gina swam up alongside and began bobbing up and down, limbering up. 'We can show all the losers at the back of the class how it's done!'

Delilah had intended to be at the front all right, but definitely not beside this leather-skinned, lemon-haired cheer-leader with those silicone tits cascading over the front of her bikini top. What kind of an unfair contents did that make it? Sam would look one way, then the other and make a choice – skinny pale flatty or impossibly tanned, Jordan-esque over-hang. Shit, bugger and sod.

The music started and a tidal wave rippled across the pool as Sam, instructing from the poolside, had them all jogging on the spot as a warm-up. 'Come on folks! Get those knees higher and higher!' he called.

'*Exactly* what he was saying to me last night!' Gina sniggered, leaning over to yell close into Delilah's ear above the thumping, pulsing music.

'*What?*' Delilah stopped bouncing and faced Gina, who carried on jogging up and down in the water. Bounce-bounce-bounce went her breasts, surely only seconds from escaping their white Lycra bonds.

'Oh after you'd gone to bed last night, I was just saying . . .' Gina's grin broadened. Such big teeth she had, all levelled off in that American way to look exactly the same in a long flat-edged row.

'I heard what you *said*. I didn't get what you *meant*.'
But she did. What lay beneath Gina's insinuation was
all too clear. Gina stopped bouncing, grabbed Delilah's
arm and pulled her across to the edge of the pool.

'Come on girls! Don't give up on me now! Keep it
going, keep it going!' Sam called down to them.

'Did he say *that* as well?' Delilah demanded.

'Oh I get it! You *like* him!' Gina laughed softly. 'I
sorta sussed that – I can see these things. Hey, I just
gave him a little road test for you! Your turn next and
you'll be fine with him, baby. Gentle or what?' She
reached out and stroked the side of Delilah's face.
Delilah flinched back. Gina didn't seem to notice and
continued, 'Sam's a real hundred per cent cutie. *So*,
like, considerate.'

'And . . . star jumps!' Sam was jumping now, arms
out then in. The wash from the jumping class crashed
against the pool wall and almost knocked Delilah over.

'Oh f*uck you*, you cow!' Delilah shrieked at Gina,
then without really being aware of what she was
doing, she grabbed a handful of Gina's long smooth
yellow mane and pulled her under the water. There
was a lot of splashing and thrashing but Delilah held
on tight.

'Oh-oh, cat fight! Go, girls!' Nick called from his
lounger, getting up for a better view. Many others were
doing the same. The class came to a halt as everyone
gawped at Delilah and the flailing Gina.

'Ladies! Please, stop this!' Michael, moving faster
than anyone would have thought possible, leapt
nimbly down from the terrace into the water, manhandled Delilah out of the way and hauled the
spluttering Gina back up for air.

'Now what was all *that* about?' he asked Delilah as
Nick offered a hand down to Gina and pulled her out

of the pool, sitting her down on his lounger and patting her back as she spluttered and coughed, his eyes on her formidable chest which heaved deeply as she fought to regain her breath.

'It was nothing. Just something. She . . .' Delilah couldn't stop the tears overflowing. She put her hands on the pool's tiled edge and dragged herself out of the water, rudely ignoring Michael even as he flung a towel round her, patting her dry and doing his best to be comforting. Delilah shrugged him off and padded quickly past Gina, muttering, 'I'm sorry Gina. I didn't, like, exactly, mean to . . . you know . . . Maybe I over-reacted . . .'

''S OK honey, I'm sorry too. Hug?' Gina opened her arms out wide.

'Um no thanks, if you don't mind.' Delilah wasn't, she decided, going to be bought off that easily. She slumped down on her lounger, hunching herself into a moody heap with her arms wrapped round her knees.

'That's OK, I so *totally* understand,' Gina sympathized. 'Feelings run high at your age. I guess I'd forgotten.'

Well you would, Delilah privately bitched to herself as she wrapped her wet body in her towel and lay back under the sunshade, feeling utterly miserable. For you it was such a very, very long time ago.

# 11

# Hot Pants

42 ml tequila
14 ml liqueur of choice
2 mint leaves
1 tsp caster sugar

Beth accepted it was a form of divine retribution,
being landed with Gina's mother Dolly to take care of
on the trip over to Dragon Island for the afternoon. She
could hardly refuse when Gina asked her to keep an
eye on the wiry old lady, not after the way Delilah had
behaved. The girl was lucky not to have been hauled
up for attempted murder.

'I'd love to come along with y'all, but I've made
plans,' Gina explained after lunch as she handed Dolly
over to Beth and Ned like a parcel being hand-
delivered. Gina was keeping to herself exactly what
those plans were. She was, at handover time, wearing
a demure pink linen short-sleeved dress and a cream
straw hat, so Beth guessed she had a secret someone to
meet in the town, though she could be quite wrong. It
was possible that Gina just fancied a spot of shopping
followed by a quiet nap somewhere under a tree.

Maybe she had booked herself in for the Cellutox Aroma Spa Ocean Wrap — who knew. If her plans involved Sam, at least she was having the grace not to mention him.

Beth hadn't yet had an opportunity to deal with Delilah. She'd prefer to do it somewhere out of shouting range of other people. Delilah had given the poolside sunbathers enough entertainment for one day without throwing in a mother–daughter slanging match as an extra. Since the incident in the pool Delilah, slippery as only a teenager could be, had made sure she hadn't found herself alone with her mother. She'd kept well out of the firing line for the rest of the morning and then avoided any chance of attack over lunch by sitting firmly between Sadie and Mark and opposite Angela, using her, to Beth's suspicious eyes, as a formidable guard dog.

Now, as the snorkelling party boarded Carlos's boat, Beth seized her chance, along with Delilah's arm, and hauled her to a pair of seats down at the front where they could be alone.

'I want a serious word with you, Delilah,' Beth began.

'Yeah but, Mum . . . look, I said I'm sorry to Gina. Like, is it my fault she's not coming?' Delilah challenged.

'Probably,' Beth replied sharply. 'After all, she's hardly going to want to go out snorkelling with a girl who tried to drown her, now is she?'

'I wouldn't have *killed* her,' Delilah said sulkily. 'It was just the way she wouldn't stop going on and on and on.'

'I should damn well hope you *weren't* going to kill her! And going on is what Gina does. She's all mouth. And she's also all-American, don't forget: you're bloody lucky she hasn't threatened to sue. You shouldn't have taken any notice of her, *and* while we're on the subject . . .'

'Which you're never going to let go of . . .' Delilah muttered.

'No, too right! Not 'til I've got to the bottom of what this fight was about.'

The boat was filling up. At the back, Ned, Nick and Carlos were helping Dolly along the narrow plank from the sand. Dolly was cackling about something and looking very unsteady. Was she sober, Beth wondered. Probably not – she did like a cocktail or six at lunchtime. She was wearing a long, voluminous kaftan constructed from extraordinary silver sequinned fabric and a matching toque. Even her shoes (mules, dangerously high in the heel for getting on and off rocky boats) were silver, the overall effect being that of a kitchen-foil space rocket made by a child.

Len, Lesley, Sadie and Mark were already aboard, settling themselves and sorting snorkel masks and fins. Bradley and Cyn had decided, at the last minute, not to come along with them, and had joined a trip to visit an old plantation house instead.

'Right. So what's all this nonsense about Sam?' Beth cut to the bottom line. 'Nick tells me you were fighting over him! I mean, how ridiculous is that?'

Delilah stared at the floor, her face pink and furious. Sod Nick, she thought, what did it have to do with him? And where *was* Gina now? How come she'd conveniently offloaded her mother and gone off on her own? Perhaps she wasn't on her own.

'What's so ridiculous? Sam can't like *her*,' Delilah hissed. 'She's like, so *ancient*. Practically *withened*.'

'*Withened?*' Beth was puzzled for a moment. 'Oh, you mean *wizened*.' It wasn't a bad word, withened, it seemed to Beth. A neat mixture of wizened and withered. Not that, in her opinion, you could apply any of the three adjectives to Gina. But she could see it might be how the American woman appeared, from that faraway viewing point of youth.

'The Sam-and-Gina situation, if there is one – which I doubt – isn't relevant,' Beth persisted as Carlos headed the boat past the reef's end and out towards Dragon Island. 'The point is that there isn't a Sam-and-Delilah situation either.' No response. Beth prodded Delilah's leg as a prompt. '*Is* there?'

Delilah's leg started jogging up and down furiously. She did this at home when she was angry, Beth thought. So many times she'd told her off in the kitchen and noticed the tiny vibrations of the table as Delilah's leg, beneath it, twitched and bounced furiously. The last time had been during the summer, when she'd caught her smoking dope out of her bedroom window with Kelly. Had Delilah really thought the smell wouldn't waft into the garden, where Beth was picking parsley to add to the Smothered Muskrat recipe? And had she really imagined her ex-punk parent wouldn't recognize that sweet heady scent?

'Is there?' Beth demanded again.

'Is there *what*?' Delilah growled.

'You know what I was asking you.'

'I don't know why; you seem to know all the answers already.' Delilah glared at Beth. Her eyes were glistening. Beth could see this was more than the effect of the salt wind. Time to let it go, she decided suddenly. It would be too cruel to force the girl to say 'No', when Sam was so obviously an object of hopeful teen desire. Nothing would happen. Glamorous Sam must be spoilt for choice among older, more experienced holiday women. He wasn't likely to waste his time feeding off the lovelorn passions of a naïve teenager. Young girls had to be more trouble than he'd be looking for at the best of times, and this one was encumbered by having her watchful parents in tow. He'd be sure to opt for a far easier life than that.

'OK, OK, we'll leave it at that. Just . . . please, no more picking fights, all right?' Beth smiled at her daughter, who scowled back. Not ready yet then, Beth understood, to let her mother off the hook.

So how come it always happened, she wondered, as Carlos carefully backed the boat up to the soft white sand of Dragon Island, that she ended up being the Bad Party. No mystery. It came free with a mother's lot, that's how.

Dragon Island was no more than a quarter of a mile long by a hundred yards' broad strip of perfect soft sand, the flecking of coral in it sparkling a fierce diamond-white. In the centre was a grove of several dozen mature coconut palms hiding a thatched bar that faced the endless ocean on the island's far side, a wooden shack laid out as changing rooms and several picnic tables beneath giant sunshades. Oversized burnt-orange hammocks, the colour sun-faded, hung from bent palms. These were usually occupied by loved-up couples who occasionally tumbled out onto the sand, as fondling that they wrongly assumed to be well out of eyeline became over-intense.

On the beach beneath a pair of symmetrically arching trees was the hotel's wedding venue: a white-painted bower like a seaside bandstand, draped with tulle and twined with jasmine. Beth tried to imagine Mark and Sadie here a week hence, all decked out in full-scale wedding finery, but could only picture the two of them as they appeared now: Sadie in a bikini and matching mini-sarong all patterned like army camouflage, and Mark in a shiny black and white Newcastle United FC vest and lime green board shorts.

At the island's southern end, a sign depicting a dancing couple wearing only floral garlands was nailed to a tree, proclaiming the far tip of the beach a clothes-free zone.

'Gross,' Delilah commented to Sadie as they padded along the beach towards the bar. 'It'll be old people showing off their flab and wrinkles.'

Sadie giggled. 'Won't matter: you won't be able to see their naughty bits for all the fleshy overhang!'

'Ugh, yuck!' Delilah shuddered. 'You're making me feel sick!'

The party laid claim to a table beneath a thatched beach shade. Hardly anyone else was around. A couple of yachts had moored a little way out to sea along the beach, and a couple lay dozing on a double hammock beneath the trees.

Ned wandered over to the bar to fetch drinks and bottles of water, while Lesley settled Dolly onto a cushioned lounger and made sure she was well shaded from the glare of the sun. With all that silver fabric, its reflection could easily, Lesley considered, set fire to the wooden table and possibly the entire beach bar. The old lady's weirdly over-white teeth flashed a glinting and intimate smile at her, and Lesley felt a sudden chill of foreboding. Why had Dolly insisted on coming with them? She wasn't intending to do snorkelling, that was for sure; getting on and off the boat was enough of a struggle for her. It unnerved Lesley that Dolly was so callously blasé about her own death. Going on about how she expected it to happen any minute now was like tempting fate, and made everyone uncomfortable. Fancy going on holiday and reminding everyone every day that the Grim Reaper was on your tail. It was selfish, that was what it was. She should either have stayed at home in Wyoming or left her death demons behind her. Surely people who had really accepted that they were about to die simply took to their beds and gave up the ghost quietly?

'This is exactly the place I always think of when I listen to *Desert Island Discs*,' Beth was saying when Ned returned from the bar.

'What's that on?' Sadie asked. 'I haven't seen that. Is it on Beeb Two?'

'It's radio, love,' Len enlightened her with exaggerated patience. 'Radio Four.'

'Oh. Right.' Sadie looked doubtful.

'Bless her, she's never heard of it! Radio Four isn't music, pet,' Len continued, trying to be helpful. 'It's mostly people talking; there are gardening programmes and plays and *Woman's Hour*. You must have heard it.'

'OK.' Sadie looked as if she was thinking deeply. 'So, like no music at all then?'

'Only theme tunes, like this, everyone knows this one, even you! *Dum dee dum dee dum dee dee* . . .' Len pranced on the sand, can of beer in hand, belting out the theme tune to *The Archers*. A pair of inquisitive faces rose from the nearby hammock, grinned at Len and settled down out of sight again. Beth saw Mark raising his eyes to the skies, his finger twirling at his temple in the universal code for 'mad'.

Dolly chuckled quietly. Beth wondered what she was thinking: you didn't get much of a clue from someone whose eyes were hidden by such very large, very dark sunglasses.

'So on *Desert Island Discs*, Sadie,' Beth told her,

'you get to choose your eight favourite records that you'd have with you if you were shipwrecked and all alone. And a book and a luxury.'

'*Eight?* Like eight songs? Er, like, *why*?' Mark interjected. 'If you was gonna fall off a ship with some music on you, you could take thousands of tracks on your iPod, no?'

'Gordon Bennet, yoof of today!' Len roared. 'What do they know? It's just the way the programme is! It's the *format*! Has been for donkey's years, you daft sod! You get eight songs. Not eighty, not eight zillion. You can't mess with a sacred formula.'

'Not until,' Beth laughed, 'some BBC spark with no sense of broadcast history updates it and we get *Desert Island Downloads*.'

'What about them books and luxuries then? That's definitely more me.' Sadie lit a cigarette. Beth guessed her luxury would be a fag machine and a smart gold Dunhill lighter.

'You get to take one book, apart from Shakespeare and the Bible. I keep changing mine,' Beth said. 'Just now it's Colette's Claudine novels, but Nancy Mitford's coming up fast on the rails.'

'I can't think of a book I'd want.' Sadie looked worried. 'Though I liked *Harry Potter*.'

'You could take magazines. Britt Ekland asked for back issues of *Vogue*,' Beth told her.

'Remember Oliver Reed, saying he'd have an inflatable woman?' Len laughed.

'What for?' Delilah asked quickly.

'To *fuck*, honey.' Dolly's harsh voice rasped out loud and laconic. 'Wha' ja think?'

'Um. Oh. Yeah,' Delilah murmured. 'Um, anyone swimming?'

'You know what, Ned?' Beth said to him as they

went down to the water. 'I reckon Delilah tried to drown the wrong one in that family.'

'I'm a good swimmer,' Lesley murmured out loud to herself. 'No I'm better than that, I'm an ace swimmer. I swam for the school. And the county. I can do this.'

She was all right in the sea back at the hotel. There was the reef not far from the shore: nothing special, just a man-made wave-breaker, a calm swimming place for nervous guests and a perch for the pelicans. When you were in the water right there it felt safe because you couldn't see the open sea over the rocks. Here on the seaward side of Dragon Island the ocean went on for ever. The next landfall from this tiny strand of sand was way out there over the horizon: it was quite probably Venezuela. If the current caught her, Lesley could be carried out to the middle of nowhere, out of sight of land and life, drifting slowly away to a lonely drawn-out death. She imagined poor Mr Benson in the grey Guernsey early-morning water, fighting to get back to land, swimming hard, some-times thrashing out in a panic, sometimes trying to be calm, to pull strongly and steadily, only to be tugged further out to cold exhaustion and defeat. Did there come a point when you gave up and gave in? What happened if you were out there till it got dark? Suppose you saw the lights of a ship and got some hope up and then watched it pass and sail away? Agonizing, that would be. Being eaten fast and brutally by a shark might be better.

She sat on the damp sand at the edge of the water and rinsed her snorkel mask out.

'Beth?' she said. 'Maybe I should just stay here and keep an eye on Dolly?' It sounded pathetic, like a plea for permission to be let off the swim. Schoolgirlish.

Any minute now, she'd be telling the others she'd got a note from her mum. 'Lesley has a slight cold and cannot swim today.'

She was a grown-up, for heaven's sake. Why not simply say she'd decided not to bother, that she'd rather lie on a lounger and stare at the sky? You were allowed to do that, when you were a grown-up. You were also allowed to have fears and to admit to them, she reminded herself firmly.

'But the snorkelling here's really good,' Beth was saying. 'That bit of dark blue water just out there, where the reef drops away – that's supposed to be one of the prime sites of the Caribbean for fabulous fish! And we might see turtles!'

'I know . . . but . . .' Lesley faltered. 'Truth is . . . I've just lately got a bit scared about the open sea. I know I'm a really good swimmer but . . .'

'Lesley, it's fine, I'll be right beside you,' Beth assured her. 'I'll make sure I stay between you and the next continent, truly. It would be a shame to miss out, you were really looking forward to it.'

Lesley pulled her mask over her head and adjusted her snorkel, trying a few experimental breaths. She felt like a small child, encouraged by her mother to go to a party where all the class mean girls would be.

'OK, as long as we don't go too far from the shore.'

'Look, I'll go one side, Len can be on the other – we can hold your hands if you like,' Beth assured her.

'No, don't say anything to Len,' Lesley said quickly, 'I don't want him to . . .'

'You ready?' Len came up and slapped her on the behind.

'Yeah, I'm ready. Don't go swimming off where I can't see you, Len,' she told him.

'What, you worried I'll be a shark's lunch?' he

laughed, patting his capacious stomach. 'Poor thing would find it'd bitten off more than it could chew.'

'Len, don't joke. You don't know what's out there.' But she did. Mr Benson was out there. A horrid, agonizing death was out there. Len thought she was over it. He'd said she was being morbid, brooding over the lost guest's disappearance. He'd even joked about it. 'You'll see,' he'd said, the day Mrs Benson had given up and gone back home. 'In a couple of years he'll have turned up in Australia with some young thing.'

'Oi, everybody!' Len did a mock whisper and waved the others closer. 'Lesley thinks there's something hungry out there, listening to us, so whatever we do . . .'

'Len! Stop it you daft sod, I only meant be careful. Stay close together in case someone gets cramp or something. And that's *everybody*, including you, Len, OK?'

Lesley splashed into the waves and ducked under the water, then rolled onto her back. Bliss. She was going to enjoy this. It was going to be all right.

Oh it was so easy. None of them were around so Cynthia could prowl where she liked. Bradley was up at the Haven having Reflexology, which gave Cyn at least a good forty minutes. And the others wouldn't be back from snorkelling for hours. Beth (sure to be Beth, in bloody charge being as sensible as ever) would hoist the blue flag requesting a return trip to the hotel, but they'd probably have to wait; Carlos wouldn't let any-one else drive his precious speedboat, and he was busy in the afternoons, zapping about in the rescue boat chasing after hopeless guests who'd sworn they were brilliant sailors but who turned out to be completely inept at handling the hotel's fleet of Hobie Cats.

Cyn strolled along the path between the lush ginger lilies and strelitzias towards the ocean-front rooms. She didn't look sideways but listened carefully and made sure she was alone. At the final turn she hesitated and peered along the open-sided corridor where she'd find rooms 1105 to 1112. There she was, the friendly cleaner who always said 'Hi' as if she was singing it, turning out the end suite ready for new arrivals.

'Er – hello?' Cyn tapped hesitantly on the open door. 'Um . . . I'm *so* sorry, but do you have a pass key? I've come back from the beach to get my sunglasses and . . . so stupid . . .' Cyn broke off and gave a small silly-me laugh. 'I've forgotten my key!'

'Sure! Which one?' The cleaner took a key from her pocket and followed Cyn along the corridor. 'Oh, this one,' she told her, indicating Beth and Ned's door.

'Thanks so much,' she beamed as the door swung open, 'I'm *so* forgetful! It must be the heat!'

A small qualm of doubt hit Cyn as she closed the door behind her. Suppose the cleaner said something to Beth? Suppose, next time she saw her, she said something about remembering her key this time? It wouldn't matter about Ned. If the girl made that kind of remark to him he'd simply brush it off and assume she'd got the wrong person. Men never did delve into things, overanalysing, the way women did. She sometimes wished she was more like that. Wouldn't it be easier just to take everything that was said at face value, without looking for hidden intricate meanings all over the place? On the minus side though, that would mean she had to accept Ned's insistence that their affair was over. But she knew he didn't mean that. He just hadn't thought things through.

Cyn stood by the door, almost afraid to move, taking in the room's layout. It was the same as hers and Bradley's but the opposite way round, with the bed on the left. She checked the mahogany bedhead. Like theirs, it was pulled a few inches clear of the wall. She remembered the first year they'd been to the Mango, Lesley in the Sundown bar one night blurting out something about how peculiar that gap was, and did they think it was to stop the wood scraping marks on the painted wall? Gina, Beth and Cynthia had laughed at her and she'd been puzzled.

'Noise abatement,' Beth had explained (of course she did). 'It's so it doesn't crash against the wall and keep the people in the next room awake,' and still Lesley hadn't got it. 'But why . . .' she'd begun. How naïve could you get?

'It's for when you're having sex, Lesley honey!' Gina had had to spell it out.

How much rocking and crashing had Beth and Ned's headboard been doing? Cyn stroked the soft silk robe that lay folded neatly on the end of the bed. It was the mauvey-grey colour of a pigeon's throat. She tried to imagine Beth in it and pictured her padding barefoot out of the bathroom with the robe slipping from one bare shoulder, her curls softly tousled, the steamy scent of shower gel in the air. I can do tousled, I can do silky robe and gorgeous scent, she thought angrily. She felt like ripping the garment in half and caught a horrified sight of herself in the mirror, actually staring round wildly, searching for scissors.

She then wandered into the bathroom and spent a few moments checking out Beth's cosmetics. She didn't seem to go for brand loyalty then: here was Clarins moisturizer, Simple cleansing wipes, Lancôme, Chanel and Max Factor eyeshadows,

Chantecaille blusher. She opened a Clinique lipgloss and tried it on. Not really her colour, she decided, peering into the mirror, a bit on the plummy side. She delved further into Beth's make-up bag, searching for more intimate items – a pack of contraceptive pills perhaps, a multi-flavour condom selection. Finding nothing of interest, she put everything back tidily where she'd found it and returned to the bedroom, then climbed onto the bed and lay down, using Beth's robe as a pillow. It was easy to tell who slept on which side – Beth's table had a heap of books, the sort that tend to come under Modern Women's Fiction, whereas the opposite table held a Psion organizer, a diver's computer watch and a copy of *Coral Reef Fishes*. No condoms there either. Perhaps they didn't do it. No, she decided, too much to hope for, especially on a hot holiday. Beth had probably got a highly efficient coil. She was the sort who'd be careful to get it changed every three years – probably using her birthday as the reminder time.

Cyn got up and went to the windows. It was tempting to open the doors and go out onto the balcony. Perhaps she could wave at the snorkelling party as they came back in the boat from the island. She could just imagine Beth out there, sitting beside Ned and saying, 'Third one along, isn't that our room? Who's that on our balcony?' He'd know. He wouldn't need a second look.

Time to go back to the beach. Bradley would be back from his reflexology any minute. She hoped he wasn't going to tell her all about it. Nothing was more boring (though analysis of a golf game came close) than hearing What the Therapist Diagnosed – you'd think people would want to keep it to themselves if a masseuse tinkering with your big toe noticed a malfunctioning colon.

Cynthia took her perfume atomizer out of her bag and sprayed it around the room. Beth would think the cleaner had been wearing swanky scent but Ned would know better. And in case he didn't – she slipped off her cream Myla knickers and pushed them under his pillow. With men it was no use being subtle; you just had to spell it out.

Beth watched Lesley as she waded out of the shallows and up the beach. There was such a difference. All that shrinking fear had vanished and Lesley was now laughing and happy. She even looked somehow taller, slimmer, radiating confidence.

'I did it!' she called. 'In the real, open sea! I was beginning to think I'd developed a real phobia there!'

'You did, and wasn't it brilliant?' Beth said as they walked back towards the bar.

'That big turtle! I thought, does he fancy me or something? He wouldn't leave me alone! Followed me everywhere like a puppy!'

'Anyone fancy a beer? Thirsty work, swimming.' Len came up behind them, flinging an arm round each of the women. 'Better get one in for old Dolly as well. What's her poison?'

Beth giggled. 'Better not mention poison, Len, she might start mixing up a potion. Where is she?' she said as they approached the palm grove. 'This is where we left her, isn't it?'

Dolly was nowhere in sight. Her lounger was still safely in the shade, and her sunglasses and hat were lying on it as if bagging it for later. Her shoes were neatly placed side by side on the sand.

'What's all that, under her hat? Isn't that her robe thing?' Len said, poking at the little fabric heap.

'She must have gone for a paddle. She can't be far

though, surely. I wish I'd known, one of us should have been with her.' Beth peered anxiously out to sea.

Lesley picked up Dolly's sunglasses and gingerly poked at the belongings so very neatly folded beneath. 'All her clothes are here!' she howled. 'It's happened again! She's gone!' Lesley, distraught, fell into the sand and screamed and screamed.

## 12

# Kiss-In-the-Dark

21 ml gin
21 ml cherry brandy
21 ml dry vermouth

The sun was down, gone in that swift final green flash
on the horizon that Beth loved to watch each evening.
You didn't get a lingering sunset here – darkness
almost literally fell, tumbling over the land in a rapid
half-hour as if it had a record time to break. Dusk was
also the peak time for mosquitoes to attack, and the
astringent whiff of sprayed chemicals and lemon filled
the air and mingled with the scents of assorted fruits
that were being sliced at the Sundown bar for the
early-evening drinks rush.

Beth, Gina, Dolly and Len sat at their usual table on
the beach side of the terrace, enjoying what Len called
a 'Day-Ender'. And how we deserve it, Beth thought as
she took a deep reviving sip of her Sea Breeze and
tried hard to obliterate from her mind the astounding
sight of Dolly that afternoon, strolling stark naked
along the sand in all her pale-skinned glory, hailed
back from her visit to Dragon Island's nudist area by

Lesley's sky-splitting screaming.

'That woman coulda woken the dead!' Dolly (now securely buttoned and belted into a navy blue linen dress) seemed to find this an amusing thing to say and had repeated it several times, drawling the words ever more slurringly as she made her way through her third pina colada. No-one else was laughing.

'Enough already, Mom,' Gina told her, taking her empty glass from her and returning it to the bar counter.

'Hey! Bring me another while you're there!' Dolly yelled. 'And a bowl of those peanuts!'

'You're not allowed peanuts, Mom, you know that. They're a choking hazard for you,' Gina told her patiently. 'And you've had plenty to drink. You'll fall out of your bed tonight if you have any more.'

Dolly gave a crackly snigger. 'I doubt it, honey. I have a feeling tonight's the night! And in the morning when I'm lying cold and stiff and gone you'll be filled with guilt that you denied me my last wish, one last measly cocktail.'

'Trust me, I'll deal with it. That's what therapy's for,' Gina replied. 'Now do you want dinner with me in the restaurant or in your room?'

'In my room of course, like I always do,' Dolly snapped. 'You think I want to sit among strangers all chewing and swallowing?'

'How should I know, Mom?' Gina sighed, catching Beth's eye and grinning. 'I mean I wouldn't ever have dreamed you'd take all your clothes off and go walkabout on a public beach, but hey, how wrong was I?'

'How many times, honey, it's a *nudist* beach; you *don't wear clothes.*' Dolly rapped a sharp gold-painted fingernail on the table as she spoke.

'Not the whole naffin' island, it isn't!' Len told her.

'Most people take it to mean that bit where it says "Nude bathing area", not the whole bloomin' shebang. Still, no harm done, eh?' He winked at Gina.

'No, I guess not.' Gina sounded weary. 'I'm sorry folks, I didn't realize Mom was going to be such a liability for you all.'

'No she wasn't, it's fine, no worries,' Beth comforted her. 'And did *you* have a good afternoon? Did you do anything exciting?'

'Er . . . not sure I'd put it that way; I just had some errands to run, nothing special.' She gave Beth a smile full of mystery and left them all to guess what she'd been up to. Or possibly who. Which took Beth back to the Delilah-and-Sam conundrum. Please, she offered a quick prayer to any listening deities, please don't let all that come to blows again.

Ned knew the instant he opened the door that Cynthia had been in the room. He felt his blood pressure instantly rocket to what was surely a potentially fatal level; at this rate Dolly wouldn't be the only one going home neatly boxed in a plane's cargo hold. How, he thought as he inhaled that unmistakable hint of vanilla, had she got in? She couldn't have come with Beth – Beth hadn't been back to the room since they returned from the island, but had spent a half-hour in the jacuzzi jollying Lesley along before joining Len and Gina at the bar. Had she broken in? He had a close look at the door lock – no damage that he could see, not that he couldn't imagine Cynthia jemmying the thing open if she really set her mind to it. Maybe her room key was simply the same as theirs – he supposed there couldn't be that many variations. Horrendous coincidence if that was the case – she could be in and out on a daily basis. She might follow him there when he was alone, creep up while he was showering. *Psycho* came to mind. Well it would: if she'd go this far, who knew what a scorned women was capable of? Or she could be hiding under the bed while he made love to Beth. Suppose she already had been? Oh God. Suppose she'd been watching and listening that night they did it on the lounger on the balcony? That had definitely been a bit special . . . but the thought of Cynthia spying on them from only feet away was an absolute blood-chiller.

Ned sat on the bed and wiped sweat from his forehead. He was just being paranoid. Wasn't he? Perhaps it wasn't Cynthia. It could be that it *was* her perfume but the cleaner had simply had a quick spray of it while tidying Cyn's room, just to see what it was like. Or used the same sort herself; Cyn couldn't be the only woman who liked that particular scent. But if it *was* her . . . what had she come in *for*? What did she hope to find? He looked around quickly, casing the room to see if there was anything immediately different, peering under the bed – she might have left something . . . Though what, a bomb? A recording device? *Herself?* He prodded the underside of the bed base. Nothing there, thank goodness.

Ned pushed the balcony doors open and went out into the steamy evening air. He could just make out Len sitting at the usual table across at the bar. There were trees blocking the view of the rest of the group, and he had to hope Beth was still with them rather than on her way back to the room for her bath. Ned needed time to check everything, make sure Cyn had left no more than her perfume behind.

Bath. Ned raced into the bathroom, suddenly terrified he'd find Cynthia herself hanging from the shower hook (bringing the holiday's potential body count up to three – a running total outdoing the worst sink prison and sure to cause the hotel the loss of at least one star from its rating). Nothing different in there either, but still that lingering, elusive hint of perfume. What to do about it? Nothing he could do, he concluded as he returned to sit on the bed and give in to a feeling of helplessness. He would have to ignore it – if he said anything to Cynthia she'd take it as revived interest. And suppose it *hadn't*, after all, been her? What kind of fool would he look?

Ned felt his heart rate gradually subside to something close to normal. To give it a few more recovery moments he relaxed back on the bed and reached for his copy of *Coral Reef Fishes*. That afternoon they'd seen some brilliant little fish, a shoal of the most starting cobalt blue ones, some with vivid yellow tails, close to where one of the yachts was moored. 'Hanging about where there might be food, do you think?' Len had asked him as they swam back together. Ned had agreed they probably were, not liking to point out, knowing this as an experienced diver, that the food in question was less likely to have been temptingly offered over the boat's side by keen fish-spotters than to have been stuff flushed out from the lavatory tanks. Often, in the sea, it was better not to think about how some species got by.

Feeling cramped and uncomfortable, Ned shifted the pillow behind his neck and flicked through the book's pages. Those were the ones, blue tangs. Between three and twenty-eight centimetres. That sounded about right. They were described as 'unafraid', which was rather sweet, he thought, smiling at the memory of the little fish as they crowded around the snorkellers, eager and bustling as riverside ducks sensing a toddler approaching with bags of stale bread.

Something fell softly to the floor as Ned shifted. Something made of diaphanous cream fabric and black ribbon. He reached down and picked up Cynthia's knickers. No doubt now. He even recognized them. He remembered buying them for her – an expensive, spontaneous, and so unwise present back in March.

'Unafraid'. He caught sight of the word again as he closed the book. If only. Bizarre, he thought. Never in his life had he imagined he'd really, really envy a fish.

Oh it felt so good to get out of the hotel. Beth sat back in the taxi and savoured the usual vicious air conditioning, feeling her skin tingle in the unaccustomed chill. A reggae version of 'White Christmas' was booming from the driver's radio, and he had decked the windscreen with so much plastic mistletoe and holly that Beth wondered how he was managing to see the road. It was his choice, she told herself firmly, nothing to do with her, and she looked instead at the view of the moonlight on the sea from the side window. She was not interested in problems tonight, feeling she'd already done her good-deed bit. In the few hours since coming back from the snorkelling trip, she had listened to Lesley as she'd told her all about the dead Mr Benson, reassured Gina that her mother hadn't caused rumpus and outrage and had comforted Len, close to weeping into his beer, as he confided his fears that his wife was losing her marbles. And this was supposed to be a holiday. Tomorrow, she promised herself, she would spent most of the day in the Haven indulging in full-on pampering, from Indian Head Massage down to Peppermint Foot Treatment.

Delilah sat sighing between Nick and Beth, making her feelings clear about being forced (as she saw it) to endure an evening in the town with her family.

'We *never* go out at home "as a family". We *keep* doing it here!' she'd wailed, raising her fingers in mock quote marks. 'Why can't I just stay behind and hang out with Sadie?'

'Come on, you'll enjoy it! You want to see more of the island, don't you?' Beth cajoled her. 'Anyway, *we'd* like you to come.' And then, for the first but probably not the last time, she'd pulled the big parental-blackmail one with: 'Indulge us, please, Delilah, we're getting old.'

'Oh God, don't lay that guilt-trip one on me!' Delilah huffed crossly. 'Don't tell me you're going to start on like that nutter Dolly that you're gonna drop down dead any minute! I can't handle it!'

'So come with us then,' Beth had bargained. 'There's a sort of Christmas street carnival on with lots of stalls and music. For supper we can pick up some roti from a stall and we might see nice things to buy.'

The girl's eyes had lit up briefly, tempted by the bait of shopping, but even as the car pulled away from the hotel she was looking anxiously out of the rear window, in search, Beth could tell, of the so-elusive, so-desirable Sam. If it wouldn't lead to an outburst of furious denial and an accusation of interfering, she'd tell Delilah she was wasting her angst: she'd heard the receptionist mention to another guest that it was Sam's night off from jollying the guests along and he was going into the town. Even Gina wouldn't be able to have a shot at him. Delilah, contrary as any teenager, would not thank her for pointing this out.

As they sped along the bumpy highway into Teignmouth, Beth glanced at Ned, sitting in front beside the driver. He was looking troubled, his eyes miles away, worrying about something. It made her uneasy and she'd have to be careful not to be annoyingly overcheerful to try to compensate. Since his affair, she'd tried so hard to stop taking on everything that wasn't comfortable, physically or emotionally, as if it was down to her, and only her, to sort out. Not easy, this, when every family gripe, every sulk, every problem had been brought to her to deal with ever since the children were born. But Ned wasn't a child. The affair had been a scalding reminder of that fact. After the initial almighty shock of it, apart from telling him that if it really was over, if he really wanted to stay with her, it would be OK, she had tried hard not to behave in a mumsy way towards him. He wanted a lover, he'd made that clear: not an extra mother.

It would have been easy, given the amount of sorrowful regret he'd expressed, to comfort him as if he was a hurt infant and tell him it was all right, it didn't matter, all over now. But, however over it might be, it *did* matter. The hurt to Beth had run deep and he understood that. She wasn't going to keep picking at the pain but it was still relatively recently healed and fragile. All the talking through had been done but sometimes there were questions she had to bite her tongue from asking. A few big ones came to her now: did he regret giving up the woman? Did he miss her? Stop this, she told herself. Next thing, the worst question would muscle its way through . . . and it did. Was he thinking he'd rather be here with *her*? Stop that right now, she told herself. If Ned wanted to be with someone else he would be.

The cab pulled up alongside the harbour where the first of the stalls had been set up. Beth climbed out and sniffed the hot night air, pungent with spices and exotic cooking smells from every street corner.

'We won't starve, anyway,' she said to Delilah, trying to entice her into a good mood.

'We wouldn't have starved at the Mango. I don't know why you went for All Inclusive if you're going to keep coming out for food,' was the tart reply.

'All Inclusive isn't good for the local economy,' Nick told her as they set off along the stall-lined street that was crowded with both islanders and tourists. 'You're just paying money into fat-cat hotel chains abroad rather than the island. It's your duty to go out and offload cash, put something in.'

'Thanks for the lecture Nick, but I did *know* that *actually.*'

'Well bloody cheer up and enjoy yourself then, you miserable slapper!' he teased, grabbing her from behind and tickling her.

'Nick *geroffme*!' Delilah shrieked, but he'd achieved a result, Beth could see. Despite her determination to sulk, Delilah was at last laughing.

There was a cruise ship in the harbour, a monstrous thing, towering over the small port like a giant iceberg hung with lights. It was unusual to see one staying overnight – as a rule they left the island soon after sunset, making their way out towards the horizon to invade the next island on their itinerary, sending thousands of trippers at a time to raid the markets and craft stalls of the next port. It seemed rather sad to Beth that they did all the actual voyaging in the dark and while the passengers slept, as if they should not for a moment be bored by having nothing to do except look at the ocean. She'd find that rather restful, she thought, that calm, isolated progress over the sea and out of sight of land, getting a feeling for the distances between islands rather than being presented with them like a surprise gift each morning. You might as well fly, otherwise.

'I suppose now you two are getting so *old* you'll start going for holidays on those things.' Delilah pointed to the ship.

'I don't think so.' Ned shuddered. 'It would be like taking a small city around with you. How do you escape? You can't just grab a cab or hire a car and disappear into the rain forest whenever you fancy a change.'

'You don't do much of that, Dad, come on.'

'No, but I *can*, that's the point.'

'He's right,' Beth agreed. 'And when you see TV ads for cruises, they show people doing things like rock-climbing and diving and lazing on deserted beaches – all things you don't actually do on board. Got to be a reason for that.'

Beth and Delilah inspected every stall for jewellery bargains and bought several necklaces made from intricate shell and beadwork. Nick picked up a mask carved from coconut shell. 'This reminds me of Delilah,' he said, holding it up over his own face. 'Look, its mouth is all turned down like hers is when she's in a strop!'

'I *so* don't look like that!' Delilah yelled, hitting him with her bag.

'Actually, she does a bit,' Ned whispered in Beth's ear. She felt her skin tingle as his breath wisped across her neck. She giggled and turned to him. 'Are you hungry? Shall we get something to eat?'

He looked at her as if he hadn't quite understood the question. Jesus, she thought, if only she hadn't said that. After all her no-motherish resolutions, what could be more of a lust-zapping maternal question than that? Could do better, she told herself, *much* better. She'd work on getting seductive, she vowed, and entice Ned into the Haven. Lovers' Massage, here we come.

'Yeah, sure,' he said now. 'There's a roti stall just past that girl selling paintings. Let's go. Nick? Delilah?'

Beth and her family sat in a line along the harbour wall. She tried to eat fast to avoid making a horrible mess, dripping the contents of her chicken roti as the doughy casing became soggy. It was a rich mixture of spiced chicken with vegetables, all mixed together in an unleavened wrap like a giant tortilla. The thing reminded her of a tiny baby swaddled in a blanket and she'd felt ludicrously hesitant about taking a first bite.

'Yo! There's Sadie and Mark!' Nick yelled, waving at a group of people walking towards them. And Michael, Beth could see, was with them and a couple of others. She recognized Ellis who helped with the hotel's water sports, Melina the manicurist from the Haven and also Sam. Beside her, she could feel the instant that Delilah noticed him, sensed her attention being focused. The besotted girl's hormones must be surging crazily, and Beth crossed her fingers that Sam was old and sensible enough to keep Delilah at a safe distance and that she'd go home happy enough with what might have been, rather than anything more turgid.

'Hey, all,' Nick said, jumping down from the harbour wall and greeting them as they approached. 'Whass 'appening?'

'We're going on to a club after we've hung out here for a bit,' Sadie told him. 'You two want to come with us?'

'Are all of you going?' Delilah looked at Sam, who smiled lazily. Beth thought quickly; should Delilah, so recently so very ill, have to be dragged miserably back to the hotel with her and Ned, or should she let her go and trust her to slow down when she got tired? If she overdid it and relapsed now, she could end up wasting the rest of the holiday in bed, feeling horrendous.

'Yeah, all of us, even Dad!' Sadie said, flinging an arm round Michael. 'It's a blues place and it's his thing. Come with us, bridesmaid!' she said to Delilah. 'We can make this a sort of hen night.'

'And take the stags along for the ride,' Sam added, aiming his frankly speculative smile at Delilah.

'Parents? You don't mind if we abandon you, do you?' Nick asked, already moving into the group and pulling an eager-eyed Delilah along with him.

'What do you think, Ned?' Beth asked him.

'Well, I'm not sure. I hadn't thought about going clubbing, myself, but . . .' he replied, gleefully aware he was keeping Delilah in agonized suspense.

'Like we were asking you to!' Delilah hissed at him through her teeth.

'Thanks Del!' Ned laughed, 'I'll remember that next time you want a lift somewhere and access to my wallet. Go on then, enjoy yourselves. And Michael you're a brave man, keeping up with this lot.'

'Nick – take care of her, won't you?' Beth whispered to him. 'And don't let her do anything . . . stupid.'

'Mum – hey, she's safe with us. No worries, OK?'

'Just you and me then,' Ned said to Beth as the taxi pulled up in front of the Mango hotel. 'Anything you fancy doing now?'

'Nothing particular. Do you want a drink in the bar? We could see if Len and Lesley are in there. Or we could go back to the room?'

'No, wait . . .' Ned grabbed her hand and led her towards the terrace. 'What about your stroll on the sand? Shall we do that first?'

Cynthia's knickers were stashed in his pocket. They'd been burning a hole in it all evening. He'd had to get them out of the room but hadn't yet had a minute without Beth in which to get rid of them. When they'd been crossing the road in the town, he'd thought about how it would be if he was run over and someone found them. He pictured a nurse handing over his possessions in a black bin liner, and Beth taking them all out, finding the silky pants that weren't hers. They had to be disposed of. He hadn't had a chance in the town – now perhaps he'd be able to leave them in one of the bins on the beach.

'Are we going to lie on the beach and gaze at the stars like the honeymooners do?' she laughed.

'Sure. Why not?'

Ned took hold of Beth's hand, and headed down towards the sea's edge. He needed to walk thirty or so yards further on before he could pick out which of the rooms on the end building was theirs. He wasn't sure quite what he expected to see, but he felt he had to reassure himself that Cynthia wasn't up there leaning over their balcony or exploring their room, waving the beam of a torch around. He put his hand in his pocket and fingered the silk fabric. Shame really, they'd been so very expensive but they had to go. No way was he going to join in Cyn's mad games by handing them back to her, not even by sliding them under her room door. With his luck Bradley would be on the other side, would open the door just as he was about to make his escape and all would be discovered, point-lessly and for nothing.

Beth was paddling now in the white-frilled shallows, carrying her shoes and holding her skirt up. She looked, Ned thought with a surge of affection, like a carefree twenty-something. A couple of tiny lights showed beneath the line of trees higher up the beach – the glow of cigarettes from a couple sprawled in the dark on a pair of sun loungers. Could they be Cynthia and . . . who, Ned wondered; Bradley didn't smoke. No, it wouldn't be her; it could be anyone. There were close to two hundred hotel guests to choose from. Delilah would tell him he was getting paranoid. She'd be right.

Ned looked up as they reached the spot beneath their room. No sign of life, not a flicker. Please, he prayed silently, don't let her have been roaming about in there again.

'Beth?' he called softly to her as they approached the far end of the beach and the sailing area. All the Hobie Cats were pulled safely up the beach and locked together with chains to prevent drink-sozzled guests from taking it into their heads to go out on the ocean for a moonlight sail and get themselves drowned. Beth hadn't heard him and was still in the sea, looking out at a distant ship. Quickly, he slipped Cynthia's pants into a big wooden bin beside the water-sports hut.

'Beth?' he called again. This time she heard him and padded up the beach to join him. He tried the door of the hut and peered in through the shutters.

'Ned, what are you doing? It's sure to be locked!' Beth giggled.

He grinned. 'I was just thinking about that squashy old sofa in there and the view of the ocean. Worth a try anyway.'

'We've got a lovely big comfy bed back in our room!' she laughed, pulling him away from the hut. 'What's wrong with that?'

'Nothing,' he said, putting his arm round her and pulling her close. 'But a change of venue can be very stimulating . . .'

When they reached the steps to their block, Beth turned to look back at the hut, wondering what on earth Ned would find so thrilling about making love among ropes, anchors, cans of boat diesel and racks of water skis.

'Hey look at that!' She pulled Ned into the shelter of the stairwell as she spotted movement by the hut. 'There was someone in there all the time!' And so there had been. Ned watched, feeling like a spy, as a couple slid out of the door. Please, he thought, please don't let them investigate to see what I put in the bin.

The two from the hut kissed briefly and the woman started walking (thank goodness) along the beach in the direction of the pool terrace.

'Well! You couldn't mistake who that is!' Beth said. 'That long blonde flag of hair could only be Gina's. The woman never stops!'

The man whistled softly and Gina turned, waving and blowing him a kiss before continuing on her way.

'And that,' Ned told her, 'is Carlos. I only hope she hasn't knackered him too much for the diving tomorrow. You'll know who to blame if we get washed up on the shore of Tobago.'

Delilah couldn't stop yawning. It was way after midnight and she needed her bed. Her head ached and she was starting to feel shivery in spite of the sweaty heat of the night. They were outside the club now, drinking at a table in a crowded courtyard lit with hurricane lamps. What a brilliant evening. Sam had stayed close to her most of the time, although he hadn't made a move on her. That would be down to Nick being there, she thought, because Sam was obviously interested. All evening he'd kept giving her little touches that were like small ownership gestures. Claiming her, that's how it felt – she was completely geed up with longing for him just to give in and kiss her. Now, sitting beside him, she could feel the length of his thigh against hers. Occasionally his hand brushed her leg and he was doing that teasing thing that boys at school did when they fancied girls. He'd been taking the piss about her ignorance of West Indian music. Fair enough, but why should she have heard of 2Ntrigue? Just because he said *everyone* knew about him, didn't mean that she had to.

'Sorry,' he apologized now, hugging her close to him and kissing her cheek, 'I shouldn't laugh at you, girl.'

Oh the bliss of feeling his strong body against her like that, scenting it, even though it was just for a few seconds and he was being no more than friendly. All the same, he hadn't been like that to Sadie or Melina. Just her.

She yawned again. Nick looked at her quickly. 'You tired, Del? You feeling OK? I should be getting you back to the hotel.'

She gave him a furious look. How dare he? She'd decide when she'd had enough.

'We're moving on to Ellis's place for something extra,' Sam whispered. 'Maybe you should go back, hey? It'll be a late one and the smoke's gonna be bad for you.'

'No! No I'm fine! I don't want to go yet.'

'Well I'm off to find a cab,' Michael said, looking at his watch and standing up. 'You young folk go and have more fun if you want but it's time for my beauty sleep. I'll be happy to see Delilah back to the Mango, Nick, if you want to go on with the others.'

They were talking about her as if she wasn't there, or as if she was three years old or a parcel or something. Insulting or what?

'But . . . Nick . . .' No-one listened to her. They were all getting up now. Party over. Oh, great.

But as the others went ahead through the courtyard's archway that led to the road, Sam took Delilah's hand and pulled her gently into a dark corner behind a low fan-leaved shrub. Delilah suddenly found she was being kissed, crushed firmly against Sam's muscled body. His hand was smoothing confidently down her side and finding its certain way under the edge of her short skirt, caressing the soft top of her thigh. And just as suddenly, just as she was relaxing into it, it was over.

'Hey Delilah girl, you're tired and it's late,' 'he told her, gradually letting her go. 'I like being with you but tonight you're too young for where we're going. OK? Go back to the Mango and I'll see you very, very soon,' he promised, his fingernail gently scratching the back of her neck as he walked her through the archway to join the others.

Michael had already hailed a taxi. Tingling and close to delirious with happiness, Delilah climbed inside and flopped onto the back seat.

He really likes me. He wants me, but he cares enough to keep me safe, she thought as sleep came close to catching up with her, that's got to be good. It proves he's a nice guy, not just a user. And that kiss. Just a taster for now, loads and loads more of that to come.

And Gina, she thought with delicious satisfaction, as she fell asleep against the cab's window, Gina eat your sodding heart out.

# 13

# Lady Killer

28 ml Cointreau
28 ml gin
14 ml apricot brandy
56 ml pineapple juice
56 ml passion-fruit
slice of orange

Lesley watched from behind a clump of hibiscus as Len jogged down the lane from the top of the hill back into the hotel grounds. Then she carried her cup of tea to a table on the far corner of the pool terrace beneath the tamarind tree, where he wouldn't immediately see her when he returned. He'd assume that at this hour she would still be in bed; his early-hours thinking time was, she understood, a vital and private start to his day and he wouldn't be thrilled to find her waiting to chat to him on the terrace, where he liked to do his cool-down stretches in meditative peace.

Tough, she thought as she peeled a banana and took a sweet delicious bite. Today, like it or not, he was going to have his body checked out. This overdoing the sports combined with overdoing the booze and food was getting way out of hand. Yesterday he'd come back from tennis (played in the midday sun, how stupid was that?) sweating like a racehorse and with his face the livid colour of tinned tomato soup. Suppose the heartburn he grumbled about really did turn out to be his heart – literally burning away? If he dropped dead tomorrow it wouldn't be a big surprise, but there'd be no satisfaction in being able to say 'I told you so' to the corpse of your adored husband. It looked as if it was her job to stop things going that far.

In spite of her attempts to persuade him to have his vital signs checked by the nurse in the Haven (by appealing to his instinct for getting his money's worth, pointing out that it was included), Len had stubbornly refused. In fact, he rarely ventured in there, considering men who went in for bodily pampering to be flaunting that bit too much of their feminine side. He made exceptions only for the odd deep-muscle sports massage when applied to muddy and injured rugby players, with the proviso that any essential oils be limited to wintergreen and camphor. So Lesley had persuaded Ellis to trick him into the dive shop and not let him out till he'd had the divers' BP monitor firmly Velcroed round his arm, and results duly noted and lectured upon if necessary. There were to be no arguments about it – if he wouldn't let Ellis have a look at him, Lesley intended threatening to shut up shop in the sex department for the rest of the holiday. And Len wouldn't like that one bit: he considered a good helping of the conjugals, as he referred to it, to be an essential ingredient of what defined All Inclusive.

Lesley watched from her hiding place as Len puffed onto the terrace and stood for a few moments panting and gasping, leaning heavily on a table top for support and looking frighteningly close to collapse.

She was alarmed to see him holding his chest, rubbing at it as if there was something in there to be massaged away. She hoped to goodness it wasn't clots, aneurysms and sundry other cholesterol-built nasties in his bloodstream.

Len hadn't noticed her – she was partly obscured by a couple of yoga enthusiasts with their bums in the air, saluting the sun. Just as he made a start on the calf stretches Ellis appeared, right on cue. Good man, she thought. Perfect timing – if you were allowed to buy drinks in this place, she'd owe him a large one.

'Len, my man! Just the fella,' Ellis called across the terrace from the dive-shop doorway. 'Come in here with me, I got a fancy new sport computer to show you. Come and try it, tell me what you think.'

And Len fell for it, keen as a puppy after a bouncy ball. Excellent. He liked gadgets – loved playing with the computer at the gym that told him how many calories he'd burned, how much of the virtual Tour de France he'd covered, how many kilos he'd lifted that day. Let's hope, Lesley thought as she got up and made her way across the beach for her early dip, that he'd take as much interest in what the blood-pressure monitor told him.

A blessed bit of peace. Beth stretched out on her lounger and started on the first page of a new book. There was nothing, to her mind, quite so relaxing as having a pile of reading matter and plenty of guilt-free time to get through it. It was bliss to be away from work and have no Witjuti grubs to purée, no kabanosi sausage to grill, no moose nose to de-hair for World Wide Wendy. The only hassle had been lugging a great heap of books with her on the plane, freshly trawled from the Gatwick bookstores. Next year, if they came back here, she decided she would buy her holiday selection a few weeks early, resist (with difficulty) beginning to read them and send them on ahead to the hotel by Federal Express.

Beth hoped for at least an hour's peace. Delilah had gone for an archery lesson (with dire warnings from everyone to be more careful where she aimed her arrows than the unfortunate Valerie had been last year) and would not be bothering her for cash or attention for a while. Nick was playing tennis with Sadie – his doubles partner for this week's hotel tournament. And yet ... here came Cynthia, making her purposeful way towards her across the terrace, clutching her flower-trimmed raffia-crocheted beach bag and looking as if she had something important to say. She looked perfectly put together – if a bit like a child dressed for a party by an overfussy mama – everything carefully matched as ever. This morning she was togged up in a glittery candy-pink and white spotted bikini, a short fringed wrapover cover-up in the same fabric and a pink straw hat with white ribbon. She even wore tiny white beaded earrings and a pink bracelet. Beach Barbie – you couldn't help but think it.

She could imagine Cynthia browsing in a smart boutique where the clothes were not on hangers and shelves but packaged up as entire outfits, displayed in cellophane-fronted boxes and fully accessorized right down to shoes and jewellery. Beth was loath to indulge in catty thoughts, but it did cross her mind that a glimpse inside Cyn's wardrobe might be an interesting character analysis. Did she store everything by colour? Would there be rails of, say, blue items arranged from pale baby shades through to navy, each of which had a special goody bag of matching extras and all the right shoes boxed and labelled, possibly with Polaroid photos on the fronts? She always seemed quite a sexy sort, Cynthia. She'd have imagined she'd have a certain amount of seductive element with regard to clothes.

'They could almost be brothers, couldn't they, our men?' Cyn commented to Beth as they both waved to Bradley and Ned who were walking down to the sea, ready to set out on Carlos's boat with the other divers. 'They're really quite alike.'

Beth couldn't agree at all – OK, both were tallish, similar in age, both quite broad across the shoulders and each still had their own quite acceptable teeth and hair, but apart from that, well she wouldn't have trouble telling Ned from Bradley in a bad light.

'I can't really see it myself, Cyn. Bradley's much darker and his hairline's completely different. Mind you, I suppose they all look much the same wandering down the sand in wetsuits.'

'Shows off the male body rather well, skintight black neoprene, doesn't it?' Cyn smirked, then turned to Beth with sudden curiosity. 'So what was he like, this secret man of yours? What happened?'

'What man?' Beth was puzzled, then recalled the cross-purposes conversation from a few nights ago. 'Oh I see what you mean. No, Cyn, that was a mistake; you completely got the wrong end of the stick. There's no-one.'

'Mistake? They're *all* a mistake . . . Well nearly all,' Cynthia said rather bitterly, her eyes still on the divers who were now climbing into the boat. 'Come on, Beth,' she cajoled, perching on the next lounger and looking as if she intended to stay till she'd heard something satisfying scandalous, 'you can tell *me* about him. It's not as if you live close by and have to spend the rest of the year worrying I'll spread it around all your friends. You could think of this as a sort of confessional!' Somehow she made this sound less like something that would have priest-like secrecy and more like gossip that would be 'confided' to *Hello!* magazine.

'I might, if I had anything to confess!' Cyn's persistence was beginning to annoy Beth. Why did she keep on like this? Which part of the denial wasn't she understanding?

'I'm boringly monogamous, me. Sorry to disappoint!' Beth flicked over a page in her book, hoping Cynthia would take the hint. She only had half an hour left now till her Aroma Spa Ocean Wrap, and she didn't want to spend it arguing with Cynthia about men she hadn't slept with. Perhaps she should make up a few, if it would get rid of Cyn; possibly invent a steamy orgy with a school rugby team. Would the bloody woman then go away happy?

'All right! If you insist!' Cyn gave in with a strangely twisted smile. 'But I know about women like you, all holier-than-thou and butter wouldn't melt on the surface. Underneath, you and me, we're not that much different. You'll see.'

Beth watched Cynthia as she got up and stalked off towards the beach, swinging her girly little basket. What in the name of buggery had she been talking about with that mildly threatening 'You'll see'? Beth, completely befuddled, rather thought, and certainly hoped, that 'see', in this context, was something she wouldn't.

Time to move. Beth reluctantly gave up on the book and wandered off towards the Haven by way of the Archery field. Delilah, Michael and Mark were there, lined up with a dozen others, learning the basics of firing at the targets way down at the far end against the wall of the Frangipani bar. She stopped to watch as Jerome, the instructor, wrapped both arms around Delilah and showed her exactly how to aim. Did he really need to do that, she wondered, realizing at the same time that of course he didn't. Jerome was a one-time Olympic medallist: getting a bit touchy-feely with attractive young female guests was probably the only perk of this job. She watched Delilah giggling as she snuggled back against his body. Did she have to be quite so flirty? Perhaps she should have a word with her about the careless putting out of signals. She was a gorgeous young thing, looking so much better now from spending time in the sun – she didn't have to act as if she was either desperate or grateful for every bit of male attention.

'I'm surprised they still do this arrows business, aren't you? After that nasty incident last year.' Len caught up with Beth. He was carrying a selection of golf clubs, on his way back, Beth was certain, from smashing another unsuspecting contestant out of the Mango tournament.

'You're right – Ned and I call this bit of the grounds Val's Field, but I don't suppose it would be tactful to talk about it when Jerome is in sight.'

'Best not,' he chuckled. 'Poor bugger. They did a lovely job at the hospital on his arm though – I mean look at that: he's got a scar to be proud of.' Len pointed to Jerome as he demonstrated the firing stance to Michael, pulling back strongly on the bow with his right arm and showing a long neat line of scar tissue where one of Valerie's misaimed arrows had pierced the delicate flesh on his shoulder the year before.

'It's a lovely job. Someone up at the Teignmouth hospital really knows how to sew,' Beth agreed.

'Don't talk to me about hospitals,' Len groaned. 'Do

you know what my ever-loving wife did to me this morning? She conned me into getting my blood pressure looked at. If I'd wanted to know, I'd have gone along and queued up for my GP.'

'And? Was it all right?' Beth asked. Nice one Lesley, she thought to herself, admiring her for finding a sneaky way to sort out what had been worrying her.

'It wasn't anywhere near as bad as she thought it was going to be! So that's telling her!' He laughed. 'I mean, I'm not a complete nutter, I only push it as far as I think I can. I ran the Guernsey Marathon – I bet she didn't tell you that. Anyway, I've told her to stop nagging me now or,' and he nudged Beth in the ribs and winked, 'I've told her we'll be joining the archery class and she knows what that means!'

'Definitely! I wonder what happened to Val and Aubrey? Did anyone hear?'

'Ah – didn't Lesley tell you? Aubrey left her. Said he couldn't settle in the house. Being shot at was only the half of it – he'd got to thinking the next thing would be powdered glass and cyanide. So he packed his red spotted hanky on a stick and buggered off.'

'Oh, that's sad. So he's on his own then?' Beth pictured gaunt Aubrey, a dignified type who'd reminded her of an ex-colonial tea-planter, leaving his Southsea bungalow for the final time, wheeling a small suitcase with one hand and his enormous, all-leather, state-of-the-art golf bag with the other.

'On his own?' Len gave a great hoot of laugher. 'You're joking! Last we heard, he'd been taken in by a blonde widow with a chain of jewellers all down the south coast. On his own! Ho ho!'

And, still gleefully laughing, Len wandered off in the direction of the bar, ready for a mid-morning sharpener to set him up for water volleyball at noon.

Beth walked on to the Haven, thinking about what would have happened if she'd thrown Ned out of the house after discovering his affair. Even if he hadn't chosen (assuming he'd *had* the choice) to go and live with The Woman, he wouldn't have been on his own for long. Attractive men, obviously even quite elderly, only borderline-attractive men – as the fate of the shot-at Aubrey proved – rarely had to exist alone for long before some female took them on, adopting them like winsome cats in need of home comforts. How different for women, she thought, her mind on whether plank-thin Valerie regretted the attempted murder of her dull husband, now that she'd lived through months of meals-for-one and a chilly solitary bed. Probably not, she then decided, as Juliana greeted her at the spa entrance. Who knew? Valerie might have booked herself a permanent berth on a cruise ship, acquired a wardrobe full of glittery cocktail frocks and be having the time of her life.

'And it's all down in the book?' Angela was shouting as if Miriam was stone deaf. 'Hair? Manicure? Full make-up for Sadie, me and this scraggy little brides-maid she's insisting on?'

Beth's ears pricked up. She was supposed to be at the relaxing stage, drifting into semi-consciousness to the inevitable Enya soundtrack. She was lying on the massage table, slathered in mud and wrapped in what looked and felt like turkey foil. Beneath it all she was stewing slowly, not so much oven-ready as slowly melting. Her face was rigid beneath a mask of muddy clay. It smelled disgusting (if Delilah was here, she'd be wrinkling her nose and screaming 'rank'), possibly taking the concept of 'organic' a stage too far, for this reeked like something scooped up from an estuary close to a sewage outlet. No wonder Juliana had worn plastic gloves and a surgical mask. Anyone in their right mind would. If she caught Weil's disease from it, she'd sue.

In spite of the 'Quiet Please' notices on the wall, the strident tones of Angela making a fuss in reception would have been enough to shatter concrete. Beth lay seething in Treatment Room 4, swaddled in her foil and mud wrap as the bride's mother slagged off Delilah, following up on 'scraggy' with 'bony'. Bloody nerve – of course the girl was a bit thin – she'd been ill for weeks. And was that any way to talk about someone who would be a major factor in your only daughter's wedding? Who would be smiling alongside her in the wedding photos? And all this from a woman who had laughed and revelled in the attention as she'd dropped her frock to the floor in the bar the other night.

'And not only her . . .' Angela as in full spate now, grumbling to poor Miriam about arrangements. 'But her brother's been coming on to my Sadie like you wouldn't believe, angling for an invite, obviously. You'd think when Sadie said "family only" she'd have meant her own – not everyone else's that she could pick up on the beach.'

Miriam's reply could not be heard, but she was a woman used to guests being difficult – complaining that treatments were booked up leaving only inconvenient times, assuming you could swap a Life and Sole foot treatment or an Indian Head one at the very last minute, men thinking (wrongly) that their call would not be traced if they phoned from their rooms asking if, among the massage menu, there was one entitled Relief.

'So that's three manicures – French for me and

Sadie, don't know what the girl will be wanting. I hope she's not a biter, nothing worse than a bridesmaid clutching a bunch of flowers with her fingernails all ragged at the ends. And hair – put Sadie down to go first, I think, then me. The girl can sort herself out – she's got nice hair, I'll give her that.'

Well thanks a bunch, Beth thought, wriggling indignantly under the foil. 'The girl', indeed. She needed to break out of her wrapping, go and give the woman a few home truths. At least her family knew how to behave and didn't deliberately shed their clothes in public places or drunkenly slosh drinks all over themselves. The urge passed, which was just as well, she conceded, as how would she have looked, emerging mud-smeared and naked (apart from skimpy paper pants) from the treatment room like something that had rolled in a swamp?

'How're we doin' in here, honey? Y'all relaxed now?' The slow melodic voice of Juliana reminded Beth that yet again she'd wrecked the calming aspect of her treatment so far. But there was still the massage bit to go, time enough to chill during that if she could evict Angela from her brain.

Juliana carefully unwrapped the crinkly foil and inspected the odorous mud beneath. 'You been sweatin' here girl!' she said. 'That's ex-cell-ent! You'll be inches slimmer after this! Rinse off in the shower now, then we rub in the scented potions, and you'll be smooth and soft – that'll get your husband goin'!' she promised.

Delilah's archery lesson was over and she now sunbathed by the pool, watching Sam from behind her sunglasses. He was over by the Sundown bar chatting to Jim the barman and drinking water from a bottle. He had a towel round his shoulders and looked as if he'd just finished a class, so she guessed it must have been his turn to take the Legs, Bums and Tums session in the gym. She was trying to make out she hadn't noticed him, just to see what he would do. Would he come over and talk to her? She hoped so – and he should do if he'd meant what he'd said. She hadn't seen him since The Kiss and had spent every hour in an agony of waiting for whatever would happen next. What was it going to be? At worst, it could be an embarrassed half-nothing – the sort of pathetic keep-a-distance backtracking that boys at school did after they'd got you in a clinch at a party and wanted to rub it in that you'd be wrong to assume one snog meant you were going out, like permanently. At best it would be something moonlit and romantic on the beach late at night.

Somewhere in between the two was a haze of mild dread based on her own sorry lack of experience. There were girls in her year at school who'd done everything, according to hints they dropped. Two had left to have babies. Delilah felt way behind – she'd never given anyone a blow job, for instance. Suppose Sam wanted her to and she a) hadn't a clue how to do it right, or b) felt mildly sickened at the thought. Or suppose he wanted to go down on *her* – was she ready for that? And how embarrassing would that be? Out of ten, probably a nine. She could feel her face going red at the thought.

Right now, though, he was still at the bar with Jim and she was still on her own on the far side of the pool. He couldn't miss her – she'd made sure of that and had pulled her lounger away from the line along the terrace by the beach so that she was out there by herself, right on the pool's edge, posing as a bikini babe concentrating on writing a postcard to her best friend. Not that she could bring herself to write more than Kelly's address and 'Hi!'; she didn't want to risk Sam coming over, grabbing it off her and reading (out loud) something juvenile like, 'I met someone and he's, like, *sooo* completely gorjus', even if that came close to what she'd eventually send.

She was in her red bikini, sprawled out for maximum effect on the pale blue seat cushion, on her front, propped up on her elbows which she kept as close in to her sides as she could without looking as if she was impersonating a chicken, so as to make the most of her pathetic cleavage. It was hardly worth calling it that, really, that sad broad vale down the front of her top. With luck, Sam was more of a leg man. Hers were stretched out elegantly behind her, one of them bent up with her long slim foot flexed and waving slightly as if she was wafting away a mosquito. Her tan was coming along well – luckily she was the type who went quite evenly brown, not all patchy and pink like Sadie was going. If Sadie's wedding dress really was the full-scale white, she would look like a raspberry ripple in it if she wasn't careful. And only a couple of days away now. Would Sam be there on Dragon Island with them all? He might be – suppose Mark had picked him out as best man? He'd be forced to kiss her then, if he didn't before, because that's what happened with the best man and chief bridesmaid.

'Hey babes, how're you going?' And suddenly, in the one second she hadn't been concentrating, Sam was there, squeezing onto the lounger to sit beside her and stroking the back of her thigh. She squirmed with a mixture of pleasure and nerves as his finger casually traced along the inside of her thigh, stopping just short of her bikini edge and fondling the soft skin there. She looked round quickly. Would her dad do something stupid if he saw where Sam's hand had so nearly gone, like grab him and give him a thumping? She doubted it; her dad was a laid-back sort, hardly likely to throw Sam into the pool yelling, 'Hey, get yourself cooled off!' or anything equally mortifying. But you never knew – he hadn't been faced with seeing anyone touch up his daughter before.

'Hello Sam. I'm fine – just doing a couple of postcards.'

'Oh, right. Hey, let me see what you're telling them back home!'

'Nothing about *you*!' she was glad she could say as he grabbed the cards from her hand.

'Nothing about anything! You haven't got very far. What have you been doing all this time? I saw you – you've been here a while!'

Delilah felt caught out. 'Nothing. Just literally nothing,' she told him. 'It's too hot to think.'

He leaned close in and whispered. 'Then come into the shade.'

For a moment she couldn't work out if he was simply giving her sensible advice, then she looked into his eyes. Wicked thoughts were lurking there, she could tell. She smiled at him, waiting for him to suggest a suitable cooling venue, though exactly for what, she preferred to keep unclear for now. She'd wing it, somehow, when the time came.

'I have to work the rest of the day and tonight,' he said, taking her hand and kneading her palm gently with his thumb. 'We could get together later tomorrow though, after the great Mango Experience weekly barbecue?' He laughed. 'You can't miss that, it's one of the highlights of your trip!'

'Mmm,' she agreed, nodding eagerly like a toddler

promised an ice cream. Why couldn't she be like a grown-up, as if this was just a perfectly everyday kind of thing for her?

'I'll catch you in the Sundown bar, round about nine? I have to do the early greeting and seating shift but I'm off by then.'

'Fine. See you around nine or so.' She tried not to squeak, but to sound more casual this time, as if she *might* happen to be around then, but couldn't be sure. Of course she'd be there, no question. Or rather *big* question, several of them – what would he expect from her, and was she up for whatever it was, really?

I must be very wicked, Beth thought, as Juliana smoothed dollop after dollop of unguents (sweetly scented this time) into her skin, because I'm getting no peace at all. In spite of the lavender candles, the sub-dued lighting and the hushed music (they were on to Sea Sounds now), Juliana was in full conversational flow on her favourite topic: the fickle nature of men.

'On this island, they don't want to settle down with a nice local girl. They wanna travel, find a rich lady from Miami and get a job over there.'

Beth made a few noises of sympathy, which was all she could do under the increasingly furious kneading as Juliana warmed to her topic.

'And they never stay faithful neither. Too many holiday girls for that – they collect them like badges so they can spread the seed!' Juliana's hearty laugh almost blew the candles out. 'I had a friend,' she went on. 'She had one man; three years he stayed with her, gave her two children. And one day she came home and he's there doing his thing with a woman from Denmark. In my friend's *own home*!' She gave Beth's thigh a slap to underline the outrage. Beth grunted her sympathy, which Juliana took as an OK to continue.

'And *on their bed*!' More slap. 'So my friend . . .'
Rub-rub-slap. 'My friend . . . she took an axe!'

Beth's eyes flew open and she stiffened. 'She did
*what*?' she said.

'She took an axe and she killed him!' Thump went
Juliana's big hands on Beth's shoulder blade.

'Like that!' Whack on her lower back.

'Dead!' Juliana slathered on another palmful of oil.
'You OK? We're nearly done now, honey. You feelin'
nice and relaxed now?'

Was it likely? 'Mmm. Er, yes I'm fine,' Beth thought
it wisest to say. She sighed, relieved it was nearly over.
After this she needed to go and have a lie-down, or a
swim, anything that really *was* restful. Juliana
certainly put her all into her work. She'd hate to catch
her on a bad day.

'Course you know what, don't you? You're ahead of
me, I can tell!'

Beth wasn't, and wondered with some dread what
was coming next.

Juliana laughed. 'I can tell because you've gone
tense on me!'

Oh really? Amazing, Beth managed not to say.

'That wasn't no friend I was talking about, not really
– that was me!'

Beth almost held her breath in horror while Juliana
did the final gentle pitter-patter with her fingers, and
at last the little finishing-off bell was tinkling.

'You enjoy that, honey? You're looking good. Now
remember, take care and for two hours it's no sun, no
drink, no tea or coffee, and drink plenty of water. I'll
leave you to dress now . . .'

But Beth was already on her feet, ready to go with
her wrap and her sandals on.

'Hey you're fast! You gotta man to meet?' Juliana grinned. 'You know I better tell you something, case you go reportin' me to Miriam and tellin' all your friends. I didn't kill him. Not quite,' she admitted, leaning close to Beth and half-whispering, as if this was secretly more shameful than if she had committed murder. 'I just gave him the big fright – and the Danish woman a big one too. Men need that sometimes, when they step out of line. You remember that, honey, if your man ever lets you down. You go get yourself a big axe and you remember what Juliana told you!'

# 14

# Sex on the Beach

28 ml peach schnapps
21 ml vodka
cranberry juice
orange juice

Delilah twisted round to look in the bathroom mirror, studying the back of her knee where she'd been scratching. The whole area – from mid-calf to halfway up her thigh – was swollen with bites, livid scarlet, mottled and agonizingly itchy. She blamed her mother, whose brilliant idea it had been to go out that afternoon and wander round the swampy woods. Why hadn't she warned her about the fifty zillion billion mosquito population that existed up in the rain forest, all hungry and desperate to munch on fresh young skin?

'It's only a twenty-minute trip in a cab and then a short walk in the rain forest,' Beth had suggested to Delilah and Nick. 'It won't make you tired, Del, and the scenery is so beautiful, definitely not to be missed.'

Oh and it was, Delilah conceded, thinking of the great hanging liana tendrils, the slender waterfalls tumbling over the mossy rocks, the giant ferns and the unexpected orchids crowded onto twisted branches. It was fabulously beautiful, like something off wildlife TV programmes but with the added mildly delicious smell of something soggily rotting. It was also sweltering and steamy and frighteningly full of things that might want to kill you – weird monkeys (unseen but heard scarily cackling in the trees), huge lizards whizzing up and down branches, checking you out; mongooses scuttling through dripping undergrowth like long rats; the terrifying suspicion of snakes – as well as things that just wanted a nourishing nibble, like the mozzies.

'Didn't you use the anti-mosquito spray?' her mother had asked, the moment she saw Delilah scratching and slapping at her legs as they followed the guide along the trail.

'You might have told me I'd be eaten alive,' Delilah had complained. 'How was I supposed to know?'

Her mother had been typically sensible and worn trousers – her legs safely protected under her beige linen and her arms out of range under a long-sleeved white shirt. Even Nick had worn his combats for protection. All right for them.

And what did she let me loose in the jungle wearing? Me, her precious daughter? Delilah grumbled to herself as she rubbed ineffectively at the worst of the bites. A little pair of denim shorts and a sleeveless tee, that's what. Why didn't she say something before they left the hotel? Why didn't she send me back to get something more covering? Does she want me to die of some mozzie-borne tropical disease?

A little corner of Delilah's mind came close to admitting that something *might* have been said as they waited for the taxi: something along the lines of

212

'There's still time to run back to your room and put some trousers on' or words to that effect. Unfortunately, Delilah had translated those words into critical mother-speak, as in 'You're not going out dressed like that, are you?', had gone into a huff and refused to change. It wasn't her fault. The hazards should have been explained more clearly. What use was a mother who couldn't make herself understood?

Sam was going to love this, she thought miserably, imagining his hands on her skin, encountering nothing but ugly oozing lumps and bumps. How sexy was it (not) to have one big fat swelled-up leg and huge bites on the inside of both elbows? Great. And they'd only get worse, Delilah realized gloomily as she ran the shower at a cool and soothing temperature, quite probably there was another giant crop of bites lurking in her skin that hadn't got round to showing themselves yet. She would be one huge scarlet splodge. Not to mention the next stage when they went blistery before turning into disgusting crunchy scabs.

'Thanks a lot, Mum.' Delilah scowled at the mirror. 'Are you always going to pull stunts like this so that I'll never, ever get it on with a boyfriend?'

The weekly Barbecue Night at the Mango Experience started early. The Frangipani restaurant was closed for the night and instead big circular tables were set up in front of the Sundown bar close to the beach, and a buffet was arranged in an open-sided marquee close to the pool. The idea was to get everyone to mingle, to have them sitting in random groups and bonding with strangers so that when they returned home they'd be able to spread the word about what a friendly place it was. Sports trainers and spa staff joined in too, distributing themselves around, eating starters at one

213

table, moving round to a main course at another, and having to smile and be scrupulously polite as guest after guest whinged that tennis courts had to be booked two days in advance and why didn't manicures come under the All Inclusive tariff.

Guests liked to make an early start bagging a table for themselves and their friends and a cocktail or two at the same time, while the barbies were being fired up in big oil drums and the steel band tuned up on the terrace. A stage was set up for after-dinner entertainment and a limbo bar was already in place to which, following a demonstration of spectacularly costumed skill, guests would be invited to try their own luck.

'There you are Lesley, your speciality!' Len called to her as he carried a tray of drinks to the table he'd chosen under the tamarind tree.

'I don't know about that,' Lesley demurred, taking a pina colada from Len's tray and choosing a chair facing the ocean.

'But you did really brilliantly last year!' Beth told her. 'I heard you were the winner by miles!'

Delilah looked at Lesley in undisguised amazement. 'What, you, like, you actually go up on the stage in front of *everyone* and wiggle under that bar? *Really?*'

'Yes really, Delilah!' Lesley assured her. 'I was a very bendy ballet dancer in my day, believe it or not.'

Delilah gave her another look, one that said she'd believe it when she saw it, but would, frankly, rather not have to be there when it happened.

'You should try it, love,' Lesley told her. 'I could do with the competition. You might need to wear something longer than that little skirt though. I've come prepared – got my stretchy Calvins on. Last year there was a woman giving it a go in a micro mini-skirt and a thong and showing the whole pudding. We didn't know where to look, did we Len?' Lesley gave a hoot of laughter while Beth fired a warning glare at Delilah, wondering if they'd done the right thing.

In past years on barbecue night, she and Ned and whoever else fancied avoiding the rather holiday-camp compulsory-jollity atmosphere (Cyn and Bradley last time), had taken the opportunity to go out to an elegant seafood restaurant along the coast and stay there until all danger of being hauled up to make fools of themselves on stage had passed. This time, with Nick and Delilah's entertainment to consider, they'd decided to give the barbecue a go as it was more likely to appeal to the younger ones. Perhaps, she thought, she and Ned should simply have gone out anyway and left them to it. She had run the idea of escape past the two of them but Delilah in particular had been really keen to stay, in spite of still giving Beth a hard time over the mosquito bites.

'Why would I want to miss it? You're such a snob Mum! It'll be fun. We have barbies at home all summer and you don't get sniffy about those.'

'True enough,' Beth conceded, not really minding either way. For one thing, if Lesley really was going to shimmy under a low bar, she'd quite like to be there to cheer her on.

'Got room for us?' Cynthia drifted over to the table, bringing with her a cloud of her perfume and a large rum punch.

'Of course! I saved seats for you and Bradley – unless you want to sit with your in-laws?' Len said, pulling out a chair for her and exuding bonhomie like a first-class host.

'That witch Angela? No way! I'm not sure where Brad is, actually,' Cynthia said as she sat down. 'He was having a treatment – one of those seaweed wraps

215

like you had earlier, Beth, and it was all running a bit late. I think he's on his way. Never mind,' she said, smiling brightly at Beth and Ned, 'I can choose another man to sit beside, can't I? Beth, you won't mind if I borrow yours? Come on, darling,' she called to Ned, patting the chair beside her. 'Come and be with me tonight. Beth can have Brad when he gets here. If she wants him, that is.'

'*Swingers*,' Delilah muttered to Nick, covering the end of the word with a cough.

'Don't even joke!' Nick said, looking round to see who else, as the terrace began to fill up, was likely to join them. Sadie and Mark were with Angela and Michael and a selection of the vast Americans, a couple of tables away. Michael waved to them, indicating a couple of vacant chairs.

'Do you want to go and sit with them?' Nick asked Delilah. 'Because if you do, I could come too.'

Delilah grabbed his wrist and pulled him away from her parents' hearing range. 'Nick. Just leave her alone. I know what you're doing, I've been watching you.'

'Doing? What, me? What *could* I be doing? Truly Delilah,' and he put his hand to his heart, 'Angela so isn't my type.'

Delilah tried to stay serious. 'You know I don't mean Angela, you idiot!' she said, hitting him on his arm, 'I'm talking about Sadie!'

Nick looked mystified, giving away his guilt by overdoing a bizarre grimace to indicate denial. '*Sadie?*' he said. 'I can't do much about Sadie, can I? She's getting married the day after tomorrow.'

'Er, like I know that, Nick? Duh? I'm the bridesmaid?'

'Mark asked me to be best man, actually.'

'He didn't! You never said!'

'It's OK, I turned him down. I thought, like tradition has it that the best man cops off with the senior bridesmaid and I thought, nah. You're not bad for a sister but neither of us is that desperate. So he's asked . . .'

'Who?' Delilah almost spat the word.

'Eager, aren't we? He's asked . . . *Sam*. That good enough for you?'

Delilah shrugged and tried to look casual. 'Yeah, I suppose. He's all right.'

'All right!' Nick teased. 'You were practically all over him the other night when we were out!'

'Er, actually . . .' She didn't go on. It might not be such a good idea to point out that Sam had been all over *her*, not to her brother. You never knew with brothers – they could come over all unexpectedly boring about these things. Kelly's brother than threatened serious violence to Micky Martin in year ten who'd put it about (untruthfully) that he'd scored a BJ off Kelly down behind the school footie pavilion around Easter time. Kelly hadn't been thrilled about the brotherly concern because at the time she was working on turning the unfounded rumour into reality. The last thing Delilah needed was Nick pointing out that Sam was in his mid-twenties and she was only sixteen and that there could only be one thing he was after. Like she didn't know? She wasn't completely stupid. They'd all be going home in a few days anyway. She needed to have this maximum fun while she could, especially after being ill for so long. She deserved it. But instead he did something she'd never have expected from her brother.

'Del, seriously,' he began, taking her arm and leading her away from the table towards the far side of the tamarind tree on the beach, out of range of the string of lamps hung from tree to tree. 'I want a word.'

'Why? Now what have I done?'

'Nothing. At least I hope you haven't, not without being safe.' He put his hand into his pocket and pulled out a small folded square of foil. For a second she thought he was giving her his spliff supply.

'Not without using one of these,' he went on, handing it to her and then gazing at the sand. If she didn't know him better she'd have sworn he was actually embarrassed. 'What's . . . ? Oh!' She hadn't actually seen condoms before, not in their packaged form. Oliver Willis had done the mortifying thing of fumbling about with the crinkly wrapping that time they'd done it at his house (taking so long about it she was surprised he was still in a suitable state to apply it), and at school when they'd had the lesson about putting the condom on the Perspex willy, she'd managed not to have to do hands-on. Probably a mistake, that.

'Just in case you *do* do something daft. Don't feel you have to, but if you do, then do it safe.'

'Safe-*ly*,' she corrected him automatically, glancing back at the table where all the grown-ups were getting on the outside of yet more drinks. Were there no responsible adults? No, she decided, seeing Cynthia's hand sliding up her dad's leg and him trying to flick it off again, definitely not.

'God I felt such a first-class tit!' Bradley was telling them as they all tucked into the barbecued jerk chicken, steaks, swordfish and spiced pork. His hands covered his face in mock shame. 'But how was I supposed to know? Dolores comes into the treatment room and tells me to get undressed and says, "Take all your clothes off and put this on" and hands me this papery thing.'

'Oh the paper pants?' Beth cut in. 'Horrible aren't they? They disintegrate.'

'Pants. Well I know *now* that they're pants,' Bradley said. 'But the other time, back on Thursday, when I was in for a facial, she'd put a paper hat over my head, to keep the stuff off my hair, so you know, like, I thought . . ..' He groaned and took a long sip of his wine. 'Anyway this afternoon, after a few minutes Dolores came back in and I'm lying there face up in all my naked glory and she does this great long shriek and runs out laughing, yelling to the world I've put paper knickers on my head.' Another groan, another slurp of wine. 'I'll never live it down. I'll be hearing all those Haven harpies howling with laughter in my sleep for years to come!'

'Sympathies, mate.' Len patted his shoulder and then winked at the others. 'Mind you, you've got to ask yourself what she found so funny, know what I mean? Couldn't you even have managed to get a semi on just to be polite?'

'Len!' Lesley prodded him hard, and glanced across at Delilah. 'There are young folks present!'

'Oi! It was cold in that room! My blood wasn't up.'

'Not the only thing that wasn't!' Len hooted.

Beside her, Beth heard Delilah murmur 'gross', but the girl was smiling. A good thing; she wouldn't expect to have produced a daughter who couldn't enjoy a bit of bawdy fun.

'It's funny here, all these men getting beauty treatments,' Delilah said to Bradley. 'I mean, Dad never does when we're at home. Do *you*?'

'*Me?*' Bradley immediately looked, Beth thought, as if he'd rather saw off his own leg than undergo trial-by-beautician ever again. 'No, never. It wouldn't occur to me, apart from the odd sports massage down at the gym, and even then only if I'd tweaked a muscle. I suppose we do it here because it comes with the package, but I'm not likely to start hanging out down at the salon in the high street. Did you see that American guy, by the way?'

'What, Fred Flintstone? Do you mean his nails?' Delilah said. 'He's very proud of them! He's had them all done in different colours.'

'That's OK for here,' Ned commented. 'But how much do you bet that he doesn't have the nerve to travel home with them all like that?'

Ned shifted in his seat, feeling crowded. Cynthia might have sounded as if she was joking when she'd claimed him to sit beside her, but right now she was being touchy-feely under the tablecloth and making him edgy. How could she think he'd want this? And what if any minute Len, who was only a chair away, saw what she was up to? No way would he keep quiet – he'd make a big daft joke of it, shouting the odds about Cyn mauling the goods that someone else had bought. She was such a cool one – which he should have remembered from all those sessions in the back of the Audi down at Oxshott, especially the times she insisted on parking too close to the dog-walkers' route. 'Give them something to talk about back home,' she'd joked. Except it probably wasn't a joke. At the same time as managing to carrying on idly chatting to Lesley and Beth, Cyn was kneading Ned's leg like a dough mix and letting her hand drift much too far north for comfort. He tried to move away a little. If she could just for a second loosen her grip, he'd be able to cross his legs and deny her access. Time it wrong and he'd have her hand trapped, smack up against his balls.

'I might just go to the bar and get . . .' he began.

'Oh you don't need to.' Cyn got in fast, looking into his face, all steely-eyed and calculating. 'Jim's on his way over.'

Defeat. Or possibly not. He slid his hand down to cover hers, twisted her big diamond ring round and squeezed it tight. Very tight. There was a sharp squeak of pain from Cynthia and he let go. She withdrew her hand and rubbed her fingers. Mission, he prayed, accomplished.

Gina was a late arrival. She drifted over to their table carrying a large, ornate cocktail and wearing a floaty white combination of floppy trousers with a top that looked like several silk squares randomly sewn together for maximum drifting effect in the breeze.

'Dolly is ailing,' she announced, sliding into the seat next to Beth. 'She says to tell you all goodbye.'

There was a shocked hush for a moment, penetrated only by the insistent chirruping of tree frogs.

'Oh Gina, I'm so sorry,' Beth said, taking her hand and feeling her eyes beginning to fill.

'Hey, don't be! She's fine, truly. She's just angry with me because I won't let her call down to room service and demand a Cocksucking Cowboy.'

'A *what*?' Cynthia spluttered. 'I didn't see *that* in the brochure!'

'It's a cocktail, apparently,' Gina explained. 'But I won't have her talking dirty like that to the bar staff. If she wants to drown herself in booze, I told her, it's gotta be done ladylike. So I've disconnected the phone and come down myself to get her a Sea Breeze.'

'Don't you want to stay and have some food while you're out?' Beth asked her. 'It's really good, especially the chicken.'

'Honey that's sweet of you, but I can't possibly eat barbie food while I'm wearing white! I'll grab something maybe later. Gotta get the drinks in – see you guys in a while!' She got up, flashed a smile round the table and walked over to the bar.

221

'Beth, you're so *nice* and so *mumsy*,' Cynthia said. 'There's her old mother dying alone up in her room and here's you, all concerned that Gina's missing a meal.'

Beth frowned, unsure how to take this. 'I was only inviting her to join us. And only after she'd told us Dolly was OK. What's so mumsy about that? Gina must get lonely, always by herself.'

'Gina! Lonely! Never knowingly short of company, I'd say.' Cynthia gave a hollow laugh.

Beth watched as Ned shifted uncomfortably. Sitting beside Cyn, he looked as if he was perched on broken glass; his left leg – closest to Cynthia – was crossed awkwardly away from her over his right. Body language, Beth wondered, how much can you tell from it? If she was the interpreting sort, she'd guess he was reacting negatively to what Cyn had just said. Very supportive of him, if so, very reassuring. It showed he was on her side – whether he was actively conscious of it or not. Nick, on the other hand, was leaning back in his seat with his hands clasped behind his head and gazing across at the bar, where Gina was sharing a joke with Jim the bartender. Beth watched as Nick's eyes narrowed, then, and she could sense the moment he made his decision, he got up from his seat and said casually, 'If it's OK with you, I think I'll just give Gina a hand. She's got a lot to carry.'

'That's true, most of it at the front,' Cynthia murmured nastily. Beth looked at her, watching her flick her fuchsia-pink nail up and down on the table. It was sad to see her so tetchy and dissatisfied. Something was bugging her – something to do with that lack of 'fireworks' in her life that she'd talked about before, perhaps. Whatever it was, it had to be a bigger problem than being married to a very sweet man who mistakenly put paper pants on his head.

It was all going off on the stage. The drums were pounding away, building up an atmosphere of anticipation. The lights were dimmed, leaving only a red spotlight, flickering in time to the throbbing beat. Delilah threaded her way through the candlelit tables on her way back from the loo and waited behind a pillar to get a good view of the team of limbo dancers. There were six of them – five girls and one man – dressed in green and scarlet glittery costumes, barely more than strips of fabric edged with feathers and beads. The bare-chested man had a tall headdress of feathers trimmed with horn, and he wore a kind of raggy loincloth made of bead-trimmed chamois leather, reminding Delilah of the window-cleaner back home who always sneaked silently as a cat up his ladder early in the morning in the hope of catching her getting dressed. Not a picture you wanted with you when you're anticipating the sight of an exotic dance act, she decided, not fat Bill heavy-breathing at the top of his ladder, all sweaty and grinning through the glass, leering as he splattered sickeningly symbolic soapy water all over her windows.

'You think you'd be any good at that? You should try it.' the voice of Sam was so close she could feel his soft breath on her neck and the swish of his beaded hair against her.

'I couldn't do that. I don't have the muscles for it!' Delilah laughed, watching the taut-thighed lead dancer flexing herself gracefully beneath the bar. Behind her, Sam edged his hand hard up the length of her leg. 'You feel fine to me, girl,' he said. '*Niiiiice* and tight.'

Delilah caught her breath. Suppose her parents saw? Her mum would go mental. Right on lousy cue, her

223

mosquito bites started to itch, exactly where Sam's hand had been. It was a sign – he'd definitely warmed her blood.

On the stage the drumbeat speeded up to frenzy level and the male dancer emerged from behind a screen, holding flaming torches. The limbo bar was now only inches from the floor, and, touched by the flames, had become a line of fire.

'Is he mad?' she murmured to Sam. 'It's too low!'

'No – he does it every day. Don't you worry about him. Do you want to stay and watch?'

Or what? That was the question. Or go and have sex on the beach? Had to be. And did she want to? Yes and no, well yes and maybe.

'I'll stay for a few minutes. 'Til this bit's over.' Delilah wondered what she was hesitating about. She touched the little foil square that was sharp-edged in her pocket. Maybe it was something to do with not wanting to look like a slag, like she was gagging for it. Boys, Kelly said, didn't like that really – they wanted to think you might not be quite in the mood, but that when you were (like twenty seconds into them snogging you, you were supposed to be gasping and squealing), it was all down to their stunning powers of sexual persuasion. 'Makes them work at it' she'd said. Like she'd know.

'Honey, I can wait. But not too long.' Sam stroked the bare flesh beneath the edge of her top and she felt her skin tingle. 'See you later? I'll be waiting for you – just along the beach?'

And he'd gone. Off to do his job, mingling with the punters and jollying them along. He was good at it – every time he stopped to chat to someone he had them smiling, had the women give small touches to a piece of his sheeny skin, making each of them feel special, like if he could choose any of them it would be *her*.

The dancer made it safely under the bar – of course he did. From the crazed applause, as Delilah made her way back towards the lamp-lit terrace and her parents' table, anyone would imagine he was a complete beginner and had never done it before. Ridiculous.

The music slowed and the feathered dancer invited volunteers to try their own luck with the limbo bar. Delilah stopped and watched as Lesley, cheered on by the others, leapt to her feet and started pushing her way between the tables towards the stage.

'What about you, Delilah? Come on girl, give it a go with me!' Lesley called as she approached, reaching out to grab her hand. Other people around made encouraging noises. There was a danger of being kidnapped and hustled onto the stage, however much she protested. Absolutely not.

'Um no – can't, sorry,' she said, wriggling out of Lesley's grasp. 'I have to be somewhere. Meeting Nick,' she mumbled, turning and fleeing into the night.

'Lesley? Are you all right?' Beth found Lesley halfway along the beach. Lesley was lying in the dark, flat out on a lounger to which she'd fled from the stage. Her hands were hiding her face and someone's abandoned beach towel was round her shoulders.

Beth pulled up another seat and sat beside her. 'Don't take any notice of Cynthia, she's being a real bitch tonight. I don't know what's got into her this year. I do know it's something from home bugging her, nothing to do with you.'

'I've never felt so fucking *humiliated*,' Lesley spluttered, wiping her tears with a corner of the Mango Experience tee shirt she'd just won for her limbo efforts, and blowing her nose on it noisily. 'Why did she have to say that? I know I made a twat of myself, falling over like that, but ...'

'But you still did better than everyone else! No-one got the bar anywhere near as low as you did!' Beth tried to jolly her out of the doldrums.

'I still fell over in front of the whole hotel though, fat clumsy lump that I am. And it was true what she said, if I hadn't put on so much weight this year I'd have got under that bar, no problem.'

'You look fine, honestly Lesley. Don't forget Cyn was also bitchy about Gina's tits and my mumsiness. *She's* the one with problems, not us.'

'I don't think I want to come back here any more.' Lesley's tears welled up again and overflowed. 'And that's sad, because now I'll be taking away a bad memory instead of all the good ones.'

Beth squashed onto the lounger beside Lesley and put her arms round her. 'Hey, whether you come back here or not, one comment from Cynthia mustn't wipe out all the good times! You really can't let her get to you. She's dropped a few hints that she's been going through a bad patch at home, so put it down to that and forget about her. That's what I'm doing.'

'You're a kind woman, Beth, you see the good in people.'

'God, I must be very irritating. And it isn't always that easy.'

'No? You make it look easy, as if things go right for you. Stuff I worry about seems to tag along with me wherever I go, even when I know it shouldn't. It's why I show off a bit, like tonight. Trying to keep my demons away. And then Cynthia sticks a pin in the balloon.'

'Actually, Lesley, this is how "not easy" things are: Ned had an affair earlier this year.' Beth, feeling rather surprised, heard herself come out with it for the first time. It sounded odd, too real, spoken out loud like that.

'*Ned?* No!' Lesley's teary eyes were wide with amazement.

'Yes. It wasn't for long, nothing serious and it's all over. I'm not even sure why I'm telling you, really, except I don't want you to imagine your life is the only one that isn't completely perfect.'

'Goodness – I hardly know what to say. You never do know about people do you? Did Delilah and Nick know?'

'No,' Beth said quickly. 'They don't need to. I don't want them to despise their dad – *I* certainly don't, but with young ones things are all black and white.'

'And everything's really over, all fine now?' Lesley asked.

Beth smiled. 'Yes. Yes, I'm sure it is. Nothing's the same, obviously, but that doesn't mean that it's changed for the worse.'

Lesley giggled suddenly. 'She was probably right, really, Cynthia. If she hadn't shouted it out so everyone could hear I might have forgiven her. It *was* my fat arse scraping the floor that pulled me over, and my great big tits knocking the bar down.'

'Which is more than her skinny ones would do,' Beth laughed. 'I'd say you were the winner there really, wouldn't you?'

It was a busy place, the beach, even this late at night. Perhaps it was the aftermath of the barbecue's party atmosphere that had people wandering about in couples on the sand, trying to work out how to inject some romance into the evening, the way holiday adverts always portrayed it. Beth felt a bit out of place, walking along on her own while pairs of people snuggled and giggled. Ahead, up on their balcony, she could make out Ned leaning on the rail and looking for her. She waved, and he waved back. She carried on towards the doorway that was closest to the steps to their corridor, past a couple lying flat out on the sand staring at the sky, enjoying the moonlight.

Up by the low-growing shrubs close to the building, someone with more than hand-holding in mind had made a nest from pulled-together loungers, with sun-shades dug low into the sand, more or less obscuring the view of whoever was beneath. Just as well, for the sound effects from that direction reminded Beth of the Nick-and-Felicity nights at home. Didn't they have somewhere more private to go to? It could be Gina, she guessed, catching sight of some white fluttery clothing, then quickly looking away and walking on past. That would make at least, what? Three scalps so far? Carlos in the water-sports hut the other night, Sam (the cause of the row with Delilah), and whoever this was. No-one could accuse Gina of failing in the Mango Experience (Sport 'n' Spa) ethic – making friends and joining in.

Beth turned to go up the stairs and saw shadowy movement from beyond the boats outside the water-sports hut – someone tallish and slender and unmistakably Delilah. Beth waited and watched as she and Sam, holding hands, ran down to the sea, jumped into the shallow waves and kicked water at each other, laughing and shrieking. Well, that was something to look forward to in the morning, Beth thought happily: Delilah in a good mood.

# 15

# Double Standard Sour

28 ml blended Scotch
14 ml gin
Juice of one lime or lemon
Half tsp grenadine
Half tsp caster sugar

Beth could hardly believe it. There was Delilah in the Wellness pavilion, first to arrive at the early Stretch class and already on her mat, legs crossed and her arms stretched out along the floor as far as she could get them in front of her, as if she was praying devoutly to an unknown deity.

'You're up early – couldn't you sleep?' Beth asked, placing her mat on the floor and sitting down rather heavily. At what point in mid-life, she wondered, did the grace of youth turn into thumping awkwardness? How was it that when she was in her thirties she could still, like Delilah, simply cross one foot over the other and sink down elegantly into a cross-legged position, whereas now, achieving the same thing involved sending her left arm to the floor first to take the weight before letting the rest of her body tumble heavily into place as gracefully as a fully stuffed bin-bag?

'Just fancied getting up and doing a class.' Delilah looked at her, big-eyed with *faux* innocence. 'Got to make the most of it, haven't I?'

What a lovely smile she had – and such a rare sight from a sixteen-year-old before midday. Was that all it took? A bit of attention from a boy she fancied? If so, Beth prayed for a constant succession of attentive and attractive young men when they got home, enough to see Delilah through the rest of her teen years and well on to even-tempered maturity.

'You certainly have,' Beth agreed. 'There's only a few days 'til we go home. It amazes me how quickly the time seems to pass.'

Delilah frowned. 'Don't talk about going home. I don't want to think about it.'

'And you were the one who didn't want to come!' Beth teased her. 'You've had a good time, haven't you? In spite of being stuck with us oldies?'

'Not bad. Could've been worse.' Pushed that bit too far, Delilah retreated. You couldn't, Beth thought, accuse the girl of overdivulging her feelings. She wouldn't ask her about being on the beach with Sam last night, as Delilah would, and who could blame her, interpret that as spying. So what if she'd had a bit of a snog with him? Wasn't that the whole purpose of a holiday when you were a teenager? There was no harm in Delilah having a romantic memory to take home and impress her friends with.

Beth remembered a school trip to Italy when she too had been sixteen. The party had trailed around all the sumptuous treasures of Florence and Verona, soaking up centuries of culture, but what had made the trip entirely memorable had been the night she and three friends had shoved decoy pillows down their beds to fool any patrolling schoolmistresses, then climbed out of their hostel window to meet boys in the piazza and snog in a shop doorway till dawn. Only vaguely did she recall Verona's famous amphitheatre or the cool pale marble of *David*, but the cigarette tang of Luigi's mouth and the combined terror and elation as his confident, eager hand slid into her bra, well, that definitely stayed with her. Remembering now, it still made her smile. Perhaps she could go back to Italy one day with Ned, she thought, and catch up on all that culture she'd so crassly deleted from her schoolgirl memories.

Beth stretched down to ease her hamstrings, while Delilah lay on her mat and closed her eyes. The room filled around them. Sadie came bounding in and sat on the far side of Delilah and prodded her in the side. 'Hey, what happened to you last night?' she hissed in a whisper piercing enough to have everyone turning round, agog for any possible reply. 'I saw you, sneaking off with Sam! *Tell!*'

Beth busied herself with calf stretches, silently sympathizing with Delilah. Whatever she'd been up to with Sam on the beach (and it had looked more playful than passionate from what she'd seen), Beth understood Delilah's frantic attempts to keep Sadie quiet. Some aspects of absorbing the local culture you definitely didn't need your parents to know about.

'You do realize it's Cassandra taking this stretch class today, don't you?' Beth asked Delilah, mischievously risking fury.

'*Yeah*, like *so*?' was the instant snappy response. Own fault, Beth conceded cheerfully, her own fault for knowingly dangling a snack to a piranha. Beside her, Delilah now sighed grumpily and clambered (moving

231

less gracefully than before) to her feet as Cassandra bounced up the steps, greeted her victims and started the music going.

'Mum? I think I might just go and get breakfast and give this a miss,' Delilah whispered to Beth as Cassandra started the first deep-bend-and-stretch movements.

'Don't be daft, it's only forty minutes,' Beth told her. 'You're doing this for *you*, aren't you?'

'Yeah, I suppose.' Delilah reluctantly caught up with the stretch.

Excellent, Beth thought. Lesson number one with men: they can wait.

'See you in the morning' had been the last thing Sam had whispered to her before he left last night. So where was he? What was with the last-minute class change to Cassandra? Delilah went through the motions of the exercises, miserably certain she'd been stood up. Hell, it was only eight hours since he'd been kissing her goodnight, all afterglowy and affectionate. What could have changed in that time? Perhaps he'd been seen by one of the hotel managers, coming back from the beach with her, and been fired. He'd already told her he was risking his job by getting too close. Staff were meant to hang out with the guests but not . . . and she hesitated to put the words 'have sex' into her head . . . not to get involved with them. That was why he wouldn't go to her room – someone might have seen them. A relief, that, she'd thought. She'd felt she had to invite him up but really that would have seemed an intimacy too far, not to mention her mum would have killed her if she'd found out. The room was full of home possessions: her clothes, her books, make-up, shoes. Delilah-and-Sam was too 'other' for such dullness. No way was he going to be part of how ordinary, how normal, her real life was. So it was the water-sports hut, just as she'd pictured, scuzzy in its way, but excitingly dangerous at the same time.

She shouldn't have come to this early class. Even if Sam had been taking it she should maybe just have kept away, not been sitting there on the floor waiting for him like some sad, hopeful little puppy. She could imagine Kelly back home, tutting and shaking her head at her overeagerness. But where *was* he? She hated this – he might have had second thoughts, third ones even. Perhaps he'd decided she was just too young. Or maybe – and this was the bit she dreaded thinking about – maybe it was the sex. Was she no good at it? Before, with Oliver Willis, she'd assumed it was their joint lack of practice that had made it a bit of a non-event. It was OK, but mechanical: no sparks, even though she was quite fond of him in the way you are with someone you've known since reception class.

This time, well, it started off great, much more thrilling than it ever got with Oliver, but then it sort of finished too soon, almost as if Sam had gone way ahead of her to somewhere by himself and just wanted it to be over, all rushing on before she got a chance to work out what she was feeling. What would a more experienced woman have done? Was it all right to ask a man to slow down a bit, or were there things she should have been doing that would have made it better?

It wasn't very comfortable, that sofa in the hut. That hadn't helped. Something under the rug that covered it had been digging into her hip and when she'd suggested moving, he'd just murmured, 'Yeah, babes, great,' as if he wasn't really listening. The room smelled of engine oil and seaweed and she kept wondering if someone would look in through the shutters. If they did it again (and she'd like the chance – her mum had always said you didn't get better at anything unless you practised, though Beth might have claimed she meant piano and ballet rather than sex) she'd rather it was out along the beach, up towards where the hotel grounds finished and no-one could see them. That was how she'd always pictured tropical sex: warm sand gently chafing her back as she lay under the stars being pleasured (one of her favourite words, like something from a rude eighteenth-century novel) by someone adoring and considerate.

He hadn't been happy about the condom either, which was worrying. Didn't he do sex education when he was at school? It couldn't have been that long ago, surely.

'Babes, it's like eating candy with the wrapping on,' he'd tried to persuade her as he nuzzled her neck. But he'd given in over that one, because otherwise it was no deal, and also, she suspected, to shut her up from going on and on about safe sex, so he must care about her. He must – but where was he?

'Lesley? I just want to apologize.' Cynthia caught up with Lesley and Beth after breakfast as they walked towards the loungers on the beach. 'I was feeling a bit down last night and I wasn't being very nice to any-one. I'm so sorry.'

'You're right. You were absolutely horrid, Cynthia – you were behaving like a bitchy schoolgirl,' Lesley said coolly. Cynthia blinked, taken aback. Beth guessed that she'd expected Lesley, usually such an easy-going, accommodating soul, to let her off the hook far more easily than that.

'But as we've only got a couple of days left here and I want to enjoy them . . . and as I don't like atmospheres, we'll forget all about it, OK?' Lesley relented at last and smiled at her, though not quite with her usual radiance.

'Oh. Oh good. And I really *am* sorry. Um . . . would either of you – or both – like to come into town this morning while Ned and Bradley are out diving? Sadie needs a few last-minute things for the wedding.' She laughed and looked around sneakily. 'You'd be doing me a big favour – otherwise I'll have to be on my own with Sadie and Angela and they fight like cats!'

'Oh, OK I'll come,' Beth said. 'I expect Delilah might, as well; it's her last chance to shop for Christmas presents for her friends back home.'

'And I'm already on the trip – Angela invited me earlier,' Lesley told her.

'Did she? I didn't know.' Cyn looked surprised.

'No – well, what she *actually* said was that we "lard-butts" – borrowing your elegant turn of phrase from last night, Cynthia – we *lard-butts* should hang out together. Charming I thought, but I'm in a mood for assuming it was well enough meant. So I said yes.'

'She can be a bit blunt, my sister-in-law.' Cynthia sighed. 'I should probably tell you sorry on her behalf, I think.'

'I wouldn't do it just yet,' Beth suggested, still mildly seething from Angela's comment about Delilah being 'scraggy'. 'I should wait till the last day and assemble everyone in the hotel for a mass apology. By then, I doubt there'll be anyone left she hasn't insulted.'

Low profile. Nick now understood, almost literally, what the phrase involved. That had been a close one, on the beach. Who would have thought that his own mother would take to going for moonlight strolls on the sand by herself in the dark? What had she been doing out there? And as for Gina, Jeez, talk about up for it! They should have gone back to his room right from the off, not started diddling about on the loungers. He'd only intended to get through the openers on the beach: conversation, a bit of a snog, just to see how the land lay. He should have realized she wasn't going to be the stopping sort, not once she'd got revved up – not that the revving had taken long. Nought to sixty in about ten seconds, a real Porsche of a woman. What did she do, save up all her sexual energy for holiday time? Did all American women launch themselves so enthusiastically into sex, like they were trying out for Cheerleader of the Year? He'd always assumed that women started to wind the pace down a bit by the time they got to her age, whatever her age was – for who could tell under the make-up and the silicone? (No flop-quality in those tits, most strange.) He could hardly keep up. But he was young – he'd managed, and scary though Gina was, she'd been pretty fantastic.

Nick wandered along the beach towards the watersports hut. It might be an idea to keep out of the way for a bit, in case Gina was prowling around in search of a morning rematch. He certainly wasn't. In fact he was, to be honest, pretty sore in the trouser department. What he really fancied was some time out by himself, where no-one could get to him. He looked towards Dragon Island. It was more or less deserted at this time of the morning. Most of the snorkel parties went over in the afternoons and only a few nudist stalwarts would be there, up at their end of the island sunning their parts. He fancied taking a boat, sailing

236

over and simply parking himself under a tree, perhaps with a quiet beer and no company.

Carlos was in the hut, feet up on his sofa but keeping an eye on the punters out on the water, one of them roaring around like a maniac on a jet ski.

'Come on in, man. What do you want? Sail? Waterski?'

'Just a nice quiet sail by myself out there where it's peaceful,' Nick said.

Carlos laughed. 'Hey man, you look like you got woman trouble. Am I right or am I right?'

Nick grinned. 'Not trouble, exactly. Just sometimes you want time on your own, know what I mean? Just chill time.'

'Sure thing. Nothing like sailing a boat around for clearing your head; just you and the wind and the ocean,' Carlos told him, clambering up from the lumpy old sofa. 'You hang on here for a minute or two while I just go and sort out the crazy guy on the jet ski and I'll be right with you.'

Nick perched carefully on the sofa's arm and looked around idly while Carlos went down to the sea's edge. Hanging off the end of an oar propped against the wall was, to his surprise, a slinky, silky pair of very definitely feminine knickers, all creamy see-through lack and black ribbon. Expensive, he'd have guessed, thinking back to the photos on the Agent Provocateur website he'd looked at when he'd (briefly) considered treating Felicity. He wondered whose they were, and what they were doing there. A trophy perhaps?

When he was at school, there'd been a boy who collected a pair of knickers from each of his conquests – he'd shown them to Nick once, all folded neatly in a box. There'd been about twenty-five pairs and Nick was supposed to feel envy and admiration rather than

237

the mild disgust he'd actually felt. The boy had said they'd been the ones the girls had been wearing at the time: but Nick, sharp-eyed, had pointed out that at least three pairs still had the price tags on them. What a div. Had the boy really expected him to believe that either most girls carried spare knickers in their handbags, or that all twenty-five had cheerfully agreed to hand over their pants and go home commando-style?

There was a large chart on the wall, with the names of all the male sports and spa staff across the top and different countries alphabetically listed down the left side. The UK, he noticed, seemed to have the greatest number of ticks in the relevant box beneath each name, with dates alongside. Germany and the USA came next: several of the staff names had scored there. What was that about, he wondered. Something to do with the weekly sailing regatta, staff against the guests?

'Got you a nice little Sunfish out here, sails real smooth,' Carlos said, coming back into the hut. 'Hey, you looking at our sweepstake chart? Only one clear winner this season! He'll collect ten dollars off each of us by Christmas, easy!' He pointed to Sam's name and laughed.

'What's it about? What are you betting on?' Nick asked. He glanced at the pants dangling from the oar and back at Carlos, who was now looking rather sheepish.

'Just a bit of fun among the boys, you know?' he said, shrugging. 'No harm. Ladies of all nations and that, you know? Hate to say it to you, man, but your Brit girls are the easiest. A pushover, no, a *fall-over*.' Carlos tittered.

'Found those.' He pointed to the silky pants. 'Found those in the bin outside where the returned beach towels go. People get up to all sorts here,' he chuckled, shaking his head. 'Stuff you wouldn't believe.'

'Oh, yeah right.' Nick grinned at him, lamely trying to do man-to-man. He left the hut and ambled down to the sea to take his boat out.

It was the underwear guy from school all over again, another of those notches-on-the-headboard thing. And was he, Nick, really any better? If only, he thought as he pushed the small boat out into the waves and climbed aboard, if only he hadn't caught sight of the last UK entry under Sam's name, dated the day before. Delilah. His lovely, naïve, trusting little sister reduced to a felt-tip tick on a wall chart and a cheap sweepstake bounty. If he felt a bit queasy out there on the boat, it wasn't because of the sea.

'Orange! I can't wear orange. *Nobody* wears *orange*!' Delilah protested in the middle of the shop. Any minute now, Beth thought, she's going to stamp her foot like a toddler, hurl herself to the floor and scream and scream till she's sick, like Violet Elizabeth Bott. And who could blame her?

'But it'll suit your colouring, and it'll match Sadie's flowers!' Angela was trying to insist as she held up a long limp dress, a shiny man-made fabric, patterned with vast orange daisies and green tendrils. It reminded Beth of cheap ironing-board covers from a market stall.

'And you're very pretty, you're the sort who'd look good in a bin-bag.' Cynthia added her rather ill-considered opinion.

'Mum, Cynthia, don't be ridiculous. It's completely gross,' Sadie declared firmly. She took the offending dress from her mother and hung it back on the rail. 'There isn't anything good in here – it's all tee shirts and tourist tat. Let's try somewhere else, OK?'

'I suppose so. Maybe . . .' Angela said, giving Beth and Lesley a sly glance, 'maybe just Delilah, Sadie and Cyn and I should go by ourselves. Perhaps it's a case of too many cooks?'

Delilah got hold of Beth's arm. 'I want Mum to come too. She's good at clothes.' Beth blinked, unused to such a compliment. Back in England, she'd remind Delilah of this, if they ever had occasion to fall out over skirt length in the middle of the Kingston shopping mall.

'Is she?' Angela questioned rudely, looking Beth up and down. 'Oh, well, if you insist. Though if we can't find a dress this morning, then that's it. Sadie will have to get married without a best woman. After all, it's what you wanted in the first place, isn't it, darling? No fuss, no guests, no *hangers-on*?'

'Certainly is,' Sadie agreed, teeth gritted as she exchanged looks with Delilah.

The shopping party left the store and returned to the small, busy street and the scorching heat.

'I need a cold drink,' Lesley gasped, fanning herself with her hands.

'Me too,' Beth agreed. 'And as soon as Delilah's found a dress I'm happy to go and get one with you. There's a lovely little bar down by the harbour – Ned and I went there the other day. Just one more shop, OK? Do you want to go on ahead and I'll meet you there?'

'I think I will. There's a gallery I want to look in. I'd like to take a local painting back home. I'll hang it in the dining room so I can look at it while I'm clearing the guests' breakfast things, and remember having nothing to do but lie around in the sun under palm trees, reading.'

Beth laughed. 'And you could get a matching one for

Len: a sort of collage of trainers, bicycles, the scent of the Abs and Tums class, a volleyball . . .'

'. . . and a dozen shots of Jim's rum punch! That's my Len, never knowingly underdoes it. I bet you right now he's in the gym, giving the punchbag what for and sweating like an old gorilla.'

Delilah found her dress in the next shop, tried it on and twirled round for everyone to have their say.

'Well it's almost orange,' Angela conceded. 'Peach, anyway. Looks all right with her tan, but it won't suit her when she's pale again.'

Neither Delilah nor Beth cared – for now the dress, strappy, plain, lightweight linen, would be fine.

'You can always spark it up with accessories,' Cynthia suggested, searching through a rack of shell necklaces and bracelets. 'This one's pretty.' She held up a long triple string of coral-coloured beads against Delilah's neck and said, 'You do look lovely. I wish I'd had a daughter. You can't dress up boys once they're past three or so. They're all mud and football after that.'

'Even your Simon?' Angela said, laughing. 'I always thought gay boys loved shopping with their mummies.'

Cynthia looked as if someone had hit her. 'You might think you're being amusingly clever, Angela, but don't you think it's just a bit insensitive, given that Simon lives half a world away from me?' She turned and slammed out of the shop.

'Shall we go after her?' Lesley murmured to Beth.

'I'll go,' Beth said. 'You go and get your painting – I'll see you down at the Harbour bar.'

'Cynthia can't say I didn't try to find her,' Beth said later to Delilah and Lesley as their cab trundled down the steep, bumpy track to the Mango Experience. 'I wonder where she went to?'

'I don't know why you bothered,' Delilah said. 'She's a grown-up. If she wants to go off by herself, that's her choice.'

'You're right,' Lesley agreed. 'She's probably already back here, in the Sundown bar having her lunchtime rum punch.'

The taxi pulled over by the gate, allowing an ambulance, on its way from the hotel, to drive out.

'Goodness, I wonder who that was for?' Beth said. 'Surely not . . .'

'Dolly?' Lesley said. 'I never really took her seriously, she can't really have . . . ?'

'Died?' Delilah blurted out, matter-of-fact as only extreme youth would be on this subject. 'Why not? She was really old.'

'Lordy, poor Gina,' Beth said as the cab pulled up at the reception area. 'Do you think we'd better go and find her?'

'I'll come with you,' Lesley said, shoving her painting and her bags at Delilah. 'Here, darling, take this lot up to 112 for me and see if Len's in there. If not, leave it outside the door and I'll be along in a while, OK?'

'Sure,' Delilah agreed, looking round and wondering if Sam had shown his face in the hotel yet. 'I'll . . . um go right now.'

'I'm not sure of Gina's room number,' Beth said. 'We could ask in reception.'

'I tell you what though.' Lesley hesitated. 'It might not be Dolly. We shouldn't maybe race up to Gina's room if it isn't, because Dolly might be out some-where, maybe in the Haven, and then we'd have panicked Gina for nothing. Let's just go and see if she's in her usual spot on the beach first, in case it's nothing at all. If she's there, we can just ask her if she fancies some lunch.'

The two women set off along the beach to the far end, where Gina liked to doze the morning away under the last palm tree. Someone was there, that was clear, lying stretched out on a lounger, wearing no more than the tiniest bikini bottom.

'Is that her?' Lesley squinted at the woman. 'I can't see her hair, so it's hard to tell from here.'

'We should be able to tell from her tits,' Beth said, laughing. 'I know I shouldn't be thinking it, if Dolly *is* dead, but you know when Gina's lying down and they stick right up, no flopping sideways? I always wonder, if you got close enough, if you could see the seam where they bunged in the implants.'

'You should ask her. I bet she'd show you.' Lesley giggled. 'Yes it is her, look – you can see her blonde hair hanging out from under her straw hat. So I wonder who the ambulance was for?'

'Beth! Lesley!' Ned came jogging up behind them. 'I saw Delilah – she told me you were up here. Um . . . look, Lesley, something happened, nothing to worry about, but it's Len . . .'


'Len fell off the Swiss ball? What in the name of buggery is a Swiss ball?' Michael asked Delilah as they strolled together up to the Haven spa.

'It looks like a giant beach ball. You use it in the gym for exercises. Apparently,' Delilah explained.

She didn't want to talk to Michael or to anyone. She just wanted to go and have her facial in peace and lie in the dark not thinking about anything. There'd been no sign of Sam all day. She'd been to ask at reception if it was his day off, but the woman there had just smirked at her like she was the tenth one to ask the

243

same thing since breakfast. Perhaps she was. There was no message for her, no 'See you tonight', nothing. So where did that leave her? Dumped? It wasn't as if they were even, like, going out. This was like some horrible teen-mag cliché – the Holiday Romance Gone Wrong. There was only tomorrow and a bit of the day after left, and tomorrow was going to be mostly – well, the afternoon, anyway – Sadie's bloody wedding. She wished she hadn't agreed to be her stupid best woman, bridesmaid, whatever, now. She should have said, 'Hey, you know what, Sadie, a wedding with just you and your man and nobody else, that's an ace idea. Go for it.' Now they were all going and it would be all afternoon wasted over on Dragon Island. Sure, Sam would be there (if he ever came back, that is), but they wouldn't be able to be on their own.

It was blissfully cool in the Haven. Delilah and Michael went and sat on the cream sofa, waiting to be called in to the treatment rooms – Delilah to her facial (Exfoliate and Enrich), Michael to his Swedish Massage.

'Lucky he wasn't badly hurt.' Michael was still, Delilah realized, going on about Len, had he been rattling on for ages? She'd taken no notice. 'I suppose they have to get the ambulance in case he sues,' Michael said. 'But I heard the Haven nurse had his ankle bandaged by the time they'd got here. Gave poor Lesley a turn though. She thought he was a goner.'

I'm *so* not interested in Len's bloody ankle, Delilah thought, feeling mournful tears starting to gather. What kind of idiot had she been?

'Oh Lordy, you're crying.' Michael put a tentative arm round her shoulders. 'Is this where I give you a hug, is that allowed?'

'I suppose.' Delilah put her head on his chest. He

smelled of fresh laundry. 'Why did you ask, is it because I'm young?'

'Well . . . yes, I suppose so, in this day and age. But mostly because you're a moody teenager and might bite.'

'I think *he* thinks I'm too young.'

'Is it that lad with the beaded hair, the one who takes some of the fitness classes?'

Delilah gave him as sharp a look as she could, through her tears. 'What do you mean?'

He laughed, but not, she realized, as if he was laughing at her. 'I wasn't born yesterday! I saw you, the way you are with him. And he likes you too, so what's the problem?'

Delilah sniffed. 'He *did* like me. Not now. He's not even *here*. He said he would be.'

'Maybe he's ill. Maybe it's his day off and he forgot,' Michael suggested. 'No need to get all chewed up about it.' He reached across the table to a box of tissues and handed her some. 'Here, have these. You've got to stop crying before your treatment or you'll mess up the creams and potions, won't you?'

He was kind, surprisingly comforting. Delilah really didn't mind him trying to jolly her along.

'I just want to tell you one thing, from the horribly patronizing great height of being an aged fart who's lived a bit,' Michael said. 'And I don't want to pry, so please don't tell me anything alarming . . .'

'Oh I won't!' Delilah assured him, trying to smile.

'Just don't regret things, OK?' he said. 'I don't mean you shouldn't recognize when you've done something silly, if you follow me, but don't waste time regretting. You can't change anything, after the event. It's over, move on and try to make the best of it. And when you get older, you'll find it's the things you *didn't* do –

maybe out of, I don't know, timidity, idleness, fear of the unknown and so on – that you regret. Are you with me?'

Delilah frowned. 'I'm not sure. I might be, once I've thought about it.'

'Exactly. Give it time. At least you've got plenty of that,' he said, smiling and giving her shoulder a final squeeze as Dolores opened the door of Treatment Room no. 4 (Geranium) and summoned him to his massage.

# 16

# Thunder and Lightning

14 ml Parfait Amour
14 ml blue curaçao
14 ml amaretto
21 ml vodka
56 ml sour mix (lemon/lime/dash sugar syrup)
28 ml soda

'Len's blaming me for his sprained ankle, you know. Can you believe that?' Lesley said to Beth as they made their selections from the breakfast buffet.

'How does he make it your fault? You were out in the town with us!' Beth sympathized.

Should she have grapefruit and papaya plus a heap of toast today, or pineapple juice and a poached egg with bacon? Beth dithered over so many delectable choices. She'd miss this back home each bleak winter morning when she was shoving a bowl of virtuous dull-beige porridge into the microwave. Every year, after the overindulgence of a gorgeous holiday, she would stock up with plenty of exotic fruits to concoct these lazy, luscious tropical breakfasts, and every year she was disappointed that somehow those fresh tangy flavours couldn't quite be reproduced. Whether it was to do with the way the food was chilled for air transport, or something about the grey British mornings, she didn't know. It just didn't work. A Tesco banana didn't taste anywhere near as sweet as one freshly picked on its home ground. Supermarket mangoes and pawpaws, chilled to sterility, seemed always sourly underripe or close to mouldy, and even in midsummer there was that essential factor missing: the sultry, steamy climate.

Lesley's hand, waving the metal tongs like a wand, hovered indecisively over a heap of crisply grilled bacon.

'Nobody really diets 'til after Christmas, do they?' She murmured her habitual mantra as she scooped up a substantial portion and moved on to consider the hash browns and fried plantain.

'Len thinks that it's because I'd been going on about him being more careful, you know, with his health,' Lesley continued as they made their way to their table. 'He says he'd decided not to go out for a long run for once, out of consideration for me. So that's why he was in the gym, doing things with that stupid Swiss ball.'

'And he fell off . . . because he was balancing on it? Is that what you're supposed to do with them?'

'I'm not really sure.' She giggled. 'Try to lie on them, maybe? Whatever it was, he did it all wrong. And that's because he won't ask anyone. Just goes his own sweet way, like with the rubbish he eats and the amount he drinks.'

Beth imagined Len on top of a large glittery ball, walking it across a circus ring under a spotlight, possibly accompanied by a team of performing poodles, dressed in pink frills and up on their hind legs. In her head she had Len kitted out as a clown complete with huge curled-up shoes, scarlet nose and full white-face make-up. He wouldn't need to stuff his costume to look clownishly rotund – in terms of comedy shape he was almost there. No wonder Lesley worried. Why did men cause so much hassle? You shouldn't have to be looking after their well-being as well as your own. She thought of Ned, who occasionally, since the affair, she hadn't been able to picture leaving the house without including in her imagined scene a tempting line-up of alluring women that he'd be helpless to resist. What *had* his woman had going for her? She wished she didn't still wonder. And when did the wondering stop? Ever? She certainly hoped so.

There was no sign of Delilah this morning, which was probably, Beth thought with some dread, because there'd been no sign of Sam all the day before. He hadn't even shown up in the evening. Poor Delilah's mood, which had started off so confident and bouncy in the morning, had declined like a water-starved flower in a vase, and she'd trailed off to bed early following a sulky after-dinner session in the bar with her brother, during which he'd tried to jolly her along by teaching her to play poker.

'You know, we haven't had a karaoke night this year, have we?' Lesley said. 'There's no time now unless it's tonight. Remember we were going to do a load of Kinks numbers this year? Len's been threatening to put one of my dresses on and do "Lola". Your Delilah would die of embarrassment.'

'There's a lot of things I meant to do; always are,' Beth sighed. 'I haven't had a tennis lesson, haven't been out sailing, haven't had a go at the archery.'

'Yes, well you're not missing much with that one:

you might have had Valerie's kind of luck and shot your husband!'

Hmmm, Beth thought, if this had been three months ago, she might well have aimed at him.

'I'm only hoping Delilah will get over her Sam passion quickly and take home some happy memories. She only had about half an evening with him. It can hardly have been the big love of her life,' Beth said.

'A lot can happen in half an evening,' Lesley commented wryly, then, seeing the look on Beth's face, backtracked quickly. 'Oh she'll be fine! Don't you worry about it – give her a week with her mates back home and she'll have deleted all the bad bits from her head and reworked it into a bloody good time. And there's the wedding to look forward to this afternoon – we can all go out on a good one with that!'

Ned swam slowly upwards, letting the current drift him towards the underside of Carlos's boat. Bradley was just ahead of him, holding onto the ladder that hung from the stern, waiting for his dive-buddy. Their two heads broke the water's surface and Ned pulled his mask up.

'What's wrong?' Bradley asked. 'You're looking a bit down. Not looking forward to going back to work's grindstone? I know I'm not.'

'OK for you – you've got another three days here,' Ned said, trying to sound cheerful. He would miss his annual diving with Bradley. They'd probably never meet again now and it was all his own fault, his and bloody Cynthia's. It might have been OK if she'd simply got over it. She'd been the one in the first place who'd been keen on the no-strings element. Why on earth had he believed her and ever thought that dabbling in sexual shenanigans with her (or anybody) would be a painless and uncomplicated event? Why didn't he *think*? Just shows, he thought, what a naïve idiot he'd been. He'd have done better, if he really wanted a sexual adventure (and had he really? It hadn't even crossed his mind before Cynthia showed up in Harrods and started pushing his buttons) to visit a professional and get it over with, swiftly and anonymously. Not a scenario any man would dare to run past a wife as being a sound option, but true all the same when you broke it down to basics. He wouldn't have done that, of course he wouldn't. It had only happened with Cyn because it had somehow all fallen into place without him having to make any effort. He realized now that effort *had* been made. By Cynthia: she'd arranged everything, been the one to travel out of her way to see him, the one to book restaurants, hotel rooms.

No excuses, he told himself as he gazed across the sea's shimmering surface. He was about thirty-five years too old to plead that he was Easily Led.

'Going to be a bit stormy, later,' Bradley commented as they climbed aboard the boat. 'Carlos says there's a wind getting up and rain due. Hope it's all right this afternoon for Sadie and Mark.'

Ned peered at the sky. It all looked the same as usual to him – clear blue but for a couple of tiny puffs of cloud. There was a small whisk of breeze though, and the surface of the sea was rilled up like cat's fur being stroked the wrong way. It made him nervous, suddenly. As if trouble was quite literally brewing.

Well if Sam didn't want her, all done up like this, then it was definitely, no question, totally over. Delilah looked in the mirror for the thousandth time and admired her own gorgeous face. It was almost time to go – she wanted to keep how she looked in her head (uncanny resemblance to Kate Moss), so she'd stay feeling confident when she saw him.

'It didn't feel like Melina put much make-up on me, and yet I look completely different,' she said to Sadie, who was twirling the final section of her hair with the heated tongs.

'I suppose that's what they mean about all the trouble you have to go to to get the natural look.' Sadie giggled. 'You don't actually look so different, Del, just more . . . well *more*. Your eyes have got . . . what's the word, a bit of *smoulder* to them.'

'You have scrubbed up quite nice, I'll give you that,' Angela said. 'I still think that dress lacks a bit of pzzazz though.'

That would be the contrast with Sadie's, Delilah thought, watching Angela begin fastening the fifty buttons down the back of her daughter's wedding dress. There was enough fabric in it, Delilah calculated, to build a marquee, complete with ruched lining. Sadie was going to look fantastic, in a Cinderella-at-the-ball sort of style, but no way would Delilah ever have chosen a dress like that. Whether she was destined for the Samson-and-Delilah outcome or whether she ended up making do with trusty old Prince William, she would never wear a fat white meringue.

It was now just the three of them. Everyone else had already crossed to the island to wait for the bridal party. Sadie, Michael and Delilah were helped up the gangway into Carlos's boat (scrubbed clean and strung with ropes of paper flowers for the occasion), and turned to wave to the many hotel guests who, curious and well-wishing, had assembled on the beach to photograph the bride and wave her off to her romantic desert island wedding.

'It'd better not rain,' Sadie said, glancing back at the pale grey line of clouds that had gathered over the island's hills.

'The island has a rain forest: you get rain.' Michael shrugged. 'Even if it does, it'll only be for the usual few minutes. And you'll be under that arbour thing.'

'I'm not worried about the dress, Dad,' Sadie said as the boat lurched across the water, 'I just think it'll be unlucky.'

'That'll be nearly every English wedding then!' Delilah said, sensing it was her job to keep the bride's mood buoyant.

Delilah felt weak with nerves. She could see Sam as the boat approached the island, waiting beside Mark, the sun glinting off new silver beads in his braided hair. How was he going to be with her? Maybe he'd ignore her, which would be the worst case. Or maybe he'd be ordinary and normal like nothing had happened. None of it. That was how she'd play it too, she told herself; it seemed the grown-up option. All the same, she couldn't help the way her insides felt – as if she was about to take all her GCSEs all over again, this time with no revision.

Carlos handed a small bag to Michael after he'd run the boat up onto the Dragon Island shore. 'The blue flag is in here,' he said. 'When you're ready for me to come back and get you, just run it up the pole by the bar and I'll see it from across the water, OK?'

Mark, all got up in a morning suit, as formal as if this was a country wedding in an Oxfordshire village, stepped forward to claim his bride as Sadie climbed carefully down the plank from the boat. Angela rushed forward, fussing at Sadie's dress and brushing sand off the hem. Beth stood on the foreshore beside Ned and caught Nick looking at Sadie with a blatantly greedy expression, as if there was something he wished he'd done. She could guess what it was. He'd have to learn, that boy, and he would, in time: you can't have every chocolate in the box.

'Ah, doesn't she look lovely?' Lesley sighed next to Beth. 'Weddings always make me want to cry. I've brought a box of tissues in case, so if anyone needs one, you know where to come.'

'Mine always made me cry, that's for sure,' Gina agreed as they all began walking, following the bride and groom with Sam and Delilah, across the island to the wedding arbour where the preacher waited.

'How many have you had?' Cyn asked. 'You've never said.'

'She doesn't like to have her past failures dragged up. That's why,' Dolly said, with her cackly laugh. 'Three times wed, three times divorced and never enough alimony to keep a cat in cream.'

'I don't need alimony, Mom,' Gina said patiently, 'I make my own way.'

'That's what I mean. You shouldn't need to, all those husbands. I blame myself.'

'Well that's good.' Gina patted her mother's arm. 'Lets me off the hook.'

'I'll be gone by morning Gina, then you'll wish you'd spoken good of me.'

'Mom, you've said that every day this trip till we're all sick of it. You'll still be saying it this time next year. If you wanna vacation with me next year, I'm telling you now, it'll be to an African safari. And if you're still sure you're gonna die, you can just go walkabout with the lions.'

Sadie promised to love, honour and cherish Mark,

and Mark promised to share all his worldly goods with Sadie, and they all waited as the happy couple kissed – for slightly longer than was comfortable for their audience. Beth watched nervously as Sam and Delilah eyed each other speculatively from their respective sides of the bride and groom. She hoped there wouldn't be either coolness or a row between the two of them; a wedding was no place to fall out and this was a very tiny island.

The first specks of rain started to fall as everyone gathered beside the bar and the first bottles of champagne were uncorked.

'Oh bring on the drink,' Cyn demanded, impatiently. 'It's the only thing that makes a wedding bearable.' Beth looked at her sharply – Cyn, she realized, was clearly already on the outside of a couple of lunchtime cocktails.

'Cyn the cynic,' Len teased, leaning heavily on the stout stick he'd been given by the Haven nurse. 'What have you got against weddings? You've got a lovely man there.'

'I know that. Brad's a darling. He's just the *one* though,' she said with a brittle laugh. 'Not really enough for a woman of healthy appetite, is it Beth?' Cynthia downed half a glass of champagne in one.

'Don't drag me into it!' Beth told her. 'One husband is plenty for me.'

'Are you sure, darling?' Cynthia leaned forward. 'That's not what you were saying before, was she Ned?'

'What? Sorry, wasn't listening.' He backed away, looking worried. 'Just going to have a word with Michael.' And he scurried away, looking, Beth thought, like a fox fleeing a hound.

* * *

'Delilah, I really like you, but . . .' Sam had at last approached Delilah, edging her away from the party by the bar.

'But,' Delilah repeated. 'That "but" says it all. What did you think I want, Sam? All this?' She waved her arm to indicate the wedding arbour, where the rain was weighing down the garlands of flowers. She almost overbalanced and steadied herself against the bottle-palm tree. Three glasses of champagne had kicked in fast.

'What *do* you think I want from you, Sam? Do you think I want a big white beachfront wedding, with *you*? Is that why you stood me up yesterday?'

'Um . . . well. You're very young and I shouldn't, maybe, have . . . Anyway, I'm sorry, I don't know what else to say.' Sam smiled apologetically at her. She sensed insincerity, a punt for easy forgiveness and permission to start again with the next silly victim, presumably cleared for take-off while Delilah was still on Mango premises.

'I'm going back home tomorrow, Sam, and you won't have to deal with me ever again. You had *sex* with me.' She almost spat the words, somehow trying to convey that this *wasn't* an insignificant event for her.

He looked around, worried who was within hearing range.

Good. Let him worry, Delilah thought, as, gleefully, it occurred to her that he might even suspect, in spite of the hotel's over-sixteens policy, that she was under age. Why put him right?

'You could have pretended just for forty-eight hours, you know. That would have been kind, after what you did,' she went on. 'You could have just turned up for a while yesterday and, like, said hello, even. How much could it have hurt? God, you're so conceited!' A small part of her conscience told her that she wasn't exactly blameless here. She'd hardly been ravished against her will in the scruffy little hut. Was he going to point that out?

He shrugged. 'Guess I am. Sorry – and yesterday, well I had things to do, like unexpectedly. You're really sweet you know.' He reached out a hand to stroke her hair and she pushed it away.

'Oh spare me that crap,' she said furiously. 'It's so ... so *patronizing*. You just collect girls who are on holiday, like for fun. You do it because you *can*.'

She felt treacherously – and unexpectedly – close to tears. Now *that* she definitely *didn't* want. She was just starting to enjoy herself, to get into her stride, telling him what she thought. It would be good practice for when she was older or dealing with some hopeless, useless boy from school. Except what she'd told Sam wasn't what she thought, not really. If, after the wedding ceremony (which she'd found quite moving) and the toasts and the speeches, if he'd come over to her, led her away from the others and put an arm round her, apologized, kissed her a bit, all that, then she'd have let him take her down to the fenced-off nudist end of the island and do whatever he wanted to her, down and dirty in the sand. She'd *wanted* him to, far more than she'd wanted it the other night. It would – and she knew for sure from how her body felt as she'd watched him during the wedding blessing – be loads better than that pathetic effort in the water-sports hut. She was ready for him this time. But no. What had he done instead? Shuffled about looking like he'd rather be anywhere but here, chatting with the bar staff and joking with Michael. Making out like he was anywhere but on the same deserted half-mile stretch of island as her. She was angry.

Back home, when she told her about telling Sam what she thought of him, Kelly would be so proud of her. She could imagine her, almost see her here, rising from the waves yelling 'Go girl!' and punching a fist into the air.

'I don't know what to say,' Sam told her, shrugging moodily. 'I keep saying I'm sorry – you're great, that's it. I didn't mean to hurt you.'

'No,' Delilah said sadly, 'I don't suppose you did. I don't suppose you gave it a thought. But do me a favour will you, please?' She'd almost run out of steam now.

'Anything. What is it?'

'Think about it, next time you pick up some little holiday girl. There aren't many of my age who come here, so when they do, just, like, leave them alone?'

'You got it.'

She hadn't, she knew that. What did it matter? After tomorrow it would be back to school and the likes of Oliver Willis for her. Oh joy, something she could really look forward to. Not.

'And you know . . .' Sam was giving her that special smile now, sure he was safely off the hook at last. 'You know, there's still tonight back at the hotel? I could make it up to you?'

The clouds closed in, dark grey and purple-tinged and fast-moving. The rain, which had fallen in short sharp bursts, now tumbled hard and persistent from the sky. Thunder rumbled from far away and Beth counted the seconds between lightning and the distant rolls. It was coming closer.

'I love this kind of weather,' Lesley said, as all the older ones sheltered on seats beneath the bar's verandah, clutching glasses of drink and eating chunks of chocolate wedding cake. All the younger ones were smoking and chatting further up the beach, under the trees and the wedding arch.

'It reminds me of being a child,' Lesley went on. 'My mum used to tell me that thunder was God moving the furniture about.'

'Mine told me he was throwing cabbages,' Ned said. 'Funny, I never thought to ask why he'd want to do that.'

'Didn't want to eat them, I expect,' Michael suggested. 'Not everyone likes cabbage.'

'His fault for inventing them then!' Len said, slapping his leg and roaring with laughter.

'Not the maddest food he's come up with though. You've cooked some weird stuff for that Wendy woman, haven't you Beth?' Lesley said. 'What's the worst?'

Beth thought for a minute, wondering if it was the champagne making her brain feel like a wet sponge. Food – cooking – that wasn't something she much cared to think about right now. It went with the Going Home idea – which she was reluctant to face before she had to.

'Oogruk flippers,' she came up with, eventually. There was a silence, as well there might be, Beth thought; then, 'And what the fuck is an oogruk when it's at home?' Cynthia asked. She was slurring now, Beth noticed, but she herself probably wasn't much better. Much longer on this island and they'd have to be carried off.

'An oogruk,' Beth said, standing up as if to deliver a lecture, 'an oogruk is a bearded seal. So first you take your oogruk. Then you cut off its flippers.'

'Ugh! I couldn't!' Lesley pulled a face and shuddered.

'No — neither could I,' Beth said. 'Neither could Wendy even, if you can believe that. Anyway, then you put them in fresh blubber for two weeks.'

'Then what?' Cynthia asked. 'Is that it? How dull.'

'More or less. Then you take them out again, take off the loose fur, cut the flippers up and eat the meat. *Voilà!* An Inuit delicacy.'

'I'd rather be here, eating Caribbean crayfish,' Bradley commented, passing round another bottle. Thunder crashed again, closer this time.

'Look,' Ned said, 'I hate to be a party pooper but it's not getting any better, this thunder, do you think we should maybe be summoning our good boatman and heading back?'

'Good plan. Who's got the blue flag?'

Nick found Delilah in the sea, paddling around by herself, up to her thighs, her linen dress soaking wet and clinging to her. Her hair was drenched, and all her carefully applied make-up was trickling down her face. Rain or tears? He couldn't begin to guess.

'I don't think you should be in the sea when it's thundery, Del. Lightning might get you,' Nick called, wading in and taking her hand to lead her to shelter. 'Hey, you're a bit cold. Are you all right?'

'Yeah. I suppose. Just a bit . . . you know, empty-ish.'

'Is it the wedding? All that lovey-dovey stuff? Can't be doing with it, me.'

'Liar.' She punched him gently. 'Don't tell me Felicity didn't get to you — that's why you came running over to St George, to be in the comfort of your loving family!'

'Now you're really ripping the piss, Del.' The two of them walked up the beach and sat together beneath a clump of trees. Mark and Sadie were now on their own in the wedding arbour, having a romantic moment alone with cake and champagne. Sam was spark out in a hammock, his long beaded hair hanging over the fabric and a couple of spliff roaches lying dead on the sand beneath. The rain was easing off now, but the sky was still a menacing, thundery colour.

'I heard you ripping into Sam. Nice one.' Nick passed her a can from his beer stash and she opened it and took a swig.

'I thought I'd feel better after that, but you know, he's so *arrogant*,' she said. 'He still thought I'd like, *go* with him tonight, even after he'd kind of admitted that he's a total waster with all women.'

Nick wondered for a moment – should he mention the sweepstake in the water-sports hut? Would it make her laugh or make her cry? Cry, instinct told him.

'It's partly my fault. You'd never have . . . without a condom . . .' he stammered.

'How did you know I did?' Delilah said quickly.

'Oh . . . just, um, guessed. You wouldn't be so upset if it was only a quick snog. Hey!' Nick said, a tiny spark of an idea forming. 'I've just thought of something. You got mad – now you need to get even.' He got to his feet. 'Wait there a sec.'

Delilah leaned against a tree and watched her parents and their holiday friends round their table near the bar. Completely wrecked, every one of them, she thought, feeling strangely affectionate.

She looked across to where Sam was sleeping peacefully. Probably, she thought, because he spent all his nights *not* sleeping.

'OK – I got these from behind the bar.' Nick came back, whispering excitedly to her and presenting her with a large pair of scissors.

'What do I do with these?' she said, feeling confused.

'You are Delilah,' he said, pointing to the recumbent form in the hammock. 'There's Samson. Think about it?'

'I was sure I had it, somewhere.' Michael patted his pockets and eventually pulled out the bag Carlos had given him.

'Well thank goodness you've found the flag, otherwise we'd have been cast away here for ever,' Angela said. 'Not that I wouldn't put it past you to have lost it,' she added. 'You were always hopeless with any responsibility.'

Michael put his hand in the bag and a look of confusion flashed across his face. 'Um . . . what's this?' he said, pulling out the bag's contents and brandishing a pair of cream and black lacy knickers.

'Yours, aren't they Cyn?' Bradley said, taking them and turning them over. 'You been catting about again?'

There was an embarrassed silence. 'So where's the blue flag?' Lesley asked at last. 'Are we supposed to run Cyn's pants up the flagpole and hope someone salutes them?'

'Many have,' Bradley said with a sigh.

'*Are* they yours?' Beth asked her. 'How come Carlos had them?'

There was another silence and she realized she'd asked the question everyone else had been dying to ask.

'Yes they are mine,' Cyn hissed at her. 'And no, I haven't been doing anything with bloody Carlos, OK? Anyway you can talk. You're not such a goody-goody yourself.'

'Cynthia . . .' Bradley warned, but she wasn't listening. Cyn leaned across and grabbed Ned's arm.

'Your *wife*, Ned, we had a conversation about "fireworks", we did. And wouldn't you be surprised . . .'

'OK, this is getting too personal,' Michael said, leaning back from the table with his hands raised. 'Shall we stop now? Before someone says something they'll regret?'

'I don't have any regrets. Not like *some* people.' Cynthia's eyes filled with tears and she rooted about in her bag for a tissue. Too late, Lesley passed her own pack over.

'I had some in here . . .' Cynthia banged the bag on the table, before turning it upside down so everything fell out, much of it onto the floor. Beth, being nearest, leaned down to gather up Cyn's wallet, purse, chequebook and keys which were strung on a key ring with a horribly familiar tag – one from Tiffany's, engraved with the single word: 'Darling'.

'This is yours?' she heard herself say.

'No.' Cynthia almost spat at her. 'Actually,' and she pointed to Ned, 'it was meant to be *his*.'

# 17

# Corpse Reviver

30 ml brandy
20 ml sweet vermouth
20 ml Calvados

Was she supposed to feel like this? There should, Beth
thought as she slid out of bed, be an instruction book
for cheated-on wives. If she could be bothered to look
on the Internet, she'd probably find there was.
Somehow, though, she doubted there'd be a chapter on
this bizarrely blissful feeling of relief that she was
experiencing. Perhaps a support group would be better
than a book – then she could talk it through with
people who'd nod and look serious, and she'd find out
if her reaction to discovering about Cynthia was totally
abnormal.

Beth opened the double doors wide and went out
onto the balcony to breathe the humid early-morning
air for the last time on this trip. No, change that, she
thought, this was going to be the last time ever in this
place. Not only did she not want to be reminded of the
Ned-and-Cyn events, but she doubted the management
would welcome the return of guests who'd assaulted

the fitness trainer's hair with scissors. It was almost Valerie and the archery class all over again.

'Beth?' Ned called from the bed. 'Beth, are you OK?'

'I'm fine, Ned, fine,' she told him – again. She wished he wouldn't keep asking. It must be the twelfth time since they'd come back from Sadie and Mark's wedding. It wasn't surprising he'd asked, though. You probably weren't supposed to find it hilariously funny, not supposed to laugh yourself almost sick, when you discovered the identity of your husband's erstwhile mistress.

So it had been Cynthia all the time. Well, for a pretty short time – even Cyn had admitted that. Not some work colleague, not the young, slinky, minx that she'd been imagining with Cat Deeley's body, Scarlett Johansson's mouth and all the sexual tricks of a top-class Parisian hooker. Just ordinary (well, reasonably attractive, she'd admit if pushed) old Cynthia. Who'd have guessed? Ned didn't even like Cyn that much. Well he didn't now anyway, not this holiday, that had become pretty clear. All this trip she'd vaguely wondered why he'd tried not to be close to Cyn, why he'd looked so uncomfortable when she'd grabbed him to sit beside her at the barbecue, why he'd looked so astounded, shocked even, that she and Bradley had turned up at all. Now it all fell into place.

'She told me they were going east somewhere this time,' he kept saying, as if she was going to accuse him of planning to meet up with Cynthia here at the Mango Experience (Sport 'n' Spa). 'I didn't think she'd want to trail here after me.'

'Are you sure you aren't flattering yourself?' Beth had asked, as they'd sat side by side on rain-soaked beach loungers after dinner. 'Wasn't it Sadie's wedding they'd come for?' No, she hadn't believed that, even as she'd said it – and saying it was probably not a good idea, for after all, why shouldn't Ned be desirable enough to be pursued?

But when he'd told her about finding the knickers Cyn had sneaked in and hidden under his pillow, and about how he'd stuffed them into the used-towel bin . . . Was she supposed to find that funny too? Possibly, not, but she did.

'You can laugh . . .' he'd said, dourly. 'You try being chased by a mad stalker.'

And so it was, as ever, that she somehow ended up being the one who had to make it all right. To tell him it would all be fine, really, once they got home, just . . . fine.

'Aren't you glad I'm not like that?' Lesley said to Len as she helped him limp across the terrace to his favourite seat at the Sundown bar. It was almost lunchtime, and it was the last day. Another round or three of drinks wouldn't make any difference now. When she got home though, that was going to be different. Even if he was the only man in the group, she was going to force him to go to Shape Sorters every week with her till the two of them had lost enough weight to fit comfortably into airline seats again. She'd threaten him with extra poundage – this time of the wallet sort, if they didn't lose the weight: no way was she going to travel in the back of the plane when they went away next year. He'd have to fork out for an upgrade.

'Well, what do you think, Lesley?' Len chuckled. 'Course I'm glad. But it's Bradley I feel sorry for. No man could be happy with a wife who lists "shagging any bloke with a pulse" under hobbies.'

'I don't know – it seems like he's put up with it for

years. I mean,' she said, 'you either get out or shut up, I suppose. She's got away with it this long . . .'

'I don't think she'll get away with this one though. I bet they're not back here next year, don't you?'

'You know, Len, I don't want to be either. It's time for a change. We should go somewhere else – there's a whole world out there. In fact . . .' She waited a moment while Jim brought their drinks – a creamy, calorie-stuffed pina colada for her, a Corpse Reviver for Len.

'Go on . . . I can see a plan already formed. Just tell me where I'm going!'

'Well . . . I was reading in one of the travel mags in the Haven about this place that's being all done up out in the Seychelles. Another spa, a bit like this. And it's got a gym to die for.' Lesley crossed her fingers quickly – that wasn't the term she should have chosen. 'What do you think?'

'Book it, sort it. You know me, Lesley – I'll be happy anywhere. As long as you're there, I'll just tag along.'


Delilah packed quickly, hurling her clothes into her bag and cramming all the free toiletries she'd collected from the bathroom into pockets and corners. She was almost looking forward to being home, to seeing her friends again and even to going back to school. She hadn't intended to go back 'til after Christmas, but she felt so much better now and she had so much to tell her friends. Her mum would probably faint when she appeared at breakfast on Monday, school books all ready and well in time for the bus.

Everything was done, packed and sorted. The room looked empty and cold now that all her possessions were stashed away, as if she had never inhabited it and it was waiting, all anonymous and uncaring, for its next occupant. She opened the door, took a quick last look round and placed her bag out in the corridor, reading for the trolley to collect it and take it to the baggage room behind reception. Time for one last swim in the pool. She would not behave like a jealous brat, not try to drown Gina or anyone else, nor would she be looking over her shoulder to see if Sam was around. He didn't have the same appeal for her, somehow, now his hair was so messily chopped off. Funny how much truth there still could be in those mad old biblical stories. Whoever would have imagined it?

Cyn's head was under her pillow. She didn't want to emerge until Ned and Beth's plane had taken off later this afternoon and she'd never have to face them again. How stupid she'd been. How pathetic, desperate even. What had she imagined would happen? That Beth would say in her usual reasonable, no-fuss way, 'Oh it was you all the time, was it? OK, here have Ned, here you are, take good care of him,' as if he was a puppy who needed a more sympathetic owner? What she hadn't expected her to do was fall about with laughter. So humiliating.

And Bradley – how could she have done this to him? Again. When would she stop? She *would* stop – right now. She was getting too old for this; it was ridiculous to keep boosting her ego with short-term sex with spare (and not-so-spare) men. She should take the Gina route and go for surgery instead. She was sure that in the long run it would be far less painful.

Bradley had gone. Not left her, but out diving as he always did. He'd said he'd miss Ned. If *she* went, would he miss her? She doubted it – only a devoted fool would. She'd been an idiot.

Cynthia emerged from beneath the pillow and considered getting up and dressed, then possibly sitting in the sun on her balcony. She would wear her sunglasses and her big straw hat, so even if every hotel guest came to point the finger from down on the beach she wouldn't have to see them. She would shower, slap on the factor fifteen and keep out of the way till the coast was clear. Brad might hate her, might want her to move out of their home, but they had three more days in this place. Three days of polite nonconversation (they'd done enough, thank you, to entertain their fellow guests) and then it would be back to freezing England with possibly a curt note from divorce lawyers by way of a Christmas present.

Cynthia climbed out of bed and yawned. There was something unexpected on her bedside table – a cold cup of tea. Bradley must have made it for her before he left for his dive. She felt a tiny quiver of hope. Surely you only made gestures like that for people you cared about? It was like an expression of sympathy to someone suffering. Maybe there was still that remote chance. Her spirits lifted a little more as she opened the terrace doors. Beautiful day – she loved the heat, this sticky climate. Next year, she very nearly dared to plan, she and Bradley would go somewhere different, to a place where they knew no-one and had no history. That place in the Seychelles should be up and running again by then. When they got home, she'd make a start on checking it out. Just the two of them, she thought, no complications, absolutely no messing it up this time.

'She's gone!' Gina came running across the pool terrace to where Lesley and Len, Ned and Beth sat under the tamarind tree. 'Dolly has gone! Can you believe it?'

Gina looked furious. Nick and Delilah, hearing the commotion, climbed out of the pool to see what was happening. Without being asked but sensing drama, Jim and barman brought Gina a large Sea Breeze and pulled out a chair for her, gently pushing her down into it.

'God! Are you sure? Gina I'm so sorry!' Beth came over and hugged her.

'Whatever happened? She seemed fine yesterday, in really good form.'

'She just went!' Gina looked stunned. 'In the night, just went. I can't believe it. Why didn't she say anything?'

'Um . . . well she sort of *has* been saying, hasn't she? All along?' Ned ventured. Beth kicked him under the table. 'Sorry,' he said. 'A bit insensitive.'

'Huh?' Gina gave him a puzzled look. 'Ah no! She hasn't gone, like *gone* gone. She's not dead. At least, not 'til I catch up with her anyway. No, I mean she's left the hotel. I called down to reception when I'd found her room empty and they said she'd checked out. She didn't even leave a note, just her death outfit, all laid out on the bed, shoes too. How selfish is that?' Gina was getting more furious by the minute. Jim brought her another drink.

'Checked out? What, like she's just taken it into her head to go home?' Lesley asked. 'Maybe she had a message from someone and had to leave. She'd have told you though, surely.'

'She hasn't gone home, apparently,' Gina explained, stopping for a second for another big gulp from her glass. 'She took a cab to the airport, they said, to catch a flight to Miami. And she hasn't gone by herself,' She looked at Delilah. 'You won't believe this, honey, and I'm really sorry to be the one to tell you, but she's taken that young Sam with her.'

The airport was hot, crowded and sweaty. The check-in lines were slow, and Delilah, as ever when things weren't moving fast enough, was getting impatient.

'We should have got here earlier,' she whined. 'There won't be time for any last-minute shopping.'

There was still the queue to pay the airport tax after check-in, and then only one X-ray machine on the way to the departure lounge. She fancied some duty-free vodka. If she could get away with it, she could just about afford a really big bottle of the cheaper sort. It was time she organized another party. Sukinder had a large house – her parents were always going out to visit various family members. There was sure to be a night near Christmas when she'd have a free house and they could ask a few people round. Delilah might even consider getting to know Oliver Willis a bit better. Perhaps they could try something unusual this time, something called 'conversation'.

'Next year . . .' Ned said to Beth as they inched their baggage trolley forward in the line, being careful not to run into Lesley's legs. 'Next year, where would you . . .'

'Where would I like to go? I'm not sure. But I tell you one thing, it'll be anywhere but here,' she told him. 'Actually . . . a month or so ago, on one of those TV holiday programmes I saw a fabulous place, a sort of spa and sport type of thing, a bit like the Mango but all being newly done. We could go there, I'll look it up as soon as we're back.'

'Great idea. A lovely relaxing place where we don't know anyone,' Ned said.

'Exactly,' Beth agreed. 'The Seychelles it is then.'

THE END

# SIZE MATTERS
## Judy Astley

**Big and beautiful? Or thin and miserable?**

Jay has always envied her cousin Delphine. While Jay was
brought up in a large, noisy and chaotic family, Delphine
was indulged, perfectly dressed with a co-ordinated
bedroom, an immaculate wardrobe, dancing lessons and
monogrammed silver-backed hairbrushes. Now Jay lives
happily with her architect husband and their three teenage
children, running a succesful cleaning company and trying
to keep some kind of order on her disorderly household,
while Delphine has long since disappeared to Australia
with her second husband. But Jay does sometimes wonder
whether she should be more like her cousin — utterly well-
organised and with a size ten figure.

So Jay decides to diet. But what should it be? High carb, no
protein? High protein, no carb? High fibre? Wheat free? Fat
free? Food free? She tries them all, with a variety of
successes and failures. But then Delphine reappears, with a
third husband in prospect and the same old air of
apparently effortless superiority. Jay never considers that
perhaps Delphine is the envious one . . .

'AS IRRESISTIBLE AS TRIPLE CHOC FUDGE CAKE —
WITH EXTRA CREAM'
*Mail on Sunday*

0 552 77185 6

**BLACK SWAN**